D0172742

For J.M.W.

Confessions of a Reluctant Recessionista

Amy Silver

arrow books

Published by Arrow Books 2009

4 6 8 10 9 7 5 3

Copyright © Amy Silver 2009

Amy Silver has asserted her right under the Copyright, Designs
and Patents Act 1988 to be identified as the author of this work.

This book is a work of fiction. Names and characters are the
product of the author's imagination and any resemblance to actual
persons, living or dead, is entirely coincidental.

This book is sold subject to the condition that it shall not, by way of
trade or otherwise, be lent, resold, hired out, or otherwise
circulated without the publisher's prior consent in any form of
binding or cover other than that in which it is published and
without a similar condition, including this condition, being
imposed on the subsequent purchaser.

First published in Great Britain in 2009 by
Arrow Books
Random House, 20 Vauxhall Bridge Road,
London SW1V 2SA

www.rbooks.co.uk

Addresses for companies within The Random House Group
Limited can be found at:

www.randomhouse.co.uk/offices.htm

The Random House Group Limited Reg. No. 954009

A CIP catalogue record for this book
is available from the British Library

ISBN 9780099543558

The Random House Group Limited supports The Forest
Stewardship Council (FSC), the leading international forest
certification organisation. All our titles that are printed on
Greenpeace approved FSC certified paper carry the FSC logo.
Our paper procurement policy can be found at
www.rbooks.co.uk/environment

Typeset by SX Composing DTP, Rayleigh, Essex

Printed and bound in Great Britain by
CPI Cox & Wyman, Reading, RG1 8EX

PL NOV 12
OY MAY 2015
SU JAN 2016

Confessions of a Reluctant Recessionista

Amy Silver is a writer and freelance journalist, and has written on everything from the diamond trade to DIY dog grooming. She lives in London and has a penchant for vintage clothes and champagne cocktails, but she always pays her credit card bills on time. This is her first novel.

1

Cassie Cavanagh *loves her Louboutins*

God, they're beautiful. They are quite possibly the most beautiful shoes I have ever seen in my entire life. Last night, after I'd come home and tried them on with just about everything in my entire wardrobe (there is nothing they don't look good with), I put them on the coffee table in the middle of the living room and just sat there, looking at them. They were still sitting there when Ali arrived.

'Bad luck,' was the first thing she said when she came into the room.

'Bad luck?'

'Shoes on the table,' she said, knocking them to the floor.

'You're just jealous.'

'Jealous, my arse. You won't be able to walk fifty yards in those things. They'll cripple you.'

'They're taxi shoes, Al. I don't intend to walk fifty yards in them. It's just taxi to bar, bar to taxi, taxi to front door. That's about thirty yards max over the course of an entire evening. Anyway, Dan can always carry me . . .'

Ali slumped down onto the sofa, stretching out her legs and kicking off her own rather elegant heels.

'You're right, you cow. You are lucky, having someone to spoil you, even if he is constantly admiring his own assets. I *am* jealous. Some days I feel like no one would notice if I turned up at the pub barefoot.' This is not true. At five nine with a pair of legs to make Gwyneth Paltrow turn green with envy, Ali never passes unnoticed. She's just so used to being one of the boys, which is virtually a job requirement when you do what she does, that she sometimes forgets the impact she makes on the opposite sex.

'You had a long day?' I asked, handing her a glass of champagne.

'The longest. Had to get up at quarter to five in order to get a decent run in before I left for work, got stuck on the Northern Line for twenty minutes on the way in which meant I missed half the morning meeting, got bollocked by Nicholas, had endless calls with impossible-to-please clients, no time for lunch, no time to pee . . .'

Ali and I met at Hamilton Churchill, the investment bank where we work. She's the high-powered one – she's a trader – and I'm just a lowly PA, but I know whose job I'd rather have. My boss might be a complete pain in the arse, but I don't have to be at work at six thirty every morning, I don't have to spend all day

2

yelling into a phone, I don't have the responsibility of buying and selling millions of pounds' worth of stock, of trying to call the market, to sort the good tips from the bad, trying to please my clients while also pleasing my bosses. Granted, I don't earn a six-figure bonus either, but I get by. Plus, I am fortunate to have a boyfriend, Dan, who is also a trader – and in addition to being extremely attractive he's also very generous, hence the Louboutins.

Generous as he is, I have to admit that the shoes came as a bit of a surprise. It wasn't as if it was my birthday, or an anniversary or even Valentine's Day – just a plain old Wednesday in October. We went out to dinner and when we got back to his flat, there they were, all wrapped up with a crimson bow, sitting in the middle of the bed. My friends won't believe it, but he can be very romantic.

Ali and I were having a girls' night in – Dan was out with clients – so we bought three bottles of champagne (Ali can put them away when she's in the mood) and ordered takeaway. Not that I was really in the mood for food. I was much too hyper, and not just about the shoes: it was only two days to go until possibly the sternest test of my professional career, the night of the annual Hamilton Churchill drinks party which I, to my amazement, had been tasked with organising. To be perfectly honest, I was slightly terrified. My boss, Nicholas, is almost impossible to please at the best of times – and I had gone ever so slightly over budget. But you don't get the bar at the Hempel Hotel, all the champagne that a room full of investors and traders can drink, and canapés from the trendiest caterers in town, for nothing.

'It'll be great, Cass,' Ali reassured me, draining her glass and getting up to open another bottle. 'You were born to plan parties. Just as I was born to go to them, drink too much and go home with someone completely inappropriate.'

'Any potential candidates for Mr Inappropriate this year?' I asked, but before she could answer we heard the key rattle in the front door.

'Oh, hell,' Ali hissed, rolling her eyes dramatically. 'I thought she was out for the night.'

'So did I,' I whispered back, shrugging guiltily.

Ali can't stand my flatmate Jude to whom she holds a diametrically opposed world view. Ali is a pure capitalist, she believes in the power of the market and the virtue of hard work. She's working class – her father is an ex-printer turned cab driver, her mum was a nurse until she died a few years ago – and pulled herself up by the bootstraps, worked incredibly hard at her crappy East London comprehensive and ended up doing maths at Cambridge.

Jude, by contrast, is upper middle class, had a pony for a best friend between the ages of eight and eighteen and politically stands a few paces to the left of Karl Marx. As far as Ali is concerned, everything Jude owns has been handed to her, largely courtesy of her father's extremely successful architecture practice. It drives Ali insane that despite all her privileges, Jude still behaves as though she spends every day struggling against injustice.

Jude, of course, thinks Ali is materialistic and selfish, motivated solely by making money without any concerns about where that money comes from. If only she could see the error of her ways, Jude says, Ali could use her numerous talents to make the world a better place. Personally, I try to stay out of it.

'Hi, guys,' Jude said, popping her head round the door and smiling at us sweetly. 'Oh, champagne! Are you celebrating something?'

'We're celebrating the fact that it's Thursday,' Ali said drily. 'D'you want some, or would a glass of Laurent Perrier contravene some principle or other?'

'Oh, I can't, thanks very much, just came home to change and then I'm off to yoga.'

Jude is pretty good at ignoring Ali's barbs – a committed pacifist, she believes in turning the other cheek. Then she spotted my shoes, still lying on the rug where Ali had dumped them so unceremoniously.

'Oooh, those are pretty,' she chirped, picking one up and surveying the glorious red sole.

Oh, Ali, please don't say anything, I thought.

'They cost five hundred quid,' Ali said, giving me an evil little grin.

'Five hundred pounds!' Jude exclaimed. 'For shoes! Honestly, Cass, that's ridiculous. You could feed a family in Africa for months on that. Hell, in some places you could probably feed a family for a year.'

Ali poured herself another glass of champagne and settled back into the sofa cushions, enjoying a ringside seat to my dressing down.

'I know, I know, it is a bit much,' I admitted. 'But I didn't actually buy them. They were a present from Dan.'

Jude sighed, cocking her head to one side and gazing at me, an expression of slight disappointment on her face. She doesn't approve of Dan. Jude doesn't approve of lots of things.

'Really. And what's he apologising for this time?'

'He's not apologising for anything, he's just being sweet,' I replied, a little unconvincingly.

Ali gave a disconcerting snort. She's not Dan's greatest fan either – it's the one thing she and Jude can agree on.

'Of course he was. And where is Prince Charming tonight?' Jude asked.

'Spearmint Rhino?' Ali suggested.

'He's out with clients!' I said indignantly. Probably at Spearmint Rhino, but I wasn't about to admit that.

The thing with Dan is that, like most traders, he plays as hard as he works. And City boys play in a certain way – one that involves copious quantities of champagne, the occasional line or three, and the odd evening in what you might term gentlemen's establishments. But they have to do that – it's expected of them, to show their clients a good time. Not that Jude understands that – the City is all a bit of a mystery to her. And after the best part of a bottle of champagne,

I was not in the mood to get into the age-old debate about Dan's suitability.

Luckily, yoga beckoned and Jude reluctantly resisted a comeback and headed off to get changed. Ali sighed heavily, and not for the first time I wished that my two closest friends could get along better. After all, they can't be that abhorrent to each other. They have me in common.

I've known Jude for ever – we were at school together although we were never really close. I wasn't really part of the horsey set. We'd lost touch for years, but she was one of those people who popped up on Facebook asking to be friends and I felt it would be rude to say no. I would never in a million years have pictured myself living with her, but about a year ago I found the perfect flat, a smart little two-bedroom place above an art gallery just off Clapham Common. There was no way I could afford it on my own, and I happened to know (through the power of Facebook again) that she was looking for a place, and I just thought, what the hell. At first, she was sceptical.

'I'm a student, Cassie,' she said. 'I shouldn't be living in a soulless new-build with a plasma-screen telly and a Smeg fridge. Wouldn't you rather find somewhere with a bit more character?'

'If by character you mean damp in the bathroom and carpets from 1976, then no, not really,' I replied.

Eventually I talked her round. And our place is not soulless. OK, so it does have laminate flooring, which I have artfully covered with rugs from Heal's and

Designers Guild, and there is an excess of gadgetry – the kitchen taps have lights which make the water look red or blue depending on temperature (ideal for when you've taken so much cocaine you can't tell hot from cold, Ali once remarked) – but I love the newness of everything.

'It makes it really easy to keep clean,' I said to Jude a month or two after we moved in.

'Particularly when you have a cleaner who comes once a week,' she replied. She thinks having a cleaner is self-indulgent; I think life is too short to clean skirting boards.

Clad head to toe in the Stella McCartney yoga wear I bought her for her birthday (she'd die if she knew what it cost), Jude popped back into the living room to pick up her keys. She frowned at the overflowing ashtray into which Ali was squishing her cigarette.

'I'll just empty this for you, shall I?' she asked.

Ali pulled a face at her back.

'Have you tried the Allen Carr method for quitting?' Jude asked as she returned the emptied ashtray. 'I hear it's very good.'

'No, I fucking haven't,' Ali mumbled and promptly lit up again.

Jude sighed and headed off to her class.

I served up the takeaway (sushi and sashimi, Ali's favourite), and resumed my investigation into the state of Ali's love life, which is frequently a complicated business.

'Mr Inappropriate?' I asked again. 'Anyone in mind?'

Ali laughed. 'Not at the moment, no,' she said, but I noticed that as she said it she couldn't quite meet my eye. 'We should go on holiday,' she announced suddenly.

'Uh-huh,' I said, now very suspicious at the way-too-abrupt change of subject.

'I haven't been anywhere for ages – we could do a spa thing or something. It would be fun. I could look for some cheap deals on the Internet.'

'We could . . .' I said, a little non-committal.

'What? You don't fancy it? Or you have to ask Dan's permission?'

'It's not that,' I said. 'Just that I was sort of planning a surprise for him. I was thinking of taking him away for our anniversary.'

'What anniversary?'

'It'll be ten months in a few weeks,' I said, slightly sheepishly.

'Your ten-month anniversary?' Ali looked unimpressed. 'And where were you thinking of going?'

'Rome. I've found some amazing places on the Internet – I'll show you.' I grabbed my laptop from the kitchen counter and brought it over. 'This is my favourite,' I said, bringing up the site, 'Hotel de Russie. It's just across the road from the Spanish Steps and it looks totally amazing. And it has the best spa in Italy, apparently.'

Ali nearly choked on her champagne. 'Yeah, for over four hundred euros a night I would bloody well hope so. Can you seriously afford that, Cass? You do know we're heading into a recession, don't you?'

'Yes, I know. But we'll be all right, won't we?' I said. 'We've got good jobs, we work for a profitable company. Anyway, it probably won't last that long, will it? These things go in cycles.' I tried to sound as though I knew what I was talking about. Ali gave me a rueful little smile.

'Well, I hope he appreciates it,' she said. I didn't say anything. Sometimes it's better not to discuss Dan with Ali when she's had a few.

I put Ali into a taxi at around ten – ridiculously early, but then she does have to be at work by six thirty. I rang Dan once or twice (oh, all right, three times) but his phone was off. So I put my shoes on (they even look great with my pyjamas) and, fuelled by an excess of champagne and armed with my credit card, decided to book the trip to Rome. Shunning Ryanair (it doesn't really set the right tone for a romantic weekend away), I found some not-too-exorbitant tickets on Alitalia and a special three-night deal at the Hotel de Russie which I'd only be paying off for a couple of months. Maybe three.

Just as I clicked on 'confirm' to purchase the tickets, my mobile rang. Snatching it up in eager anticipation of seeing Dan's name come up on the screen, I was mightily disappointed to discover that it was Celia, my older sister. I toyed with the idea of ignoring her, but as usual, my guilt got the better of me.

'Hi, Cee,' I said, with as much cheeriness as I could muster. 'How's it going?'

'Why aren't you coming up this weekend?' she

snapped, immediately on the offensive. Despite its suddenness this attack was not entirely unexpected. The coming weekend was my parents' twenty-eighth wedding anniversary, and my sister had been planning the party for months.

'Celia, I told you I can't come this weekend, I've got plans I made ages ago and I can't change them now.' This was not entirely true. I did have plans to spend the weekend with Dan – he'd been away on two stag trips and one weekend training session in the past four weeks and I felt as though I'd barely seen him. 'In any case, Cee, it's not like it's their thirtieth. Twenty-eight isn't really a big deal, is it? Bet you don't even know what gift you're supposed to give for twenty-eight years.'

'I've looked it up. There isn't one.'

'There you go then.'

'For Christ's sake, Cassandra,' she said, knowing only too well that the use of my full name sets my teeth on edge, 'it *is* a big deal. It's twenty-eight years of marriage. And I've booked the function room at the Holiday Inn in Corby! You can't do this to them, they'll be *heartbroken*. Particularly after what happened at Dad's birthday.'

My sister knows exactly how to push my buttons. Bringing up Dad's birthday debacle was a masterstroke.

It happened a couple of months ago. My father had a birthday barbeque in the summer, to which Dan was invited.

'We're ever so keen to meet him, love,' my mother had said on the phone. 'You've been seeing this chap for months now. About time he and your father got acquainted, isn't it?'

Not in my opinion it wasn't. If it were up to me, Dan and my parents would never cross paths. Here is the awful truth – and it is *really* awful – I'm embarrassed by my family. I know that everyone goes through a stage when the idea of bumping into their friends when in the company of their parents is the very definition of hell, but you're supposed to grow out of that stage when you're about seventeen. I never did. And I don't know which is worse: the embarrassment they cause me or the burning shame I feel because I am embarrassed by them.

My parents are not unpleasant people. They are kind and respectable, active members of the Kettering Rotary Club and their local Conservative Party. But they are unworldly. They live in a Britain which most of us left behind a long time ago, the Britain of the 1970s, the Britain of avocado bathroom suites, prawn cocktail starters and mushroom vol-au-vents, the Britain in which holidaying in Spain was seen as exotic and adventurous.

The Cavanagh family didn't even get as far as Spain, in fact. When I was a child we stayed at the same bed and breakfast in Bournemouth every single summer with one exception. When I was fourteen I persuaded them to take us to France, on the pretext that it would be a good opportunity for Celia and me to practise our

French. We drove to Portsmouth and took the ferry to Le Havre (my mother and sister spent the entire four-hour journey throwing up in the toilets), and from there to a place called Granville, where we stayed in a tiny two-bedroom apartment with a view across the bay towards Saint-Malo.

On our second evening in Granville, we ventured out to dinner in a picture-perfect little brasserie near the harbour, complete with blood-red awning outside and a long, copper-topped bar. I vividly remember my parents' terrified expressions as the stereotypically snooty waiter presented them with menus written *entirely in French*; Celia and I did our best to translate but we were not exactly what you might term proficient. We did, however, recognise the odd word – *agneau* and *côte de boeuf* stood out – and so Dad, Celia and I opted for the beef, while Mum ordered lamb. When it arrived she looked at it suspiciously; the pale, slightly spongy meat on her plate did not resemble the traditional roast to which she was accustomed. Gingerly, she took a bite. Then, her face blanching, she returned her fork to her plate and summoned the waiter.

'Excuse me,' she said, loudly and slowly so that he was sure to understand, 'but are you sure this is lamb? *L'agneau?*'

'*Oui, madame, ce sont des cervelles d'agneau.*' He smiled at her warmly, enjoying the moment. 'Zees are ze brains of lambs.'

And my mother was back in the toilet, throwing up

again. For the rest of the holiday we ate spag bol and fish and chips back at the apartment, with Mum complaining bitterly that it wasn't much of a holiday if she had to cook all the time.

My parents are provincial. They are petit bourgeois. I love them dearly. But for as long as I can remember I have wanted to get away – not from them so much as from their life. The idea of Dan sitting on the sofa in the peach-themed living room of our mum and dad's 1930s semi in the Kettering suburbs, drinking a pint of Tetley while admiring my mother's collection of Royal Doulton figurines, or discussing the front-page story of the *Daily Mail* with Dad, was just too awful to contemplate. So when they invited us down for the birthday party I lied and said that Dan couldn't make it – he had to visit his grandmother in Edinburgh who had taken ill.

I'd told Dan that he was invited but that he needn't bother to come because he'd find it boring, and he put up no argument at all. However, for some inexplicable reason he decided that he'd earn some Brownie points – perhaps for use at a later meeting – by ringing up halfway through the afternoon's festivities to apologise for his absence and to wish my Dad a happy sixtieth. He was so sorry he couldn't make it, he said, but there was just no getting out of the annual Hamilton Churchill team-building weekend. The look on my father's face will stay with me for a very long time.

And Celia knew it. With a resigned sigh and a heavy heart, I conceded defeat.

'All right, Celia, I'll cancel my plans. I'll get the train up on Saturday. Can you pick me up from the station?'

'Not on Saturday, Cassie. The party's Saturday and I'll be busy all day getting things ready. Come up Friday night. I'll come and get you and we can go for a bite at the Harvester with the kids.'

Oh, joy . . .

2

Cassie Cavanagh *is homicidal*

How would I like to kill him? Let me count the ways: stabbing, shooting, poisoning, shoving him beneath the next DLR train . . . I was ten minutes late this morning. Ten. And of course it wasn't my fault – if you live in London, it genuinely almost never is. It's typical though. I actually woke up before my alarm went off so I decided to set off for work earlier than usual so that I could finalise party plans and get a jump-start on the day. Ha. So much for early birds and worms and all that.

It was a glorious October morning, the air crisp and the sky cloudless, the kind of morning which absolutely demands that you don your brand new, bright red trenchcoat and enormous Marc Jacobs sunglasses even though it is only six fifty in the morning and the sun is barely up yet. Although I was unable to wedge myself onto the first two Northern Line trains to arrive at Clapham Common, I was still ahead of time when the third one arrived and, miraculously, I was actually able to get a seat, on which someone had kindly left a copy of *Metro*, allowing me to catch up on world events before I got to the office.

I was just flicking through the paper reading yet another Cheryl Cole story (the only woman in Britain, Ali once said, who has worse taste in men than I do), when, between Oval and Kennington, the train came to a sudden, shuddering halt. The lights dimmed. They came back up again. The temperature began to rise. I wriggled out of my coat, accidentally elbowing the portly middle-aged lady to my left and provoking an exasperated, exaggerated sigh.

I read *Metro* from cover to cover (Jude's right, there really isn't that much of interest in it), including all the horoscopes. '*Geminis in love*', of which Dan is one, '*face a turbulent week ahead*', apparently. While Virgos like me are '*going to get their just rewards*'. Sounds ominous. Fourteen minutes later the driver read out an incomprehensible announcement. Probably something about signal failure. It's usually signal failure. A few minutes after that the train began to move again, lurching forward painfully at walking-while-carrying-heavy-shopping pace.

By the time we made it to Waterloo, where I change to the Waterloo and City line, I was already running late. By some truly amazing feats of contortion (those Yogalates classes at Holmes Place must be paying off) I managed to squeeze myself onto the next carriage, bracing myself against the door and craning my neck to avoid having my face pressed into the sweaty armpit of the man in front of me. This, part two of a three-part journey to work, is usually the low point.

Part three I like. In fact, I must be the only person I know who actually enjoys their commute, or at least a part of it, to work. I love sitting at the front of the DLR train as it rises up out of the gloom of Bank station into bright sunshine, trundling along above the streets of East London like a particularly slow and not especially frightening roller coaster. I love the view across the water from West India Quay towards the forest of steel and glass towers rising up from the Docklands. I like riding the super-fast lift to the forty-second floor of One Canada Square, the tallest of Canary Wharf's skyscrapers and home to Hamilton Churchill's equity trading floor. This is the kind of place I dreamed about working when I was growing up: not that I pictured myself as a PA, obviously – I didn't really know what I wanted to be. But I knew *where* I wanted to be: I longed to be somewhere like this, somewhere noisy and glamorous and frenetic, a place where important, consequential things happened, a place a long way from suburban Kettering.

The second I went through the doors of our open-plan office, I regretted the choice of bright red trenchcoat that morning. Against a sea of men (and a couple of women) in sombre dark suits I stood out like a beacon. Or a red rag to a bull.

'What the fuck time do you call this, Cassie?' he yelled at me before I'd even made it to my desk.

My boss, ladies and gentlemen, the charming Mr Nicholas Hawksworth, fifty-something divorcé, father of two and all-round bastard.

'It's ten minutes past eight,' I said politely, flicking on my computer.

'Don't be fucking smart with me,' he snapped. I was *telling the time*, for God's sake, how is that being smart?

'Where the hell is that analyst's note on Vodafone? It was supposed to be on my desk first thing this morning.' Well, at least he'd switched from 'fuck' to 'hell' – it usually meant he was calming down. I followed him into his office.

'I put it on your desk last night – on the left . . .' I looked down at his desk. He'd plonked his newspaper down on top of it. 'It's under the *FT*,' I said.

'Well, that's no bloody good, is it? Get me a coffee, will you? And when I say I want something on my desk first thing, that's what I mean. Not the night before, not that afternoon. All right?'

Yes, of course, I thought as I descended the lift to go to the Caffè Nero round the corner (there's a Starbucks in the building but for some reason Nicholas won't drink their coffee), *God forbid I should be too efficient*. The thing is, I am efficient. I'm good at my job. Punctual (well, almost), organised, resourceful and very presentable, I can type one hundred words per minute, draw up elaborate charts in PowerPoint and remember every meeting he's going to have this week without looking at the diary. And I pick up his dry cleaning. I'm indispensable. He wouldn't survive a day without me.

Today, though, it felt as if he would happily go the rest of his life without ever laying eyes on me again. There was the lateness issue, the craftily concealed analyst's note, and then the coffee I got him was insufficiently strong (it's not as though I make it, for God's sake) so I had to go back and get another one which was then insufficiently hot. I thought he was going to throw it at me – I kid you not, legend has it he did just that to a previous assistant. I was saved by his mobile ringing, whereupon he spent the next ten minutes giving his ex-wife a load of abuse about the fact that his younger son had failed to make the school rugby team. Why exactly that was her fault I couldn't quite work out. Then he couldn't get an email to send (my fault, naturally), the dry cleaners had failed to get a mark out of his favourite shirt (why did I insist on taking his clothes to the worst cleaner in London?) and how on earth could he be expected to read the speech I had typed up for him for the analysts' dinner next Thursday when the font was so ridiculously small? I didn't bother to point out that it is the same font I have used for every single speech I've typed up for him since I came to the company. What would be the use?

The only things he didn't blame me for were that morning's one and a half per cent fall on the FTSE and the previous evening's four–nil drubbing of Chelsea by AC Milan, but these events only darkened his mood further. So when the food and beverage director from the Hempel rang to confirm arrangements for the party and some idiot on switchboard put them through to Nicholas's direct line I thought he was going to have an aneurysm.

'In my office, Cavanagh. Now.'

I trailed in, my heart sinking into my shoes.

'Yes, Nicholas?'

'I've just had a call from the Hempel,' he said, his voice ominously low and even.

'Oh, God, why are they calling you? I didn't give them your number.'

'I don't know why they're fucking calling me. I do know that the price they have quoted for this bloody party tomorrow is nowhere near what we agreed. Nowhere near!' He was yelling now. The other PA on the floor, Christa Freeman, glanced over nervously. 'How could you sign this off without checking with me first?'

'Nicholas,' I said, my voice trembling just a little, 'I know it's slightly over budget but I did go to a number of places and there were cheaper quotes but they simply weren't the sort of places that would impress our clients. This is one of the best hotels in London, it has a great reputation . . .' I was rambling hopelessly. 'I can show you comparative quotes,' I said.

'I honestly don't have time for that. The markets are in fucking freefall, for Christ's sake, and you want me to start planning parties? That's what I asked *you* to do.' Some of the traders were rubber-necking now. Nicholas's tantrums are legendary.

'Nicholas . . . I . . .'

'You'd better hope that this is a success, Cassie. This

better be the best bloody party we've ever thrown. I mean that. This needs to make the *Vanity Fair* Oscars party look dull.'

So, no pressure then.

Back at my desk I went over the party plans again and again. If I'm completely honest, it wasn't just Nicholas who I was looking to impress. It mattered to me that Dan thought I'd done a good job, too. And while it may sound ridiculous, it mattered to me that all his trader buddies thought I'd done a good job. I have no problem with what I do – I don't think there's any shame in being 'just a PA', but I often get the sense that his friends see me as, well, a bit ditzy and pointless. Which is completely unfair. I have opinions about world events. I read the newspapers. OK, I mostly read *Metro* and occasionally the *Sunday Times* style section, but I can name at least four members of the cabinet and probably one or two of the opposition front bench. I can point to Syria on an unmarked map of the world. I might not understand how a derivative works, but neither do they. Not really. They're just salesmen.

Not that I would ever say that to their faces – a lot of them really do think they're God's gift. I remember the outbreak of unbearable smugness in the office when it was revealed, a few months ago, that scientists at Cambridge had discovered that the higher the testosterone level a trader had in the morning, the more money he was likely to make that day. So not only could the day's most profitable trader crow about how much money he'd made, he could also crow about having the biggest balls. One night in the pub, I pointed out that studies also linked high levels of testosterone with slow social development in childhood and baldness in adults. That didn't go down very well.

I really admire what Ali and the other handful of women on the floor do, but I can't say that I envy them. They have to work seventy-hour weeks in what is sometimes an unbearable environment – the stories you hear about misogyny and bullying in the City are fairly accurate. The pretty girls spend their time fending off unwanted advances and the less pretty girls have to put up with incessant cruel remarks. I am fortunate enough never to have been the object of either – the fact that I'm Dan's girlfriend probably has something to do with it, but it's also because I'm 'just a PA', a person of little consequence and no threat to anyone's ego.

Today, egos were taking a pounding all over the place. By mid-afternoon the FTSE 100 had fallen by more than a hundred points and the Dow Jones was down nearly half a per cent. The atmosphere in the trading room was fraught, even more so than usual. A lot of the traders, who like to pride themselves on their poker faces, were starting to look very nervous. By the time the London market closed at four, the FTSE had fallen another hundred points and nervousness had given way to what looked a lot like panic. I caught Ali's eye just after the market closed; she gave a sad little shake of her head. Not a good day.

I didn't get to speak to Dan, although he did wave half-heartedly from the other side of the floor as he was heading off out the door. I couldn't tell at that distance whether his expression was similarly gloomy. But he rang me a little while later from the pub.

'How'd you make out?' I asked, with some trepidation.

'Better than a lot of the guys. Not too bad actually. Turns out my decision to short HBOS was a stroke of genius. You OK? It seemed like Nick was in a foul mood.'

'You have no idea. You going to be there long? Maybe we could go and get some dinner once I get out of here.'

'Cass, I really can't tonight. It turned into a late one last night and I'm shattered. And I want to be on form for your soirée tomorrow. I'll make it up to you, promise. This weekend, I'm all yours.'

Yeah, about that . . . I couldn't face telling him that our plans to spend the entire weekend in bed, guzzling champagne and strawberries and generally being debauched, were going to have to be put on hold.

Disappointed that I wasn't going to see Dan that night, I decided to head home via the DVD place on the high street. I was in the mood for historical romance, preferably involving Rufus Sewell or Orlando Bloom ripping someone's bodice off. The arrival of Nicholas, brandishing a sheaf of papers, drove such thoughts straight out of my head.

'Do you know who the chief executive of Private Capital Trust is, Cassie?' he asked me, perching his not inconsiderably sized arse on the edge of my desk.

'No, Nicholas,' I replied, 'I can't say that I do.'

'Well, do you know what he looks like?'

Of course I bloody don't, you moron, I've just told you I don't know who he is.

'No, I don't, I'm afraid.'

'Well, you should. When the guests arrive at the party tomorrow I want you standing at the door, looking fetching in some little black dress or other, greeting everyone by name. If you think you can manage it, you might want to add in some small talk, nothing too inane, but don't overstretch yourself. Here's the list. Names and photographs, with some brief biographical details. Some of them will be bringing wives, girlfriends and mistresses. Probably not all three at once. Well, hopefully not, anyway. I don't have *their* names and pictures, obviously, so you'll just have to try and negotiate that minefield as gracefully as possible. OK? Right, well, have a good evening.'

My heart sank. There were close to two hundred names on the list, the vast majority white, male and somewhere in their forties of fifties. They all looked exactly alike. They all looked like Nicholas.

Several hours later I passed out on the sofa and dreamed that I was on the judging panel of a bizarre beauty pageant in which all the contestants were overweight, ruddy-faced, middle-aged men. The swimsuit portion of the evening was especially painful. Nicholas came second, and I knew that I'd be in for a hard time the next day at work.

3

Cassie Cavanagh *is flushed with success*

I felt sick. I literally thought I was going to throw up all over my new Marc Jacobs dress, which would have been a shame since I paid close to a month's salary for it. Plus, much as I hated to admit it, Ali had a point about the shoes. For some reason, while I was perfectly capable of dancing around my flat in them, somewhere on the descent down the highly polished marble stairs from the hotel lobby to the party venue, they had transformed themselves from objects of desire to potentially lethal instruments of torture. I was desperate for a drink to take the edge off but equally terrified that, given that I hadn't had time to eat so much as a blueberry muffin all day, anything even vaguely alcoholic would increase the chances of me going arse over tit down the stairs.

My anxiety was only increased by the sight of Nicholas barrelling towards me, stuffed uncomfortably into a tux that looked a size or three too small for him. His face was redder than usual.

'Where the hell did you find the caterers, Cassie? The food looks . . . bizarre,' he spat the word at me, 'and the waitresses look like . . . well . . . like they're all on smack.'

Actually they looked like models but I imagine that Nicholas's taste runs closer to glamour model than supermodel.

'The food does not look bizarre, it looks extraordinary. That's the whole point,' I said, realising that in my irritation I was speaking to him in a way that I might live to regret. 'It's modern Brit with a twist. Did you really want us to be serving up the same tired chicken satay and smoked salmon blinis that they serve at all of these events?'

'I like chicken satay,' he replied gruffly, grabbing a tiny, beautifully crafted foie gras club sandwich from an admittedly anorexic-looking waitress as she slithered past us. He munched on it, glaring at me.

'Humph,' he spluttered. 'Bloody good actually. And you look nice. But I still think the waitresses look like drug addicts.'

That was a compliment! That was two compliments in one sentence. Tempered by one criticism, but still nothing short of miraculous coming from Nicholas. I breathed a sigh of relief. My nerves started to ease. I started to forget about how much my feet hurt. I drank a Kir Royal. Things were looking up.

The venue certainly looked the part, with heavily

subdued, ice-blue lighting, artful arrangements of white orchids on the tables and a huge, faded projection of *Wall Street* playing across the feature wall. I had initially been a little bit nervous about the film idea (was 'greed is good' a valid mantra in 2009?), but Nicholas loved it. The dance floor, on the far side of the room, was illuminated orange and screened from the rest of the room by a row of tall, leafy plants. To the left of the room were huge doors opening out to the stone steps which led up to the garden, an elongated rectangle of perfectly manicured lawn, subtly lit with dozens of tall church candles. Hiring the garden as well as the main venue was probably not completely necessary in October, but Ali, a confirmed pack-a-day girl, insisted that without a convenient smoking space there would be mutiny among the guests. Plus it offered a location for discreet canoodling.

And then the guests started to arrive. I had stashed the list of names and photos which Nicholas had so kindly given me just over twenty-four hours to memorise behind the little reception desk at the entrance so that I could glance it at from time to time. Mercifully, there was a surprising number of women and ethnic minorities among the early arrivals, and they of course were a great deal more memorable. Then things got a little more shaky – it's amazing how similar men of a certain age look when they're all in black tie, particularly when you've never met any of them before and you're on your third glass of champagne. Fortunately, none of them seemed in the slightest bit interested in actually speaking to me, so as long as I could get the names right I didn't have to remember anything else about them, such as where they worked or how many children they had.

But there always has to be one, doesn't there? Some guy who's already been to another bar for a sharpener or three and who decides he's going to make witty conversation with the girl on the door. In this case it was Paul Fitzgerald, an unbearably cocky hedge fund manager from Thornton & Bishop whom I had met before at one of Dan's parties and who decided he would engage me in a lively debate on the pros and cons of quantitative easing – his plan clearly being to embarrass the dumb brunette on the door in front of his friends and, as luck would have it, in front of her boss, since Nicholas had just shown up at my side and was shifting awkwardly from foot to foot like a child in need of the toilet.

'So, what did you think about the Chancellor's announcement today, love?' he asked, with a sly sideways glance to his friends, who all smirked appreciatively. 'Is £75 billion enough to counter deflationary and systemic financial risks? Or are you one of those girls who thinks it's never a good idea to print money?' He was leaning in close to me, and I could smell the gin on his breath.

I smiled at him as sweetly as I could. Had Nicholas not been standing right there I would have simply told him to get lost, he was so obviously just trying to make me feel bad. There was a moment of silence which seemed to go on for ever.

And then the best-looking man at the party came through the door, greeted Nicholas with a warm handshake and a smile, kissed me on the mouth and said, 'You look bloody gorgeous.' Then, turning to face Paul he muttered, 'Stop hitting on my girlfriend, you pillock, she's well out of your league.'

I wanted to kiss him. Again.

As they disappeared off towards the bar, Nicholas took me firmly by the elbow and steered me behind the reception desk.

'No fuck-ups so far?' he asked. He seemed to have got quite drunk very fast.

'No, of course not. It's all going really well.'

'We don't have any journalists at this thing, do we?'

'No, you told me not to invite any.'

'Good. Last thing we need is a bunch of bloody hacks here pissing and moaning about squandering investors' money on champagne. Bunch of bloody freeloaders. If any turn up, just you make sure they aren't allowed in.'

Great, so now I'm the bouncer?

'Of course, Nicholas, it's invitation only.'

'Good. You look nice,' he said, again, and stomped back to join the festivities.

Ali arrived late, looking impossibly tall and svelte in a very short black dress and sky-high red heels. If she wasn't my best friend I would be terrified of her.

'Meet you in the garden in five for a cigarette,' she said as she kissed me hello, before heading off to the bar where she was immediately engulfed by a crowd of men. Moments later I'd summoned Christa, one of the other PAs, to take over meet-and-greet duty while I slipped out.

Ten minutes later I was still standing in the garden alone, freezing to death. And I don't even smoke. I was just about to give up on her when Ali emerged.

'I see Dan's up to his old tricks,' she said, nodding in his direction. He was standing near the bar, laughing at something someone had said, his hand placed on the lower back of the blonde standing next to him. I felt the horrible, jealous twist I get in my gut whenever I see him with someone else, and tried to shake it off.

'He's just flirting, it doesn't mean anything,' I said crossly. 'It's me he's coming home with.'

'I'm only joking,' Ali said, a little half-heartedly. 'Anyway. What a great party! The place looks amazing. And you look amazing. Well done, honey.'

'Glad you think so,' I said, trying to stop my teeth from chattering. 'Now hurry up and smoke your fag before I freeze to death.' A group of traders from Hamilton came out onto the balcony. Instead of coming over to say hello they remained huddled in their corner, talking in unusually subdued voices.

'What's up with that lot?' I asked, inspecting the nearest floral arrangement, a collection of the most beautiful white orchids. I wondered whether I could smuggle it out on the way home. It would look great on my coffee table.

'They're all shitting themselves,' Ali whispered conspiratorially, 'everyone is. Even your Dan the wunderkind.'

'Why?'

'God, Cass, where have you been all day? Last week it was Allen Brothers, this week it's Grant & Waters. Investment banks are going tits up left, right and centre and even those that aren't going under are making savage cutbacks. We're next. The writing is well and truly on the wall now. Rumour has it around a quarter of the traders are looking at redundancy.'

'Oh, my God. But you'll be all right, won't you? And Dan will be? I can't believe this. It's Hamilton Churchill, for God's sake, it's one of the oldest investment banks in the UK.'

'So what? It doesn't mean a thing. Believe me, the powers that be might not let Lloyds TSB go to the wall, but that's because they aren't prepared to let Joe Bloggs lose his life's savings. If we fail, it's just a bunch of rich people who lose their money. That's the theory, anyway. No one gives a shit.' She threw her cigarette to the floor and stomped on it viciously.

'Anyway, come on, let's not let it spoil the party,' she said, trying to reassure me. 'There's a last-days-of-Rome atmosphere building in there and I for one plan to enjoy it.'

So, apparently, did Dan, who was now talking to not one but three blondes, all of whom seemed to be hanging on his every word. Just as they were all squawking at some fantastically amusing comment he had made he caught my eye and abandoned them immediately, making his way through the crowd to my side.

'Great job, babe. It's quite a party,' he said, giving me a kiss. 'And you look beautiful. Have I told you that already?' He escorted me over to a table in the corner and we sat down. He took hold of my hand but he wasn't looking at me. His eyes were constantly roving the room.

'Is everything OK?' I asked him, slipping my hand into his. His palm felt clammy against mine.

'Great, sure. Of course,' he replied, but he was shaking slightly. Whether he was on edge because of the news from the markets or the cocaine he'd no doubt been snorting off the cistern in the men's room all evening, I couldn't be sure.

'I see Ali's hunting the Fox,' Dan said, nodding in Ali's direction. She was cosying up to one of the more dashing attendees at the party, one of the few who in his tux looked more like James Bond than a waiter.

'Hunting a fox?'

'That, as you should remember from your notes, is Jean-Luc Renard, aka the Fox, ridiculously rich French bloke. One of Ali's clients. Married with three kids, not that you'd notice from the way he behaves.'

'Oh, Christ. Does she know he's married?'

Dan laughed and gave me a kiss on the forehead. 'You're so sweet sometimes,' he said. Then all of a sudden he jumped to his feet and said, 'Just spotted someone I need to have a bit of a chat with. Back in a mo'.'

I didn't see him again for about an hour, and when I did he was swaying a little, his arm draped (lovingly? or for support?) around the shoulder of a statuesque brunette in what looked from a distance like a Roland Mouret dress. I recognised her from the guest list – I couldn't remember her name but I did know she was an American, a high-flyer from one of the US banks who managed a squillion-pound investment fund. That knot of jealousy in my stomach tightened just a little. I watched them cross the room together and find a table near the bar, where they continued to talk, their heads just a little too close together.

I was debating the pros and cons of marching over there and introducing myself (pro: I could let her know that he's taken; con: I look like the neurotic jealous girlfriend), when Nicholas appeared, lurching through the crowd, clutching a pint of beer in his hand. Who drinks beer when there's champagne on tap? Boorish, charmless Nicholas, that's who.

'What are you doing over here, all on your own?' he slurred at me, slumping into the chair next to me. 'You've done the hard work, you should be having fun.'

'I was,' I said. 'I am. I'm just . . .'

'Waiting for him.' He jerked his head in Dan's direction. 'Never mind him. You've done a good job tonight. Go and enjoy yourself.' And with that he hauled himself to his feet and staggered off again, sloshing beer on to the floor and guests alike as he went.

For a moment or two, all thoughts of Dan and the American went out of my head. I did a good job. *I did a good job.* Nicholas Hawksworth thought I had done a good job. That was something worth celebrating. From that moment on, the rest of the evening passed in a bit of a blur. With Nicholas's approval gained, I was finally able to relax, hit the bar and mingle.

Ali eventually tore herself away from the Frenchman for long enough for us to have a bit of a dance, the American woman disappeared and everyone finally seemed to forget that their jobs were on the line just long enough to enjoy themselves.

Officially, the party was over at 10.30 (it was just supposed to be cocktails, after all). Dan and a couple of his trader friends, Mick and James, ushered me into a taxi at around midnight. Back at Dan's place in Clerkenwell I went straight to bed, while the boys stayed up playing poker. Dan came to bed at three. He slipped his arms around me and started kissing my neck.

'It was a great night, Cass,' he whispered to me. 'Feel like celebrating?'

'You have to be up in two hours,' I groaned, by which I meant, I have to be up in four hours.

'So I'll sleep for an hour.' He slipped the straps of my camisole off my shoulders.

Sometimes he can be very persuasive.

Cassie Cavanagh *has had the weekend from hell*

Friday was horrible. Truly horrible. I don't know whether it was because he'd had almost no sleep, or because he was so hungover, or simply because he had been on a winning streak for weeks and everyone's luck runs out eventually, but things went badly wrong for Dan.

I didn't even know anything was up until I got a text from Ali in the afternoon. I'd been so busy catching up on all the things that had been put to one side while I'd been party organising, I'd barely looked up from the desk all day. Plus, the success of the party notwithstanding, I was nervous about Nicholas – he'd spent virtually all day on the phone in his office with the door shut, a clear sign that something was wrong.

Around three, my phone buzzed on my desk.
think Dan may be in trouble
from: Ali

Nicholas's office is at one end of the trading floor and my desk is just outside it. Dan is right down at the other end, so I can barely see him from where I sit. I asked Christa, who is PA to Nicholas's second-in-command, to cover my phone for a moment while I popped out, and I quickly walked the length of the floor. I couldn't actually go up to him and have a conversation, of course, not during trading hours, but I'm pretty good at reading him, even if he does have the best poker face on the floor. But you didn't have to know him well to judge his mood today – it was written all over his face, which was deathly pale and covered with a sheen of sweat. His head rested on one hand; his second phone dangled over his shoulder while he barked into the first one.

I returned to my desk.

what's going on? I texted Ali.

not sure bad call maybe

you doing ok? I asked her.

just about breaking even

I rang my sister.

'What is it?' she snapped when she answered. I could hear kids shrieking in the background. Celia has three of her own, but is frequently to be found looking after as many as five or six; because she's a 'full-time mum', other mothers, part-time mums presumably, take advantage of her, apparently. (I once made the mistake of referring to someone as a working mother. 'All mothers work!' Celia said icily. 'Some of us just work harder at it than others.')

'I can't come tonight, Celia. I'll come up tomorrow,

but I cannot do tonight.'

'Cassandra, you had better be outside Kettering station at seven forty-two this evening or I will personally drive down to London to kill you.'

'For God's sake, why? Why do I have to be there tonight?'

'Because I've made arrangements and I'm not changing them now. Whatever it is that is *so* much more important than your family will just have to wait. I'm not arguing about this.'

And with that she hung up.

Dan didn't go to the pub with the rest of the guys after the bell rang, he stayed at his desk. Once the office had emptied out I went over to speak to him.

'How bad?' I asked.

'Pretty fucking catastrophic,' he said without looking up. 'The tip I got, last night, you know from that guy at Midas? Well, either he was trying to stitch me up or he just doesn't know what he's talking about, because I went heavily short on Lloyds TSB and Aviva and they're two of the biggest gainers of the day. Jesus, Cass, I've fucked up, I've really fucked up.' He took my hand in his. 'Can we go home, babe? I just really want to go home.'

Caught between the rock of disappointing my parents and the hard place of exacerbating Dan's misery, I foundered.

'What is it?' he asked, looking up at me. 'You still got work to do?'

'I can't, Dan. I'm really sorry, I have to go home. To Kettering, I mean. I meant to tell you yesterday but we never really got the time to—'

'Right,' he said, withdrawing his hand from mine and getting to his feet. 'All right then. I'll see you when I see you, I guess.'

'Dan, please don't be angry with me,' I pleaded, but he was already walking away, his head bowed, looking more dejected than I can ever remember seeing him. I felt awful, heartbroken. By the time I caught the six fifty-two from St Pancras to Kettering, heartbreak had turned to rage. I was furious with my sister. How dare she guilt-trip me into going to this bloody party, into leaving my boyfriend at the very moment he needed me most? Silently I fumed for the next fifty-six minutes, planning exactly what I was going to say to her when I saw her.

Frustratingly I had to rethink my opening gambit ('You bitch, Celia') when I saw her standing on the platform, the baby in her arms, three-year-old Rosie in the pushchair and five-year-old Tom crawling around on the floor pushing a small vehicle and making impressively accurate truck noises. Celia smiled winningly at me.

'Look, kids, it's Auntie Cassie! Come all the way from London to see us!'

'Hello, darlings!' I cooed back. It's difficult to stay pissed off when you have two blond angels running at you, arms outstretched, gurgling wholehearted hellos. Disentangling myself from the children, I gave Celia an unenthusiastic peck on the cheek and took Monty, the baby, from her arms.

'God, he's huge,' I exclaimed. 'I can't believe how much he's grown.'

'That's the thing about babies,' Celia replied sourly. 'If you only see them once every six months then you will be amazed by their growth spurts.'

'He looks exactly like his dad,' I said, knowing that would annoy her. The other kids have far more of their father in them than they do of Celia, too, and she hates it when people point this out. 'Where is Michael, by the way? Is he not joining us for dinner?'

'Change of plan,' she said with an air of weary resignation. 'The "quick pint" he went for after work turned into three, so I told him to just stay there. Do you mind if we get takeaway instead? Not sure I can be bothered to go out. Sorry, Cass.' My anger at her dissipated and was replaced with guilt. Celia looked wiped out. Her face was pale and her eyes ringed with dark circles. With her hair scraped back into a ponytail and wearing a less-than-flattering tracksuit she looked closer to thirty-five than twenty-seven. It was hardly surprising though. How could she not be exhausted with three children of five and under to take care of and a twenty-eighth wedding anniversary party to plan, not to mention having to cope with her feckless husband and recalcitrant younger sister.

'That's OK, Cee, takeaway's fine. It'll be nice to hang out with you and the kids at home.'

'Great. And I am sorry, Cassie, that you had to change your plans for this weekend. I know you're not keen on family things.' You've got to hand it to her, Celia knows how to twist the knife.

Dinner was a rather greasy Chinese eaten while sitting on the floor and watching the DVD of *Mamma Mia*, Rosie and Tom singing along lustily and tunelessly, getting all the lyrics wrong. Eventually, Celia put them to bed.

'Wouldn't usually let them stay up this late, but they were desperate to see their Auntie Cassie,' Celia said as I opened a bottle of Rioja. 'They see you so infrequently.'

We were sitting at her rather formal dining room table. I felt an interrogation coming on.

'How's work?' she asked. 'Are you worried, you know, with the credit crunch and this recession business? Do you think your bank's going to be OK? Because Mike was saying that quite a few of the banks are in trouble.' Michael, Celia's husband, is a solicitor with a small local firm and something of a know-it-all. He spends most of his time drafting contracts for property sales but he likes to pretend that he has insider knowledge of the business world.

'It's mostly the US ones,' I said, with a breezy confidence that I didn't feel as strongly as I might have done a few days previously.

'Really? Because Mike was saying that quite a few of the British banks are having problems, too.'

Conversations with Celia are often like this. Mike was saying this, Mike was saying that. It drives me up the wall. She appears to have no opinions of her own, except for those on what Mike would call 'women's subjects' like childcare and cake-baking.

'We're fine, Celia, really. My job's great. I'm actually in my boss's good books for a change – I had to organise this drinks party for the clients and it was a real success. It was in this amazing hotel, the Hempel, you know, designed by Anouska Hempel—'

'Ooh, did I tell you I got the function room at the Holiday Inn for tomorrow?' Celia said, cutting me off in full flow. 'It's ever so nice, actually. It's out on the A43, towards Corby. Lovely place. There's a gym and a pool and everything. I think it's a three-star. Anyway, the function room is lovely – nice views of the countryside and fields and things, and they've given us a really good deal on the buffet.'

'Sounds great, Cee,' I said, pouring myself another glass of wine. As I replaced the bottle on the table, Celia picked it up and put the cork back in.

'That's probably enough for tonight – don't want to be hungover tomorrow, do we?'

Unused to being sent to bed at ten thirty in the evening on a Friday night, I hung around downstairs once Celia had gone up to bed, retrieved the bottle of red wine from its hiding place and rang Ali.

'Where did you disappear to last night?' I asked her when she picked up.

'I went home.'

'No, you did not. I saw you with that French guy again. What's going on?'

She laughed throatily. 'Oh, it's nothing really,' she said.

'It didn't look like nothing.'

'Well, maybe it's something. I've been . . . seeing him on and off for a little while now.'

'You kept that quiet. Is that because he's married?'

'Oh, don't, Cass. It's not like I'm trying to get him to leave his wife. He's French – you know what they're like. They all have a bit on the side. The wife probably does, too.'

'And you're OK with that?'

'I'm great with that. Suits me down to the ground. Clandestine meetings, amazing sex and no relationship hassle. No meeting of the parents, no hanging out with his boring friends, no emotional dramas . . . You should try it. It's bloody fantastic.'

I was woken the following morning by Tom demanding that I play football with him immediately. I looked at my phone. Seven fifteen.

'Too early, Tommy. Let Auntie Cass sleep just a bit longer and then we'll play football, I promise.'

'But I want to play *now*,' he wheedled, pulling the duvet off the bed. I grabbed it back. Our tug-of-war was interrupted by Celia.

'Tom, what are doing in here? Leave Auntie Cassie alone and go downstairs to have your breakfast.'

'But I want to play *football*,' Tom insisted.

'Cassie doesn't have time for football, Tom. She's going to be busy with me today.' All of a sudden a kickabout in the garden with Tom was sounding rather attractive. Tom started to whimper. Celia ignored him. 'Better jump in the shower, Cass, before Mike gets in there. We've got loads to do this morning.'

I looked at my phone again. No missed calls, no text messages. I'd called Dan four times the previous evening and sent two texts telling him I loved him. He was officially ignoring me.

Why I had to be dragged out of bed at half past seven I have no idea, since we didn't actually get going until after nine. I think Celia just cannot stand the idea that I am lying in bed doing nothing when she is making breakfast, supervising baths, brushing hair and selecting outfits. In any case, I was showered and dressed and just helping myself to a second piece of toast when Mike emerged wearing a ridiculous pair of green and brown checked trousers and a brown sweater.

'All right, Cass?' he said, giving me a peck on the cheek. 'You made it then?'

'I did indeed. How are you?'

'Oh, not so bad, not so bad. Bit of a sore head this morning, you know how it is. Off to play eighteen holes at the club with a couple of chaps from work. How's your job going, by the way? You still got one? Hamilton Churchill's not gone under yet?' he enquired cheerily.

'It's going fine, Mike,' I said, gritting my teeth.

'Even so, you might want to start looking around, you know, keep an eye out for other opportunities. Just to be safe. Because from what I hear, there are going to be a lot of jobs going in your sector.'

I chewed my toast and clamped my mouth shut. Fortunately, we were interrupted by Rosie who came tearing into the room and flung herself across my lap.

'Lucy's got a party dress on,' Rosie announced proudly, showing me her doll, which had been draped in sparkly silver wrapping paper.

'And doesn't she look lovely?' I replied, thinking, *wrapping paper*. Oh, shit. A gift. I had completely forgotten to get my parents a gift. Shit, shit, shit.

Since Mike was golfing all day and therefore unable to either help out with party preparations or look after the children, Celia had arranged for Rosie and Monty to spend the day with Jo, her best friend who has kids of similar ages. After Jo's we drove Tom to his karate lesson, then into town to buy balloons and glittery, sparkly things which Celia said were for sprinkling over tables. We picked up the cake, a rather boring white square with *'Congratulations!'* written on it in blue icing and *'Tim and Susan, 28 happy years'* underneath in pink. From there we went to the dry cleaner's to fetch Mike's 'good' suit, to the florist's to pick up the fifteen floral centrepieces (it's a good thing Celia drives an Espace), and from there to the school to pick Tom up from karate. We drove him home for a hurriedly devoured sandwich, after which he too was left with Jo.

'All right then, we'd best get over to the Holiday Inn and start getting everything ready,' Celia said as we drove off, waving goodbye to a tearful Rosie who isn't used to spending quite so much time apart from Mummy.

'Yeah,' I said slowly, wondering if I should have broken the news about the present to Celia when she wasn't behind the wheel of a large, fast-moving vehicle. 'The thing is, Cee, I sort of forgot, you know, there was so much going on at work this week and worries with Dan and everything and . . .'

'You forgot what?'

'The present.'

After several minutes of screeched expressions of disbelief, Celia finally executed a furious and dangerous U-turn and we headed back into town to Peacocks, the local department store.

'You have twenty minutes,' Celia hissed at me, 'to find something decent and pay for it. I cannot believe you have done this, Cassandra. Today of all days.' Shopping, needless to say, was a fraught experience, made all the worse by the fact that everything I selected was dismissed by my sister as overpriced and useless.

'What on earth would they do with a hurricane lamp? We don't get many hurricanes around here, and in any case, they never burn candles except on birthdays.' The set of Georg Jensen silver leaf bowls was also rejected out of hand, as was a beautiful purple and turquoise glass platter. Eventually, much against my will, I was persuaded to purchase a Mini Chopper food processor which, Celia insisted, Mum had been hankering after for some time.

'Not much of a gift for Dad though, is it?' I objected.

'Of course it is,' she said crossly. 'Mum makes the food and Dad eats it, so they both benefit.' Too cowed to argue, I got out my credit card and went to the till. Fortunately they offered a gift-wrapping service in-store, so all I needed then was a card. I picked out something bland and unmemorable from the stationery shop next door.

By the time we got to the Holiday Inn, Celia was in a vile temper.

'We're an hour behind schedule,' she snapped at me as she slammed the door of the car and marched around to the boot. 'By now we should have . . .' she fished a list out of her handbag, '. . . arranged and set tables, put up the "Congratulations" banner and decorated the memory tree.'

'The what tree?' I asked as she shoved a box full of baubles into my arms.

'Memory tree. It's like a Christmas tree, only decorated with mementoes from Mum and Dad's past. Their wedding invitation, honeymoon pictures, stuff like that.'

Despite myself, I raised my eyes to the heavens. Big mistake.

'Don't roll your eyes at me, Cassandra,' she screeched at me. 'It's a lovely idea. And if it doesn't turn out perfectly it will be all your fault.'

The decorating went relatively smoothly, but unfortunately, final preparations for my parents' arrival were marred ever so slightly by me knocking over a table laden with canapés just as Mum and Dad were due to show up. In front of the assembled guests, Celia went into apoplexy.

'Cassie!' she hissed at me as I crawled around on the carpet, picking up sausage rolls. 'What on earth are you doing?'

'I'm sorry,' I huffed back at her. 'It wasn't like I did it on purpose.' Tom and Rosie, who had just arrived with their dad, had joined me on the carpet. Tom grabbed a handful of mini chicken kievs and lobbed them at his sister, who shrieked with delight, prompting their irate mother to grab each child by an arm and drag them to their feet.

'I told you not to have that second glass of wine,' Celia snapped at me. 'You're drunk already. Honestly.'

I was just about to launch into a riposte about my legendary capacity to hold my liquor when my parents marched proudly through the door to be greeted by the sight of their warring daughters and howling grandchildren. It wasn't quite the welcome Celia had planned.

Fortunately, that was the low point of the evening. Things got a great deal better from then on. My parents, decked out in what my mother might term their Sunday best (Dad in a dark blue suit, Mum in a purple dress which almost certainly came from Marks &

49

Spencer) seemed to enjoy themselves tremendously. Mum was obviously very touched that so many people had made it (there were about sixty people which is pretty good going for a twenty-eighth, if you ask me), and she seemed absolutely delighted with my gift.

'I owe you one, Cee,' I said to my sister as my mother oohed and aaahed over the range of Mini Chopper features.

'Just one? You think so?' Celia replied, giving me a dark look.

After everyone had helped themselves to a surfeit of sausage rolls and mini quiches from the buffet, Dad gave a lovely speech at the end of which he thanked his 'beautiful daughters for organising such a wonderful party'.

Celia shot daggers at me. Guilt welled up in my chest. Bad daughter, bad sister.

'I'll tell him it had nothing to do with me,' I whispered to Celia, who was smiling through gritted teeth.

'Oh, don't bother, Cassie. Why don't you run off and ring your boyfriend? Again.'

It was true that I had absented myself from the party on more than one occasion to ring Dan, but his phone had been turned off all night. Eventually, just we were leaving, I got a text, saying:

Am fine Cass, stop hassling. Cu when u get back.

My sister dropped me off at the station after lunch on Sunday. She gave me a perfunctory peck on the cheek as I slipped out of the car.

'Oh, I forgot to say,' she said with a smile, 'there's engineering works on the line today. You'll have to get the replacement bus service from St Albans to Bedford.' Then she slammed the door and drove off. Door to door, it took me four hours to get home.

When I did finally make it back to an empty flat, I collapsed on the sofa and opened my laptop, logging onto my Facebook page to see if anyone else had done anything interesting that weekend. There was a message from Ali.

Hey Cass, just tried your mobile but it went straight to voicemail. You're probably on the train. Just wanted to warn you there's a piece in the Telegraph *today about Hamilton, no source but they're predicting hundreds of redundancies. I fear bloodshed on the floor. Hope the family gathering was not as hellish as predicted. See you tomorrow xx A*

I opened a bottle of wine and fought the urge to ring Dan. I lost the battle on the third glass, but just as I had feared, he wasn't picking up. I tried to watch Sky-plussed episodes of *Grey's Anatomy* but even McSteamy couldn't hold my concentration for more than a few minutes at a time. I was filled with Sunday-evening unease, that vague feeling of foreboding so reminiscent of unfinished homework and maths tests on a Monday. For once, I was disappointed that Jude wasn't in – she's very good at pep talks, whereas talking to Ali, I was convinced, would only make me feel more nervous about the very real prospect that Dan was on the verge of losing his job.

Cassie Cavanagh *is unemployed*

I wasn't expecting it. That Monday when I arrived in the office, business carried on as usual. The atmosphere was a little subdued, but it was not as bad as I had been led to expect by Ali's rather alarming message the night before. To be fair to her, the piece in the *Sunday Telegraph*, which I called up on my computer that morning, did give serious cause for concern. It claimed that Hamilton had suffered heavy losses in recent weeks and up to a third of traders and analysts could go, as well as around a fifth of the support staff. I still didn't expect it. Dan might have had a bad day on Friday but he was known as one of the best traders on the floor and he'd made a ton of money for the company over the past year.

Now I can't believe how deluded I was. When Nicholas called me into his office that afternoon, for one ridiculous moment I thought he was going to heap more praise on me for the party success. When he told me to close the door I imagined perhaps that he was going to explain how, in the light of forthcoming cutbacks, my job might have to change. Perhaps I'd be looking at a heavier workload. Perhaps, I thought, I might even see a bit more money as a result.

I suppose the best you can say is that it didn't last long. It was over within minutes. Senior staff were now going to have to share assistants, he told me, they could no longer afford to keep one each. It had been decided that on the basis of her superior experience Christa Freeman would stay on to cover the UK equities desk. I would be paid until the end of the month, plus a 'generous' redundancy package, but I could leave straight away. My services, Nicholas said, without looking up from his computer screen, were no longer required.

I just stood there. I didn't say anything. I didn't move. For what seemed like an age, a perfect silence descended over his office. Eventually, he looked up at me.

'I'm very sorry, Cassie. That'll be all.'

And just like that, I was dismissed.

I could feel them watching me. Everyone was watching me as I emerged from his office, my face burning, desperate not to cry. They knew, I thought. They all knew. Looking back on it, they probably weren't watching me; they almost certainly didn't know. Why on earth would they care if Nicholas Hawksworth's PA got sacked? Most of them would struggle to remember my name, they wouldn't be concerned about me losing my job. But Christa bloody smug Freeman certainly knew – she gave me the sickliest of saccharine smiles and then went back to her typing. *I still have work to do*, was the subtext.

I looked for Dan but couldn't see him. I searched for Ali and caught her eye. Seeing the expression on my face she ended her call and came straight over to me – committing the punishable-by-sacking crime of leaving her desk during trading hours.

'He didn't, did he?'

'He bloody well did,' I said. 'Did you know this was going to happen?'

'Of course not, Cassie. I knew all our jobs were on the line, though. I told you that. I warned you.'

'I didn't realise you meant mine,' I said, tears welling up in my eyes.

'Don't cry,' she said, slipping her hand into mine and squeezing it. 'Cry later. Don't cry here.' She went back to her desk and I started to pack my things. Someone (that bitch Christa probably) had thoughtfully placed a couple of cardboard boxes next to my desk while I had been in Nicholas's office.

Ten minutes later I was perched on a stool in a corner of the Beluga Bar having just ordered a large gin and tonic from the beautiful Czech girl behind the bar, a favourite among the Hamilton traders. I took a gulp of my drink. I couldn't believe it. This could not be happening to me. Cast aside. Redundant. Just a few days after lauding my incomparable organisational skills, they were sacking me. I had been dumped, deemed the lesser assistant, labelled dispensable.

About halfway through my second drink, denial was replaced with rage. By the time Dan turned up, a couple of friends in tow, I was simmering with fury. Dan took one look at me and carefully steered his friends to the other side of the room before eventually coming over. He ordered a beer and another G&T for me, but only after making small talk with the pretty Czech girl. By the time he turned to talk to me I was just about ready to explode.

'I'm sorry, Cass,' he said, enveloping me in his arms. 'It's a totally shit thing to happen. Nicholas is such a prick.'

'It's unbelievable,' I hissed at him. 'I can't believe they chose to keep Christa on and they're sacking me. I'm fucking indispensable! Do they not realise that?'

'Cassie, you're not indispensable, you're a secretary,' Dan said in an unhelpfully condescending tone. I burst into tears. An expression of panic crossed his face and he glanced around the room to see if anyone was watching. Dan doesn't do emotional melodramas, particularly in front of his friends.

'Jesus Christ, Cassie,' he whispered. 'Please don't do that. Don't make a scene.' He fished around in his pocket and handed me a second-hand Kleenex. Then he said, 'You're being really selfish, you know that? You'll get another job – you can work for any type of company, you can work for bloody Sainsbury's. If I lose my job, or if one of the boys over there gets sacked, we're screwed, do you understand that? We'll never get re-hired in this market. Now go to the loo and sort yourself out, you look awful.'

I fled to the ladies. Perhaps he was right. Perhaps I was being selfish. Traders like Dan and Ali stood to lose a great deal more than I did if they lost their jobs. And my skills were a little more transferable. He certainly had a point about me looking awful. I scrutinised myself in the mirror. My face was pale and blotchy, my mascara had started to run and I seemed to have managed (God knows when) to have dribbled coffee down the front of my shirt. Fantastic. Whipping out my make-up bag I got started on emergency maintenance. I was just re-applying my mascara when the door to the ladies burst open, giving me such a fright that I almost took my eye out, and Christa marched in.

'Cassie,' she intoned mournfully, cocking her head to one side like a puppy. 'I am so sorry. You must be devastated.'

'Well, I wouldn't say devastated, Christa. It's not like it was my dream job. Plenty of secretarial jobs going around.' I sniffed, dabbing at my eyelid with a Kleenex, removing the ugly black smear caused by Christa's dramatic entrance a moment previously. And as I said this, I felt it. Dan was right. I was right. I was an extremely competent PA. I would find another job. A better job. I turned to Christa, who was still pulling her faux-concerned face, and gave her the most dazzling smile I could muster under the circumstances.

'Must dash, anyway. Meeting friends for cocktails. Good luck with Nicholas. Don't forget, just one shot in his latte in the morning or he gets very jittery.' Ha. Bring Nicholas anything weaker than a triple-shot in the morning and your chances of making it to lunchtime alive were slim to none.

Feeling better about things already, I decided that an early exit was probably best, particularly since the three double G&Ts I'd consumed in under half an hour were making me feel a little woozy. Dan was sitting on the stool I had vacated, flirting with the Czech girl. Yes, he could be romantic sometimes, at others he could be a real shit. Still, determined to save face I went over and picked up my rather forlorn little box of belongings.

'You not staying?' he asked.

'Not really in the mood right now,' I said. 'Think I'll make it an early night.'

'You sure?' he asked, putting his arm around me, but I could tell he was relieved. 'Sorry if I snapped at you earlier. We're all just a bit on edge. And I'm sorry about the job, but I know you, Cass, you'll have no trouble finding something else.' He kissed me on the forehead. I hate it when he does that. It's so dismissive, so un-boyfriend-like. It's the kind of kiss you give a child, or an ageing aunt. Determined not to let him get to me, I smiled my breeziest, haven't-got-a-care-in-the-world smile, turned on my heel and left the bar. When I glanced back over my shoulder to see if he was watching me leave, I saw that he was simultaneously waving his mates over and dialling a number on his mobile phone.

By the time I got back to Clapham I was too distracted by concerns about Dan to worry about the fact that I had just lost my job. It wasn't just the way he had acted that evening, it was his behaviour of the past few days, ever since I said I was going away on Friday night. I decided that he must be punishing me. I hadn't been there for him in his hour of need; now he was repaying the favour. There was a kind of logic to it, I supposed, but it still seemed rather petty.

Jude was in the kitchen making something that smelt deliciously of lime and chillies. I dumped my cardboard box of belongings on the floor and slumped onto the sofa. She carried on stirring, oblivious to my distress.

'I'm making aubergine and tofu satay,' she called out. 'Do you want some?'

'Is there anything to drink in the fridge?' I asked.

'Not unless you bought something. There was about a glass of that white left from the bottle you opened last night, and that's gone in the sauce.'

I groaned dramatically.

'Cassie, what's going on?' she asked, and I recounted the whole sorry tale.

Jude, as ever, was full of practical advice. Over a surprisingly tasty dinner (Jude's a good cook, but I'm always suspicious of anything containing tofu, quorn or any other weird meat substitutes), accompanied by sparkling mineral water ('So much better to make plans with a clear head,' Jude said, a sentiment with which I strongly disagree), she came up with the *Recession Buster*, a Plan of Action which I was to follow over the next couple of weeks.

Recession-Busting Action Number One: Register with morale-demolishing temp agencies.

When I tried to object she cut me off. 'This is not an easy market, Cassie. I know you think that with your skills you should walk into another job, but I wouldn't count on it. Things are tough out there.'

'Jude, you're a student,' I pointed out. 'How would you know?'

She tossed me a copy of the *Guardian*. *'Jobless Total Rises to Two Million'*, the headline read. I must stop reading *Metro*, it really is useless. All right then, Office Angels here I come.

Recession-Busting Action Number Two: Start counting the pennies (and stop having any fun).

'You could start keeping a money diary,' she suggested, 'write down everything you spend every day and see where you can make cutbacks.'

'Mmm,' I replied, non-committally, fishing around in my bag for my mobile. There was a message from Ali asking if I was OK. Nothing from Dan.

'It's a really useful way to identify areas where you're overspending,' she said.

'Yeah, I really don't think that's going to be necessary, Jude. I'm getting a pay-off, and I'm paid for the next two weeks, so I'll be fine. You don't have to worry about the rent.'

She opened her mouth to say something but thought better of it, instead spooning in a final mouthful of tofu.

Recession-Busting Action Number Three: Come up with a five-year (yawn) plan.

'This is starting to sound a bit Stalinist even by your standards, Jude,' I said.

'Nonsense. It's just being sensible. It's about time you figured out what you want to do with your life. After all, being a PA in the City wasn't exactly your dream career, was it?' she asked.

True, but then I didn't really have a dream career. I'd never given it all that much thought.

'This could be a blessing in disguise, Cassie. It might be the ideal opportunity to move into a field which really inspires you.' There was a long pause. 'What does really inspire you?'

Now there's a question. I have never had a career plan. Beyond getting the hell out of Kettering and coming to London (or going to New York, I didn't have particularly strong feelings either way) and earning enough money to keep me in shoes, cocktails and the occasional weekend in Paris or Rome, I really didn't mind that much what I did. Unlike Jude, who was taking an MA in Cultural Studies at Goldsmith as a prelude to working for some anti-capitalist think tank whose name I forget, or Ali, who did maths at Cambridge in order to pave the way for making a lot of money in the City, I had never come up with a game plan. I did a degree in business administration, mostly because my father insisted that people with degrees in business administration would never be out of work for long (about to test that theory, Dad), but I had never really pictured myself with a career. A job, yes, but not a career.

'There must be something, Cassie,' Jude prompted, fidgeting with the worry beads she wears around her neck, a sure sign that she was getting impatient.

'Well, I've always fancied the idea of doing something in the media,' I said, 'or fashion, maybe. Or design. I like interior design. But then again, I think I might have a good head for business. And I like food, of course . . . and booze, obviously, so anything in those fields, I guess. Or, come to think of it, I could do something in events organising. I reckon I'd probably be quite good at that. Perhaps I could try out for the *X Factor* . . .'

Jude fidgeted more frantically. 'OK, lots of ideas there, but I think you probably need to shorten the list a bit . . . And will you stop looking at your phone all the time, Cassie? You need to focus.'

All of a sudden, tears sprang to my eyes. 'I lost my job this afternoon, Jude – I really don't think it's the end of the world if I haven't found full employment within five hours of being made redundant, is it? I can't think about jobs now, OK? I'm worried about Dan.'

She sighed heavily and got up to clear the plates.

'Yes, I know,' I snapped at her, 'you don't like him! You've told me a million bloody times. I get it, you don't like Dan. But I do, and he's going through something, and I'm worried about him and about us . . .' I grabbed a Kleenex and blew my nose. Jude sat down next to me and wrapped her arm around my shoulder and made soothing noises.

'It'll be OK, Cass. He'll be OK. How about we go to the Rose & Crown and have a drink? I'm buying.'

I perked up a little. Jude almost never offers to get the drinks in.

I awoke the following day with a raging hangover. It turns out that one of the barmen in the Rose has a serious crush on Jude and as a result was keen to ply us with free drinks all night. For a second when I woke, all, with the exception of my aching head, was well with the world. For just a moment I forgot that I was unemployed. I even had a split second of panic when I looked at my alarm clock and realised it was almost eleven – I was late for work! Except that I wasn't. No work to be late for. I checked my phone (no missed calls), rolled over and went back to sleep.

At about half twelve, my phone buzzed. *Private number calling*.

'Hello?' I croaked.

'Cass, it's me.' Ali, calling from work. 'Are you OK?'

'Yeah, fine. Pissed off. Hungover. How are things there? Nicholas had a nervous breakdown yet?'

There was a long, ominous pause.

'Shit, are you OK, Al? They're not getting rid of you too, are they?'

'Not me, but they've already called in six or seven guys this morning. Dan was one of them. I'm sorry, Cass. Seems like that big trading loss on Friday just came at the worst possible time.'

'Oh, my God! Where is he? Is he still there? Can you put me through?'

'No, he and Mick Knight – he's also got the sack – left as soon as they were told, about an hour ago. They're probably in the Beluga. I just thought I ought to let you know. He looked pretty awful when he came out.'

I couldn't believe he hadn't called me. I hauled myself out of bed and into the shower, made a strong pot of coffee and called Dan's mobile. No answer. Scrolling down through my contacts, I found Mick's number. I knew it wasn't a great idea to try to trace one's boyfriend through his mates (particularly through his recently sacked mates), but it felt as though Dan hadn't been answering my calls for days. I was starting to wonder whether there was something up with his phone. On the third ring, Mick answered.

'Oh, hi Cassie. No, he's not here, he came for one, then he buggered off. Not really in the mood for a session, I think.'

We shared condolences and I hung up.

Turning up at one's boyfriend's flat unannounced is probably an even worse idea than ringing around his mates to track him down, but I was determined to see Dan. I knew that if I could just get to talk to him he'd feel better. I could spoil him for a day or two and, after a suitable mourning period, we could figure out what he could do next. Dressed in skinny jeans, the Chloé boots I'd got on sale last spring and a little fake-fur coat over the halter-neck top he likes me in, I hopped on the tube and made my way to Farringdon and up to Rosebery Avenue. I buzzed the intercom and waited. No answer. I buzzed again. No one came. Up on the second floor, where Dan's bedroom is, I thought for a moment that I saw the blinds move, though I couldn't be sure. I rang his mobile. I left a message.

'Dan, it's me. I've come to see you. Please ring me back. I'm going to go to the Ambassador and wait for an hour or so, so please come and find me. I'm sorry, I'm so sorry about the job, about everything. Please come and find me, I really want to talk to you.'

Eventually I gave up standing around in the street like a lovesick puppy and headed for the pub. I ordered an orange juice. Half an hour later, I ordered a coffee. Half an hour after that, I thought, oh fuck it, and went for a gin and tonic. Hair of the dog. No sign of Dan, no texts and no missed calls. Eventually, at around three, I gave up and started to wend my weary way home. The prospect of going back to an empty flat (or worse, a flat occupied by Jude, who would have me making lists and fine-tuning the Plan of Action), was too depressing to contemplate, so instead of changing to the Northern Line at Embankment, I just kept going, all the way round to South Ken. I got out of the tube, hopped on a bus, and within minutes was standing outside the gloriously dramatic window display at Harvey Nichols.

Some people drink, some people take drugs. I shop. I realise that it is incomprehensible to many people (most of them straight men), but there is something incredibly *hopeful* about buying new clothes. Yes, it is ridiculous to imagine that a garment can change your life, but there can be no doubting the mood-enhancing, confidence-boosting power of a beautiful new coat, or a killer pair of heels, or, as turned out to be the case that afternoon, an incredibly flattering pair of size eight jeans. Size eight! My heart soared. All the stress of the past couple of weeks must have been taking its toll. They weren't cheap. 7 For All Mankind jeans do not come cheap – but it could have been worse. I could have gone for the McQueen ones which were around three times the price.

I was standing in the changing room, admiring my form and congratulating myself on my thrift, when my mobile rang. At long last! It was Dan.

'Hey baby,' I said, 'how are you? Where are you? I want to see you.'

'Hi, Cass,' he said, his voice sounding small and far away. 'I'm OK. I'm just . . . out and about, you know.'

It didn't sound like he was out and about. I couldn't hear any background noise, no pub hubbub, no traffic.

'Are you going home soon? Can I meet you there? Or you could come round to mine?'

There was a long pause, so long I thought we might have been cut off.

'Dan? Are you still there?'

'Cassie, it's just been a really shit day.'

'I know, I know it has, it's awful. I just want to see you.'

Another long pause.

'Cassie. I'm really sorry.'

'Tomorrow then?'

'No, Cassie . . .' he gave a long, heartfelt sigh. 'I can't . . . do this at the moment.'

'You can't do what?' A lump rose to my throat.

'Do the whole relationship thing, you know? Things are just . . . really weird at the moment and I need to be on my own, focus one hundred per cent on myself, on finding a new job. You know how it is.'

'No, I don't know, Dan,' I said, trying as hard as I could to stop the tears coming. 'I really don't.'

There was a long, painful silence.

'I have to go, Cassie. I'm really sorry.'

He hung up.

I took the 7 For All Mankind jeans off, sat down on the floor and burst into tears. Seconds later, a rail-thin sales assistant wearing crimson lipstick yanked the curtain open, revealing me, sitting cross-legged on the floor in my halter neck and purple knickers, to most of the Womenswear (Casual) section.

'Is everything all right?' she asked, plummily.

'No, it bloody well isn't,' I sobbed, grabbing at the curtain and attempting to cover myself up with my coat.

'Well . . . I am sorry but there are other people waiting

to try things on,' the assistant huffed. 'So perhaps you could deal with your . . . problems somewhere else.'

'Yes, all right,' I sniffed. I was tempted to call her a heartless bitch, but instead I just asked, ever so politely, if she would mind closing the curtain so that I could get dressed and continue my meltdown somewhere else.

I changed as quickly as I could, wiped my eyes and, with as much dignity as I could muster, stalked over to the till to pay for the jeans. Nervous breakdown in front of snooty sales assistant or no, flattering size eight skinny jeans at less than £150 don't come along every day. You have to embrace opportunities like these when they are presented to you.

With the jeans purchased, I composed myself and ventured downstairs, to International Contemporary Collections. Since I was already here and had a perfect excuse for indulging in a little retail therapy I felt I might as well carry on. I purchased a gorgeous Vivienne Westwood print blouse and a cute pair of earrings from Juicy Couture before stocking up on some essential beauty things on the ground floor. As I left the shop I realised that I had entered my pin number at the till without even looking at the total. I had no idea what I had just spent and I really, really didn't care.

6

Cassie Cavanagh *will shop if she wants to, shop if she wants to, shop if she wants to*

Two days after Dan broke up with me, the Harvey Nicks bags still lay untouched in the corner of my bedroom. I was, I have to admit, wallowing a bit. After I returned from my shopping trip on Tuesday I'd rung Ali, who hastened round with several bottles of booze. I can't remember exactly what we drank now. I think she made cocktails of some sort. It's all a bit of a blur. At some point I crawled under my duvet and have hibernated there for the best part of forty-eight hours.

Occasionally I've surfaced to go to the loo or to pick, half-heartedly, at the contents of the fridge. But other than that I've loyally floundered in smelly pyjamas, watching DVDs borrowed from Jez, the bloke from downstairs who, fortunately for me, owns a vast collection of violent action movies and political thrillers. As far as I'm concerned, these are the only genres that can be tolerated post break-up. Far better, in the early days of heartbreak, to wade knee-deep in blood and guts than to weep for lost love, so my usual collection – *Love Actually*, *How to Lose a Guy in Ten Days* and various Jane Austen TV adaptations – has been banished indefinitely.

Needless to say I'm a terrible person to live with at the moment, but Jude has been an angel. She's brought me cups of tea accompanied by Marmite on toast (even though she loathes Marmite and just the smell of it makes her gag), she's ventured downstairs to Jez's flat to exchange *Hard to Kill* for *Kill Harder*, she even offered to do my laundry (I accepted). Apart from her initial, knee-jerk 'that sodding wanker' comment, she did not bad-mouth Dan at all, she listened sympathetically when I raged about him, she nodded dutifully when I told her how wonderful he was and how I couldn't live without him and how I must, must have him back.

However, this, the morning of day three AD (After Dan), Jude woke me at eight thirty brandishing a cup of tea and a determined frown.

'Jesus, Jude,' I complained, 'it's not like I've got a job to go to.'

'Precisely,' she said, snapping open the blinds to reveal skies that looked as grey and miserable as I felt. 'I know you're feeling down, but enough is enough. You have to get up and start putting the Recession Buster into action. I want you online by nine a.m., checking out the job sites. Register with some agencies.' She smiled at me, wrinkling her nose just a little. 'And you really ought to think about taking a shower.'

I clung on to my duvet for as long as possible, only venturing from the safety of my bedroom once I'd heard the front door slam as Jude left for college. I couldn't face any further admonishments from my well-meaning flatmate and I had to admit that she was right. It was true, joining the ranks of the great unwashed was hardly likely to help out in the job-search stakes, or more importantly in the getting-Dan-back stakes. And I had decided, over the course of my morning cup of tea, that all this wallowing was ridiculous. I could get him back. I *would* get him back. This whole break-up thing was just an overreaction – an understandable overreaction – to the shock of losing his job. I would leave him alone for a few more days and then I'd ring him. He might not agree to give it another go straight away, he was much too stubborn for that – but I'd talk him round. I can be persuasive too, sometimes.

I showered, washed my hair, put on a life-affirming outfit (the new skinny jeans might have a whiff of sadness about them, but they still looked good) and flipped open my laptop. I did not, as Jude had suggested, start looking at recruitment agency sites, but fell at the first hurdle and went straight to Facebook. I brought up Dan's profile and felt a sharp twinge of agony as I noticed that he had changed his status from 'in a relationship' to 'single'. Still, it could be worse, he could have de-friended me. There were a bunch of messages from various friends and colleagues expressing sympathy over his job loss. I scrolled down. And then my heart stopped. There, plain for everyone to see, was a message from someone called Tania Silk.

Missed you last night. Hope all's well. Later? xxxxx

Who the fuck was Tania Silk? I clicked on her name and a picture came up, a full-length shot of a tanned brunette in a red bikini in front of a turquoise sea. The picture was taken from too far away for her face to be clearly recognisable, but the body was annoyingly impressive.

I rang Ali.

'Who the fuck is Tania Silk?' I snapped at her before she'd even had a chance to say hello.

'What? What are you talking about? Market's open, Cass, can't talk now. Nick's on the warpath and my head's on the block. Ring you back later.'

I stormed around the flat, my heart beating fit to break my ribs. He was seeing someone else. He was seeing someone else? He couldn't be. I felt physically sick. I went back to my computer, looked at the message again. Maybe it was perfectly innocent. Maybe it was nothing. Maybe she was just a friend. A friend I'd never heard of. Who sent messages with five kisses at the end. I clicked on her name again and peered at her face. She was familiar. Older, in her thirties, in very good shape . . . I'd seen her before. I'd seen her recently. I'd seen her at the Hempel, at the drinks party, sitting with my then boyfriend, now ex-boyfriend, talking for too long, their heads too close.

Somewhere underneath the heap of dirty clothes, magazines and DVD covers next to my bed there lay the cheat sheet Nicholas had given me, the list of names of guests for the party. Flinging aside grubby T-shirts and copies of *Vogue*, I tore through the pile until I found it. I flicked through page after page of overweight forty-somethings until I found it, Rylance, Siddell, Silk. There she was. Tania Silk.

One of Alchemy Asset Management's rising stars, Tania Silk manages the £800 million Global Equities fund. Over the past two years, the fund has returned more than 10 per cent per annum in a highly challenging market and has a Triple A rating from FundWatch.

Tania hails from New York: she misses baseball and 24-hour pizza delivery but has discovered the joys of cricket, pub lunches and running in London's parks.

Cricket? She likes cricket? What the hell is wrong with her? (Dan loves cricket.)

She's too old for him. She must be thirty-three if she's a day. She's at least six years older than him. She's ancient. She's an old hag.

She's a fund manager. She's a rising star. She must be clever. He can talk to her, *really* talk to her, about what he does.

How long has this been going on? Did this start at the party? Did something happen at the party? In my head, I rewound the tape. Dan and I were sitting together, having a drink. He'd been telling me about Ali and the French guy. Then he got up, said he'd be back in a little while and he disappeared. For an hour. And the next time I saw him, he had his arm around her.

Oh God oh God oh God.

He was with her at the party. And afterwards he went to bed with me. I went to the bathroom, threw up, brushed my teeth and went back to bed. I lay there, for hours, not sleeping, not reading, not watching TV, not anything, just feeling as wretched as it is possible to feel. As hard as I tried, I could not stop playing things over in my head, not just the moment that I saw them together at the party, his arm draped around her shoulder, but other things, too. His mobile ringing in the middle of the night a few weeks ago, and him getting out of bed to take the call, for example. He said it was Mick, but when I asked Mick the next day in the pub about it, he just looked at me blankly, before starting to babble about a problem at work. I thought about all the nights he'd been 'too tired' or 'too busy' to see me lately, the twenty-four long-stemmed red roses he sent, completely out of the blue, after he'd been 'working all weekend'. The Louboutins. My beautiful Louboutins. It came to me like a slap in the face, a punch to the gut, the cruellest cut of all. They were a guilt gift.

Seized by a terrible and all-consuming rage, I leapt out of bed, grabbed the shoes from my closet, marched into the kitchen and threw them in the bin. I ate everything in the fridge (including an entire block of cheddar, a jar of artichoke hearts and half a tub of

Häagen-Dazs), threw up again and then went back to bed.

Ali called just after five.

'I'm so sorry, Cass, I've had an absolute bitch of a day.'

'Did you know, Ali? About her?'

'There were rumours . . .'

'You knew?' I shrieked. Betrayal by him was one thing, by her, another matter altogether.

'Rumours, Cassie, and there are always rumours about guys like him. I didn't *know* anything. I was going to talk to you about it last week, but you were so happy, planning weekends away and everything . . . And I didn't know anything for sure . . .' Her voice tailed off. Then, in a more assertive, Ali-like tone, she said, 'Get up, get dressed. I'm coming round and we're going out.'

I fished the shoes out of the bin and carefully wiped them down with a moistened sheet of kitchen roll.

Ali rang again an hour later.

'You ready? I'm outside, in a black cab.'

We started off on the roof terrace at Shoreditch House. Then there was a bar, and then another bar, and another one after that. There were peach Bellinis, watermelon Martinis, cosmopolitans and Kirs. We ended up in the Crazy Bear in Fitzrovia where I got trapped in the ladies loos, which are entirely walled with mirrors, for a fifteen minutes. Eventually, Ali came to find me.

'I couldn't find my way out,' I slurred at her. She giggled, leading me back out to the bar. I collapsed into an armchair next to the fire.

'It's not funny,' I whined. 'Everything's falling apart.' We were getting to the maudlin portion of the evening's festivities. 'I don't understand why he did it. I don't understand why I wasn't enough for him . . . What did I do, Ali?'

'You didn't do anything, Cassie, he's just a shit. I know that deep down you know that.'

'He's not a shit . . . He's just . . .'

'An arsehole.'

'No, no. I must have done something to drive him away. I just don't know what. You have to tell me, Ali, what you heard. You were suspicious, weren't you? Why? Please tell me what you know.'

'Cassie, it doesn't matter now . . .' she started to say.

'It does matter, Ali. I need to know, please just tell me.'

She sighed. 'All right, it was a couple of weeks ago. In the pub after work, some guys were talking about her. Tania. Apparently she has a bit of a reputation, she had to leave Allen Brothers because of an affair with her boss. Allegedly. Anyway, they were talking about her, you know the sort of thing, "I'd hit that," all that bullshit, and someone said something about Dan, suggesting that they should ask him what she was like.'

'Oh, Christ.'

'Anyway, the second they noticed I was listening

they shut up. And . . . I don't know, I didn't really take it seriously. I thought maybe they were talking about something that had happened before you guys got together.' She didn't sound very convincing. 'I was going to ask you if everything was OK, but when I came round last week and you were talking about anniversary weekends and things, I just assumed everything must be OK.'

'I thought it was,' I said, waving at the waitress as I polished off my drink. 'But then I'm clearly a complete idiot.'

'No, Cassie, you just see the good in people. You trust people.'

'Exactly. I'm an idiot.'

I was woken by a door hitting me sharply on the top of my head. I opened my eyes to discover that I was lying on the cold blue tiles of our bathroom floor, fully clothed, my feet in the shower cubicle. A dark-haired man was standing over me, his expression a mixture of confusion and concern.

'I'm so sorry. Are you all right? What are you doing down there?' he spluttered.

'Well, I was asleep,' I said crossly, struggling to sit up. 'Who the hell are you?'

He offered a hand to help me up, but I waved it away.

'I'm Jake,' he said, retreating slowly as I hauled myself to my feet, glaring at him. 'I'm a friend of Jude's. We came back here to work on a project we're doing together at college.'

'Well, you should think about knocking before barging into my bathroom,' I snapped at him.

'The door was open,' he pointed out.

'You could knock anyway. God, what time is it? Is it early? I feel like death.'

'It's twelve thirty,' he said. He grinned an annoying lopsided grin. 'I have to say you don't look that hot.'

'Thank you very much,' I snarled, barging past him and into the living room, where Jude was sitting on the sofa, a stack of papers laid out on the coffee table in front of her.

'Oh hi, Cass,' she chirped. 'I was wondering where you'd got to. Tried to ring you last night – I ended up crashing round Amanda's place.' She frowned at me. 'God, you look terrible.'

'Thanks.'

'No, really, you do. I've got a friend round, by the way. Jake.'

'We met,' I said sourly, yanking open the fridge. 'Oh, for God's sake, there's no bloody milk!'

'I did buy it last time,' Jude murmured, going back to her reading.

'Good for you!' I snapped.

'Cassie!' she said. 'I was just pointing out—'

'Dan cheated on me!' I yelled at her. Jude did her level best to look surprised.

'Dan was cheating on me. With an American! Some old, wrinkled, thirty-five-year-old American!'

Jake wandered back into the living room. 'Thirty-five's not really that old,' he said.

For a second I thought about throwing my empty coffee mug at him, but instead I just slammed it down on the kitchen counter.

'I'm sorry about your boyfriend,' he said. 'That's awful.'

'Yes, well, men are awful,' I retorted, shoving past him for the second time that morning.

I marched back into the bathroom and turned on the shower. Catching sight of my reflection in the mirror, I did a double take. They were right, I did look hideous – washed out, blotchy and bleary-eyed, with my hair sticking up at weird angles, thanks to a night spent, literally, on the tiles. I was mortified. I can't believe I'd let people see me like this. Oh, Christ. I got into the shower and scrubbed, trying to wash away the pain, humiliation and smell of gin.

An hour or so later, I emerged from my bedroom, with clean hair, wearing jeans, Uggs, a lovely leather jacket given to me for my birthday by the boyfriend before Dan (whom I was now seriously considering calling, just to say hello) and just enough make-up to transform my complexion from pasty to perfect. Jake, sitting on the sofa next to Jude, looked gratifyingly impressed as I swept into the room. Jude, on the other hand, eyed me disapprovingly.

'That doesn't look much like an interview outfit, Cass. How's the job search going?'

'It's not,' I replied. 'Look, I lost my job on Monday. My boyfriend broke up with me on Tuesday. On Wednesday, I did nothing but lie in bed watching rubbish films and eating cheese. That was the high point of my week. Yesterday, I discovered that my ex has been shagging some thirty-seven-year-old American woman, so today, if you don't mind, I'm going shopping. I'll start looking for a job on Monday.'

I love shopping for winter clothes. OK, I love shopping for summer, spring and autumn clothes, too, but there's something effortless about winter wear. It's so forgiving. No need for toned arms and shaved legs, it's all about wrapping yourself up in layers, swathing yourself in woollens, donning cute hats and colourful scarves and amazing, to-die-for, sex-kittenish over-the-knee boots.

On Friday, I spent a very satisfying afternoon on the Kings Road, with just the briefest of detours down Sloane Street. (I needed some gloves and they have lovely ones in Chanel. Yes, they're pricey but they'll last for ever.)

On Saturday, I went to the gym for the first time in a week. Running on the treadmill, I noticed that in my plain black tracksuit bottoms and faded grey T-shirt, I looked a little drab. Particularly compared to the girl next to me who was sporting blue leggings with a pink stripe down the side and matching pink vest.

'Like your outfit,' I gasped at her, reducing my speed from eight miles per hour to seven.

'Thanks,' she huffed back. 'Sweaty Betty, on the high street. They've got some really good stuff. Nice trainers, too.'

So on my way home I popped in to take a look. She was right, they did have good stuff. I left with two new running outfits, two sports bras, a yoga mat and a pair of trainers.

I was hoping that Jude would be out when I got home, but there she was, sitting at the counter in the kitchen, reading the paper and sipping camomile tea. I loathe the smell of camomile tea. She looked at me as I came in, sighed, shook her head sadly and went back to her paper.

'What?' I said, dropping my packages in the living room. 'What now?'

'Cassie, you just lost your job and as far as I can make out, you have done nothing but shop ever since. I'm just worried, that's all. I'm worried about you and, to be honest, I'm worried about the rent.'

God, her and the bloody rent. Anyone would have thought we had an eviction notice attached to the front door.

'Jude,' I said, gritting my teeth, 'I will have the money to pay the rent, I promise. You don't have to worry about that.' She sighed and went back to her newspaper. She was worried, I could tell, and it wasn't long before she spoke up again.

'I know that I'm nagging at you, Cass, but I am concerned. I know you're having a terrible time, but you have to remember that this isn't just about you. If you can't pay up then I'll have to find someone else to move in. Or we'll both have to find somewhere else to go.'

'I know, you're right, I know . . .'

'Maybe,' she cut in, 'maybe you ought to think about moving home for a little while, just while you sort yourself out. And we could sublet your place for a few months.'

'No!' I cried. 'Anything but that! I can't move home, Jude, I really can't. I'd go mad.' I sat down next to her at the counter.

'I will get a job. Job hunting starts Monday. In earnest. Promise. Plus, I'm not just shopping randomly, you know,' giving her arm a squeeze. 'There is a point to my purchases. This morning, for example, I was feeling really rubbish about myself in the gym, with my kit almost falling apart—'

'You bought those jogging bottoms about a month ago,' Jude interrupted, rolling her eyes at me.

'Almost falling apart,' I went on, 'and you know what it's like. If you don't feel good about yourself in the gym it's really de-motivating. Makes you not want to bother any more. And if I stopped going, it would be a huge waste of money, wouldn't it? Paying a hundred quid a month and then not even going?'

'It's a waste of money anyway. What's wrong with running in the park?'

'Park's full of nutters and dog shit,' I muttered. 'Plus it's much too cold to run outside now. I'd have to buy a whole new exercise wardrobe if I were to run in the park in winter, and that would cost a fortune, wouldn't it?'

Jude just laughed, shaking her head again.

'Jake was asking about you, by the way,' she said, tossing me the magazine section, the only bit of the paper I tend to look at.

'Who?' I asked, flicking through the magazine to the health and beauty section. There was an article on the new 'peel' treatment at Body & Soul, a day spa in Kensington. 'Oh, that sounds nice. "An Energising blood orange-scented body scrub followed by a thirty-minute massage".'

'You know, my friend from college, the guy who was here the other day? The one you could barely be civil to?'

'Oh, right. I wonder if they've got any appointments at Body & Soul today? I could do with a massage after all the stress of the past few days. Plus I'm in desperate need of a pedicure.'

I rang the spa and, incredibly, they'd had a couple of cancellations. They could fit me in after lunch. Fantastic.

'I've got to keep busy,' I said to Jude, who, I could tell, was just dying to ask me how much the treatments cost (£125 for the massage, £55 for the pedicure, not that I would have told her that). 'If I stay in I'll just be sitting around here all day, moping about Dan. You don't want me to do that, do you?'

'No, of course not. You should go out and enjoy yourself,' she said, surprisingly encouragingly. 'Actually, Jake and I were thinking of going to the Eve Arnold exhibition at the Barbican this afternoon. You should join us. It'd be a lot cheaper than going to the spa. Did I tell you that Jake's a photographer? He's really good actually.'

Aha. Now I see what she's up to.

'Mmm, not really in the mood for art right now. All that standing around and considering the meaning of things. It's just going to depress me even more.' Desperate to divert her focus from my spending habits, I brought up the only other subject she's willing to talk about ad nauseam, Matt.

'How's the love of your life doing? Hope you're not keeping news from the front from me, just because my love life's down the pan.' Matt is Jude's boyfriend whom she almost never sees – he works for Unicef and spends around nine months of the year out of the country, usually in places where there is a higher-than-average likelihood of being shot.

'Not at all. He's fine. Sierra Leone this week. With a bit of luck he'll be in London for ten days in December. I was going to ask you about that, actually – usually he stays at his brother's place, but I was hoping he might stay here this time?'

'Course he can, Jude. He can stay for as long as he likes.' I gave her a quick peck on the cheek and slipped out the door before she could start interrogating me on the cost of spa treatments.

The exfoliating scrub was delightfully relaxing, the pedicure less so. Not that the beauty therapist didn't do a very fine job, lacquering my toenails to perfection with Chanel Rouge Noir. No, it was just that my much-needed pampering session was interrupted by a telephone call from my sister.

'Are you all right?' she asked, her voice dripping with concern.

'I'm fine, Cee.'

'Mum told me about your email.' I'd delivered the bad news about my job to my parents electronically the previous evening. 'She said she tried to call you straight away.' I had then turned off my mobile phone so that I wouldn't have to field endless questions about my state of mind and my plans for the future. I was getting more than enough of that from Jude.

'I know, I missed her calls. I'll get back to her later on today. Promise,' I said, feeling guilty as I did. I had no intention of calling back later that day.

'What are you going to do, Cass? Have you started looking for things? Michael did warn you, didn't he, that job losses were just around the corner? Do you remember, he suggested that you start looking for other opportunities?' If I hadn't been in the process of receiving a foot massage I might have kicked something.

'I'll be OK, Celia. There are plenty of other jobs in London.'

'Mmm. Or you could think of coming back and living somewhere round here, couldn't you? After all, Michael says—'

'Celia?' I cut in. 'Celia? Can you hear me? I'm about to go into a tunnel,' I said, ignoring the pedicurist's quizzical look. 'You're breaking up.'

I switched the phone off and didn't turn it on again for the rest of the afternoon.

On Sunday, I met Ali for eggs Benedict and Bloody Marys at Canteen in Spitalfields market. At first she kept me amused with stories of Nicholas's very public humiliation of Christa Freeman, who, it was turning out, was perhaps not quite the star secretary he had thought, but eventually, inevitably, the conversation turned to Dan.

'Are you sure you want to hear this?' she asked me.

'Well, not really, but I'd rather find out the gory details from you than discover them some other way. It's Emily's wedding next month, there are going to be loads of work people there, it's bound to come up at some point.' Emily is a colleague from Hamilton Churchill. Her nuptials were taking place in just a few weeks' time in some incredibly fancy country house hotel and virtually everyone from the office, including Dan, was going to be there. Until the bloodbath break-up, I'd really been looking forward to going with him.

'OK. Well, I asked James Cohen about it.' James was one of Dan's best friends at Hamilton. 'He was very reluctant to tell me anything, but eventually he told me that Dan met Tania at the Alchemy summer party in August.'

More than two months ago. I took a gulp of my Bloody Mary, almost taking my eye out with the celery stick.

'Apparently they left together and he spent the night with her.'

I remembered the Alchemy party. It was on a Friday. When I asked him why he hadn't answered any of my calls or texts on Saturday he told me he'd left his phone in the back of a cab. The taxi driver didn't return it to him, he said, until Saturday evening.

'According to James, Dan felt awful about it and told this Tania woman that it couldn't happen again. James says she kept calling him but he didn't see her again until some time in September. There was that charity casino bash at the Stock Exchange and she was there.'

I remembered that night, too.

'But Dan stayed at my place that night,' I said. 'I remember – he said it was dull, that gambling for a charitable cause took the pleasure out of it.'

'I know. But . . . Are you really sure you want to know this, Cass?' Her voice was filled with foreboding.

'What? What is it?'

'Well, he didn't stay very long at the casino thing. Come to think of it, I hardly remember seeing him that night. James reckons he bumped into Tania, they hooked up, went back to her place for a bit and then he went home to you.' She said this hurriedly, taking no pleasure in being the bearer of such awful news.

A lone, fat tear splashed onto my half-finished plate of eggs Benedict.

'The next day he sent me two dozen red roses. I remember being so surprised, and so happy. My boyfriend sends me flowers, for no reason at all, it doesn't have to be Valentine's Day. He just does it, I thought, because he loves me.' I pushed away my food. 'I'm not hungry. I need another drink.'

Ali summoned the waitress.

'So they've been seeing each since then? For a month?'

'Seems that way, although according to James, Dan tried to break it off a couple of times. James was actually really shocked when he heard that Dan had chosen—'

'Her.'

The waitress brought our drinks and took away the plates. Ali lit a cigarette, ignoring the ostentatious coughing noises from the next table.

'Water's wet, the sky's blue, men cheat,' she said ruefully. 'And talking of cheating, I'm afraid I can't hang out and shop this afternoon.' She gave a cheeky, guilty little smile.

'The Frenchman, I take it?'

'We have an assignation at the Covent Garden Hotel. Actually, we're meeting in Coco de Mer, across the road. They have these beautiful embroidered blindfolds . . .'

'Ali,' I said, trying hard not to sound too much like Jude, 'are you sure this is a good idea?'

'Almost certainly not, but you know. The heart wants what it wants.'

'Oh, it's your heart that wants, is it?'

*

88

Left to my own devices that afternoon, feeling a little abandoned by my best friend not to mention steamrollered by my ex, I went a bit over the top on the retail therapy. It's hard to believe, isn't it, that shops didn't use to open on Sundays. What on earth did people do all day? Even the religious ones must have been bored stiff – it's not like church takes all day. Unless of course you go to one of those evangelical places where the services go on for hours and hours. I bought dresses and shoes and a cute little skirt suit (perfect for job interviews), a beautiful silver Paradise Orchid ring from Bower & Hall (well, no one else is going to spoil me now, are they?) and a bag full of pampering goodies from this fabulous Chinese place which sells things like 'mood-freshening body scrubs' made from bamboo and green tea. My mood was definitely in need of some freshening. Finally, I popped into Montezumas for a couple of bags of champagne and white chocolate truffles to eat on the sofa that evening. It was essential, I reasoned, if I was going to start hunting for jobs the next morning, to keep my spirits up.

Cassie Cavanagh *is feeling undesirable*

Bank balance: -£766.88
Available overdraft: £1,800
Amount of rent due in one week's time: £800

I was feeling undesirable not to the opposite sex (I had a date set up for that Thursday – exactly nine days AD – not bad going), but to potential employers. As Jude had warned, job hunting was proving a little trickier than I had anticipated. I leapt out of bed bright and early on Monday morning, eager to get started. I browsed JobSearch.co.uk, I looked at the Reed Recruitment site. I checked my emails. I had a promotional mail from NET-A-PORTER. They had Bottega Veneta bags on sale. I clicked on the link. Thirty per cent off! Bargain. I placed an order. Back to the job hunt. An ad for a PA/Events Coordinator. I dismissed it when I saw the pay they were offering. Pathetic.

There was another post, a PA to the MD and FD of a property investment company, which offered a salary more commensurate with what I was used to. The advert demanded someone who had 'superb organisational skills', who was 'very polished' and 'a true team player, not a queen bee type'. That summed me up perfectly. I filled in the application, attached my CV, dashed off a quick covering letter and sent it.

Filled with a sense of achievement, I decided to nip down to Starbucks to grab a coffee and a croque monsieur. On the way back, I collected the post from our box and sorted through it over breakfast. I sifted through the mail, which was mostly junk (newsletters from the various charities to which Jude makes regular contributions), but at the bottom were two more interesting items. A stiff, cream envelope with the familiar Hamilton Churchill logo embossed on the back, and a credit card statement.

Good news first. I opened the Hamilton Churchill letter. Very sorry to let you go, blah blah blah, please find enclosed your final salary cheque and redundancy payment in the amount of £3,000. Three thousand pounds!

'Three thousand bloody pounds!' I shrieked out loud. Thank God for that. That would last me ages! That would last me weeks and weeks! I didn't have to worry, I didn't have to feel guilty, I could buy as many Bottega Veneta bags as I bloody well wanted! And I certainly didn't have to take the first crappy job that came along. I could take my time. I had breathing room. Flooded with an overwhelming sense of relief, I flung the mail onto the living room table and collapsed on the sofa.

Just as a piece of toast will always fall butter side up, so the mail landed credit card bill on top. I glared at it. Could I ignore it? Just for a few days? Probably best not to. I should just rip it open and get the pain over with. I should do it now, now that I'm feeling better about things. Gingerly, I slipped my finger under the lip of the envelope and ripped. I pulled out the contents. It seemed alarmingly long. Four pages. Bloody hell. I looked at the total. My heart stopped.

£5,322.87.

Five thousand. Three hundred. And twenty-two pounds. Eighty-seven pence.

Holy crap.

My heart went from 0 to 120 bpm in a matter of seconds. That couldn't be right. That just *could not* be right. Someone must have stolen my identity! That was the only possible explanation. Someone has been masquerading as me, using my card, spending £74 on underwear from Figleaves! Oh, OK, that was me. They've been buying shoes at Sub Couture! No, that was me. They've been having dinner at Roka! Oh, all right, that was me, too. My sense of horror and shame growing, I realised that it was all me. Me, me, me, buying clothes and shoes and cases of wine, me, spending a fortune on cosmetics and hair products, me buying flights to Rome . . . Oh, bugger. I'd completely forgotten about the Rome thing.

I rang Alitalia straight away. No, the woman said, they didn't do refunds, but if I needed to cancel the trip due to illness or bereavement, my travel insurer would cover the cost. Bereft I might be, but travel insurance? Who the hell has travel insurance? Perhaps I could flog the tickets to someone else? Ali and her Frenchman might fancy a weekend in Rome. Or I could sell them on eBay. I might even make a profit. I rang Alitalia back. Would it be possible to issue the tickets without a name on them? The woman laughed. No, that would not be possible, she said, since airline tickets, as everyone knows, are not transferable. Great. Not only had I wasted more than four hundred pounds on tickets to Rome, but the airline woman was calling me stupid.

I rang the Hotel de Russie next, and was eventually transferred to someone who spoke passable English. Yes, they could cancel my reservation, but I would be charged for the first night's stay.

If you do not cancel your booking more than seven days before your planned arrival date you have to pay for the first night. Hotel policy. Ridiculous, thieving policy more like.

And just when I thought I could not feel any worse, something at the top of the statement caught my eye. It was dated the fifteenth of October. The fifteenth of October. That was over a week ago. Which meant that none of the many, many purchases I'd made over the past week had even shown up on the statement yet. Feeling more than a little queasy, I delved into my bag, rooted around for my purse and retrieved a handful of scrunched-up credit card slips. With a growing sense of foreboding, I fetched a calculator from the desk in Jude's room and totted up the total.

Holy, holy crap. Over the past seven days I had spent £1,433.29. Which meant that my total debt amounted to . . . £6,756.16. Oh. My. God.

I wondered if I could cancel the order for the Bottega Veneta handbag? I decided against it. Probably a false economy – the bag was on sale and if I cancelled that purchase I would most likely just end up buying something at full price instead. No, instead of thinking about saving money, I had to think about making it. I logged back onto the Reed Recruitment site and applied for every job I thought I might be even vaguely qualified for. Most of them were more senior positions than the one I had held at Hamilton Churchill, but I had to aim high now. I was going to need the money.

I was just tinkering with the wording of a covering letter for the post of an executive assistant to the head of a large multinational company when my phone buzzed in my bag. I fished it out and almost dropped it on the floor when I saw his name on the display. Dan calling.

My heart was pounding in my chest.

Should I answer it? No, I should press ignore.

No, I should answer it and tell him exactly what I thought of him.

No, I shouldn't – I would probably end up crying and screaming, which was undignified. I didn't want to give him the satisfaction.

But I didn't want to give him the opportunity to apologise to by voicemail either – he didn't deserve to get away with that.

The phone stopped ringing. I stared at it, waiting for it to buzz again, to alert me to the fact that I had a new message. It didn't. Bollocks! Why hadn't I answered it? Maybe he was calling to beg for forgiveness, to plead with me to take him back. Which was a very good reason not to take his calls. Knowing me, I'd let myself be suckered in to getting back together with him.

Feeling panicky and flustered, I decided to go for a walk. I needed some air. Leaving my phone behind so as to eliminate any temptation to take Dan's calls, I set off in the direction of the Common. I was almost there when I noticed the 'Sale' sign in the window of Oliver Bonas.

Don't go in, Cassie, I told myself. Resist! Then I saw it. In the window display was the lovely little red lacquered bedside table I'd been coveting for ages. And it was reduced, from £410 to £280. A saving of more than a hundred pounds! Cursing my bad luck (why oh why had they put *that* table in the window?) I went inside and bought it.

The man in the shop promised to deliver the table later that afternoon; I assured him I would be there to take delivery. On the way back home I bumped into Hassan, the Algerian *Big Issue* vendor who sells his magazines outside Sainsbury's. This added about half an hour to my journey: He is a very sweet man but he is also one of those people who answers the question,

'How are you?' honestly; and since he appears to be afflicted by an enormous variety of minor ailments, there is not such thing as a brief conversation with Hassan.

By the time I arrived home it was obvious that Jude had been home and gone out again, not least from the note taped to the front of my computer screen. In an angry red scrawl she had written:

We need to talk. Be in tonight. DON'T go out. Will be home 6-ish.

Next to my computer lay my credit card bill and the pile of receipts I had been going through. I had been so freaked out by Dan's call I'd forgotten to hide them. So no prizes for guessing what tonight's conversation would be about.

I spent the rest of the day procrastinating – I couldn't seem to concentrate on any one task for more than a few minutes. I did the washing, tidied the house, reorganised my wardrobe by colour and watched four episodes of *Gilmore Girls* back to back. I tried on four different outfits for the Thursday night date, but none of them looked right. I browsed job websites but couldn't find any further posts to apply for. In any case, surely one of the applications I had sent off that morning was bound to yield something?

The reason for my lack of concentration was, of course, the fact that I was waiting for the phone to ring. Waiting for it to ring, hoping for it to ring, dreading it ringing, since I had no idea what I would say, if I were to say anything at all, if it did ring. It didn't. I felt cheated, I had missed my chance for closure. Still, maybe it didn't matter. Maybe the Thursday night date would go so well that all thoughts of Dan would be banished for ever. Somehow I doubted it.

The date was Ali's idea. The man in question was a friend of one of her clients: a trainee solicitor at a City firm, he was allegedly very bright and very attractive and destined for great things. At first I refused.

'It is way too soon, Ali,' I protested. 'I'm a mess. I can't see anyone now.'

'You can and you will,' she replied. 'We both know that the only real way to get over one relationship is to distract yourself with another one – even if it's just an in-betweener thing. The moment you're shagging someone else you'll stop thinking about shagging Dan, or not shagging Dan, or the fact that Dan's shagging some Yank.' She had a point.

I was still contemplating possible date outfits when the doorbell rang – my new bedside table was being delivered. Unfortunately the delivery man had barely managed to get it through the door when Jude showed up – and she had a surprise for me. She'd brought Ali along, too.

'What is this?' Jude demanded, staring at the bedside table which was now sitting in the middle of the living room. 'Oh, please don't tell me,' she went on, 'you've been shopping!' She grabbed the pile of receipts which were still sitting on the kitchen counter (why the hell hadn't I got rid of those?) and waved them in my face. 'This has got to stop, Cassie.

This is totally insane,' she yelled.

The delivery man, who was nervously inching past her towards the door, said, 'If you could just sign here . . .'

'No!' Jude shouted at him. 'She cannot sign. Take it back. She doesn't want it.'

'But, but . . .' he stammered, 'it was in the sale. We can't take it back.'

'Yeah!' I said triumphantly. 'They won't take it back.' I signed the receipt and the delivery man fled.

Jude stood in the middle of the room, almost purple in the face. Ali stood at her side. She didn't meet my eye.

'OK,' Jude said. 'We get it. You lost your job, your horrible boyfriend dumped you for another woman, it's not very nice. But you cannot do this. You can't just spend your way out of every problem you ever have.'

She was right, of course. I had been overdoing it, but I was suddenly furious at being ambushed like this. And for some reason, it was Ali, who hadn't yet said a word, who I was furious with.

'You got anything to add, Al? Because I don't remember you complaining about my spending when we were drinking fifteen-quid-a-throw cocktails last week. What is this, anyway? An intervention? You two are ganging up on me now, are you? How did that happen? You don't even like each other.'

'Maybe we don't always see eye to eye,' Ali said evenly, 'but Jude rang me when she saw your credit card bill and all those receipts because she was worried about you. And I happen to think she's right to be worried. If you let this get out of control you could find yourself in real trouble, Cass. We're not ganging up on you, but we do feel like you've got to stop all this and start concentrating on what you're going to do next.'

'You are ganging up on me,' I pouted. I started dragging my new table across the floor towards my bedroom. Jude grabbed the other side of it, tugging in the opposite direction. 'Jude!' I yelled. 'Let go! They're not going to take it back!'

'Then you can sell it on eBay,' she said, refusing to relinquish her grasp. A futile tug-of-war ensued, both of us grunting and swearing as we tried to manoeuvre the table in opposite directions.

'Oh, for fuck's sake!' Ali snapped eventually. 'Just let her keep the bloody thing. Compromise, OK? Jude, you let go of the sodding table and in return Cassie agrees to a sensible discussion about what she's going to do about work.'

With my new piece of furniture safely installed in my bedroom, I returned to the kitchen and slumped down at the counter, feeling a bit like a sulky teenager who's been caught nicking vodka from her parents' drinks cabinet.

'I have been applying for jobs,' I pointed out. 'It's not my fault I haven't got anything yet.'

'You haven't registered with any temp agencies,' Jude countered. 'You're not following the Recession Buster plan.' I rolled my eyes at her. Ali tried to suppress a smile. I pointed out that I now had three grand in redundancy pay. They shoved the credit card bill and receipts back at me.

'Plus there's rent due in a few days,' Jude pointed out. 'And don't roll your eyes at me, Cassie. This is not just about you. We signed that rental agreement together. You default and they could come after me for the cash.'

I was going to have to make cutbacks. I had to cancel the cleaner, the Sky subscription, and 'make my own damn coffee' instead of spending seven quid a day in Starbucks. There were to be rules. I was to be allowed to go out on weekends only and there was to be absolutely no shopping. No luxuries, no indulgences, no spa treatments. Thrift was to be the order of the day. We worked out that so long as I stuck to these rules, my redundancy package would cover the minimum repayment on my credit card for this month and next, as well as next month's rent, bills and living expenses. Very basic living expenses. After that, I would be broke.

'You've got a little over five weeks to find a job,' Jude said.

'I won't need five weeks,' I assured her, 'you'll see. I'll find something in no time.'

Well, maybe not no time. Every day for the following week I checked my emails for news from potential employers. None came. Each morning I descended the stairs to the entrance hall into which our mail was delivered, each morning I sifted through bills and junk mail and letters for people who hadn't lived in this building for months, and each morning there was nothing for me. No offers of interviews, no expressions of interest. Hell, I hadn't even had a rejection letter! I was just being ignored. Even worse, the temp agencies I finally spoke to told me that they weren't taking on any new people at the moment – they had more than enough temps to cover the jobs that were out there.

I was going stir-crazy in the flat (I couldn't risk going out in case I bought anything) and Jude was making things ten times worse. Every evening when she got home she bombarded me with questions: what had I done all day, how much had I spent, how many jobs had I applied for, had I had any responses yet? It was driving me insane. I'd heard nothing from Dan since the day of the credit card bill and Thursday's date with the solicitor hadn't helped take my mind off Dan at all.

The date was, in fact, a total, unmitigated disaster. His name was Sean and he was, I have to admit, very attractive. He was also dull, pompous, completely without charm and told slightly racist jokes. Plus he turned up wearing too-tight jeans and a pink shirt with sweat patches under the armpits.

'How in God's name could you set me up with that man?' I demanded of Ali as I walked home, alone, after spending ninety painful minutes, one and a half hours of my life that I was never going to get back, in Sean's company.

'Well, I don't really know him,' she said blithely, 'but he's good-looking and he's loaded. You like good-looking and loaded, don't you?'

'Sure,' I replied, 'but I also like human.'

8

Cassie Cavanagh *is a paragon of virtue*

Bank balance: -£193.50
Available overdraft: £1,800
Weeks to go until the money runs out: Four
Weeks to go until the social event of the year: Two

No clothes, no shoes, no cocktails, no lattes, not so much as a lipstick. My anti-extravagance drive was going exceptionally well, although there was one ugly black cloud looming on the horizon in the shape of Emily's wedding. In two weeks' time I would be attending the nuptials of Emily Conrad and Tristan Pilkington-Smythe, to be held at Bramley House, astonishingly expensive boutique hotel slash palace in the Cotswolds. I would be attending the wedding of the decade and I had absolutely nothing to wear.

When I mentioned this to Jude she got incredibly irritated with me, dragging me into my room and pulling out five or six dresses that would be suitable for a winter wedding and flinging them on the bed, demanding, 'What's wrong with that one then?' over and over again. She doesn't understand.

Emily Conrad works in the corporate finance department at Hamilton. She's the daughter of Sir Peter Conrad, media mogul and patron of the arts. Emily drives a bright red Mercedes, she wears Chanel, she holidays in Mustique. Her intended, whom I've never met, is terrifyingly posh, one hundred and sixth in line to the throne or something. So far, so daunting. But among the legions of posh and rich people I'll have to face will be dozens of my erstwhile colleagues, including Nicholas, Christa and, worst of all, Dan. I'm praying, hoping against hope that he won't be bringing the American woman. I don't even know if he's still seeing her. I de-friended him on Facebook after I found out about the infidelity. In any case, I *have* to look good. I have to look great, and I can't be wearing a dress that he, or anyone else at work has already seen me in. I certainly can't wear the Louboutins, which will for ever be tainted with his betrayal.

Still, with no job on the horizon and the redundancy money fast trickling away, dress-shopping is off the agenda. Not only that, but instead of staying at the lovely country house hotel with all the rich and posh guests, I've had to book myself a room in the distinctly average-looking B&B in the local village. I'll just have to slope off quietly and hope that no one notices.

Unless of course I found myself a job quickly.

So you see, it was the wedding, anxiety about the

bloody wedding, which made me agree to Jude's ludicrous suggestion. Yesterday, she came bouncing into the room, grinning manically at me.

'Great news!' she announced. 'I've got you a job!'

'Really?' I asked, trying to sound enthusiastic but feeling deeply sceptical.

'Now, it's not the sort of thing you would usually go for . . .'

No, I'll bet it isn't.

'. . . but if you just hear me out. It's just a part-time thing, it'll give you some extra cash, tide you over until you find something more . . . suitable.'

'OK then, I'm listening.'

'Don't just dismiss it out of hand.'

'OK.'

'You'll think about it?'

'Yes, yes, all right. What is it?'

'Dog walking.'

'Dog walking.'

'Yes, dog walking.'

'Absolutely no way in hell, Jude,' I said. 'I don't like dogs. I'm a cat person, through and through. If you know of anyone who needs their cat walked, I'm there. But I'm not doing dogs.'

'You said you'd think about it, you said you wouldn't dismiss it out of hand,' she complained.

'That was before I knew what it was.'

'But I've got it all set up,' she said. 'The thing is that my friend Lucy's parents are going away for a couple of weeks, and they've got the lady next door to feed their dogs, but she's got a dodgy hip and she can't take them out for walks. They live just across the Common. It's really close. And I . . . well, I already said you'd do it.'

'Jude! You can't just hire me out to people without my permission!'

'But you need the money, Cass. And Lucy reckons there are quite a few of her parents' friends who need dog walkers – all in this area. Apparently there was a guy who used to do it for them, but it turned out that he was a member of the Socialist Workers' Party, plus someone caught him smoking grass when in charge of the dogs, so he got the sack. It's cash in hand, you'll be out and about, getting some exercise instead of just sitting around here eating junk food all day . . . Please, Cassie?'

The following day I set out to make my first dog-walking appointment. It was a bitterly cold and misty morning, the watery November sunlight barely breaking through the clouds. Cursing Jude all the way, I trudged across the muddy Common to Jedburgh Street where I was due to meet Mrs Bromell, the neighbour with the dodgy hip, to pick up the keys and collect the dogs.

'Fifi and Trixie are their names,' she told me. 'Fifi's the larger one. You'll find their leads on the hook behind the door in the kitchen and the bags are under the sink.'

'The bags?'

'You know, for the poop.'

Oh, Christ.

I let myself into the house and was incredibly relieved to be greeted by a pair of small and meek-looking poodles who regarded me benignly with sad eyes, wagging their tails gently and showing no interest whatsoever in sinking their teeth into my ankles.

Despite the cold, and the ignominy of being in the process of scooping fresh dog shit into a plastic bag at the precise moment at which three attractive young men jogged past me, dog walking turned out to be far less stressful than expected. Trixie and Fifi were docile and well behaved, they didn't make a run for it the moment I released them from their leads and they didn't get into any fights with other dogs. We walked briskly around the Common a couple of times – the first exercise I'd done in days – and I returned them home safely without incident.

I was just letting myself out of the house when Mrs Bromell appeared behind me.

'Hello, dear,' she said, 'you'll be back again tomorrow morning then? I was wondering if you could take another couple of dogs out at the same time? The lady who lives a couple of houses down mentioned she'd like someone to take hers out – she's got young children, you see, and she doesn't really have time to walk the dogs in the morning. Bit of extra cash for you.'

'Of course,' I replied. 'No problem at all.' Nothing to it, this dog-walking malarkey.

Within days I had built up a growing client base. The cash-rich, time-poor of Clapham were queuing up to have me escort their pampered hounds around the Common. I had so many requests that I had to do two shifts, one in the morning and one in the evening – the money wasn't exactly brilliant but since I appeared to have no prospect of any real employment it would have to do.

I did have a couple of other schemes up my sleeve. I had noticed that on some of the less established job-hunting sites, there were advertisements of a more unusual nature. Some of them, like the ones demanding a female masseuse (photo required) were clearly to be avoided, but others looked more promising:

The Research House is looking for females aged 30–45 to take part in a study on Mayonnaise. You must have children. The sessions will be held at our central London facility on November 10th. The time slots available are: 10.00am, 12.30pm and 2.45pm.

We are offering an incentive of £50 for your time and opinions.

OK, so I wasn't the perfect candidate – but not being aged between thirty and forty-five, not having any children and not liking mayonnaise did not seem to me to be insurmountable obstacles.

Another research study asked for people to take part in some market research for a global deodorant brand.

Applicants should have a high level of spoken English, should be confident and comfortable speaking in front of people, and should be avid users of deodorant.

Did using deodorant every day after a shower qualify one as an 'avid user'? I wasn't sure, but I put my name down for that one, too.

In the meantime, I walked dogs. It was on my fifth or sixth evening outing that disaster struck. I was taking Susie, an enormous (albeit very friendly) Alsatian, a pair of skittish greyhounds named Thierry and Theo, a fat and slow Labrador retriever called Paddington and, last but not least, Stanley, a vicious little bastard of a Jack Russell. It was pouring with rain. I had called Mrs Bromell (who, for some reason, had become my dog-walk pimp) to suggest that it perhaps wasn't the best idea to take the dogs out that night given the weather, but she insisted that a brief stroll would be OK.

'Dogs don't mind a bit of rain,' she said. *Maybe so*, I thought, *but I bloody well do*.

I picked up the dogs – who all lived on the same street – and until Stanley joined the group it was going OK. Susie was incredibly strong and was dragging us along (well, Paddington and me, anyway) a little faster than we might have wanted to go, but I had things under control. Until, on the edge of Clapham Common, completely without warning, Stanley decided to have a nip at Thierry's ankles and all hell broke lose. Theo came to his brother's aid, clamping his teeth firmly around Stanley's left ear. Susie, who is usually such a friendly hound, decided that someone Stanley's size should not be picked on, and bared her teeth terrifyingly at Theo, hackles raised. Yelling for calm, I managed to get tangled up in the leads and had to let go of one or risk dislocating a shoulder. As soon as I let go of his lead, Thierry sprinted off into the distance, yelping horribly. Theo and Susie followed at a gallop, dragging yapping Stanley, an increasingly distressed Paddington, and me, along behind them.

It had been pouring with rain half the day. The Common was a bog. We were tearing along, the five of us, skidding and sliding through the mud, water splashing up in our faces and raining down on our bedraggled heads. All the dogs were barking furiously, I was yelling at them to stop, trying to keep hold of the leads, trying to dig my heels into the grass to stop them.

In the darkness ahead loomed a park bench. The dogs were headed straight at it.

'Left!' I yelled helplessly at the leaders. 'Go left!'

Susie went left, Theo went right, Stanley charged straight underneath the bench and I ran straight into it, flying right over it and landing face down in a deep, muddy puddle on the other side. I'd released my hold on the leads, letting the dogs scatter in all directions. Paddington, who had been at the rear of the pack and had managed to stop before hitting the bench, ambled around it and licked my face affectionately.

Forty-five minutes and one nervous breakdown later I had assembled my filthy, soaking, disobedient charges and the six of us limped homewards across the Common. Mrs Bromell was waiting for me outside Susie's house.

'Goodness,' she said when she saw us, 'look at the state of them! Honestly, Cassie, you shouldn't let them get dirty like that! They're going to tramp mud all over their owners' houses.'

Caught between the urge to scream expletives at her and the temptation to simply sit down on the pavement and cry my eyes out, I apologised.

'I'm very sorry,' I said. 'Things got a bit out of control. They're not all as well trained as Fifi and Trixie,' I added, glaring at Stanley. He yipped happily, wagging his tail at me.

I delivered the dogs to their disgruntled owners. Cold, wet, muddy, exhausted and bleeding slightly from a cut above my right eye sustained when falling over the bench, I don't think I have ever felt so miserable. And my misery only deepened as I stood on the steps of number thirty-two, home to Thierry and Theo, one of the most beautiful houses on the road, a huge, imposing Georgian home with enormous windows revealing a coolly decorated interior (all zebra skin rugs and pristine white sofas). No doubt the home of some investment banker and his perfectly manicured wife. I rang the doorbell. The housekeeper answered.

'For goodness' sake!' she said when she saw the state of the dogs. 'They can't come through the house like that. Take them round the back to the utility room.' They had a housekeeper *and* a utility room. It just wasn't fair. I escorted my muddy charges around through the garden and back door, admiring the stunning glass and chrome kitchen extension, and delivered the dogs to the housekeeper, who was still muttering crossly about the state of them. She didn't show the slightest bit of concern for bedraggled, bleeding me. I started off home.

I was quite convinced that things could not possibly get any worse when, lo and behold, they did. I had just reached the High Street when I saw them: Christa Freeman and Angela Chenowith, PA to Hamilton Churchill's managing director. They were walking straight at me, huddling beneath an enormous yellow umbrella, picking their way through the puddles in their stilettos. I froze. There was nowhere to run, unless you count straight into the traffic. I considered it. Briefly, the thought of being crushed by a 4x4 did seem preferable to having to confront Christa in my current state. I dithered too long. They were almost on top of me. Christa clocked me. Her expression went from surprised to slightly disgusted. Steeling myself for what I imagined was likely to be one of the most painful conversations of my life, I tried to smile. They looked at me, then at each other.

'Hello,' I said with as much jollity as I could muster.

They walked straight past me. They did not even acknowledge my existence. I couldn't believe it. 'Hello!' I said, loudly and angrily.

Christa said something to Angela and they both laughed.

If I'd had anything to throw at them, I'd have thrown it. Sadly I had already binned the assorted bags of dog shit, so I had to make do with storming home in a terrible rage. Jude was going to rue the day she'd suggested this bloody dog-walking thing to me. I crashed into the flat, slamming the door behind me.

'Jude!' I yelled. 'Where the bloody hell are you?'

There was no answer. I stormed around the flat, trampling mud everywhere. She was out.

'I could kill you!' I yelled at no one in particular, storming back into the living room, only to discover that my Designer's Guild rug was now covered in muddy footprints. Aaaargh. I kicked off my trainers, took off my sodden clothes and stuffed everything into the washing machine. Then I took a very long, very hot shower.

Dressed in my pyjamas, clean, warm and dry, but still simmering with fury, I went straight for the fridge where, on the bottom shelf, was a bottle of champagne which Jude had bought for us to open when I got a new job. I opened it and poured myself a large glass. I flipped open my laptop and went straight to NET-A-PORTER. I was damned if the next time Christa Freeman laid eyes on me I'd be in anything less than the most amazing dress ever. The wedding was black tie, of course. I lost my heart to a Balmain embroidered mini dress, but even I wouldn't stretch to six grand for a frock. Eventually I settled on a Matthew Williamson embellished silk dress. Click. The site suggested I wear it with Jimmy Choo sandals and an Anya Hindmarch clutch. Well, I was off the wagon now. Click, click. I swigged down the rest of my champagne and poured myself another glass. Proceed to checkout. Click. The total came to £2,245. More champagne. Gulp. Confirm purchase. Click.

I got up early the next morning. I often do when I'm hungover. You wake up, you think, oh God, what the hell did I do last night, you remember that you spent £2,245 on a wedding outfit, you think, oh shit, and then you can't get back to sleep again. Given that it wasn't even seven o'clock yet, I was surprised to see Jude sitting in the kitchen, drinking a mug of camomile tea. She didn't smile when she saw me.

'You get a new job then?' she asked, indicating with a jerk of her head the empty bottle of champagne that was sitting on the table where I'd left it.

'No, I just had a really bad day. I'm sorry, I'll replace it.'

'Did you win the lottery?'

'It's a twenty-five-quid bottle of Moët & Chandon, Jude, I think I can probably stretch to that without breaking the bank.'

'Right. And what about the dress? And the shoes? And the handbag?'

Shit. I'd left my laptop on.

'I come home, I see empty champagne bottles, mud all over the place, all the lights left on, and then I go to check my emails and I find out that you have spent more than two grand – two fucking grand – on a dress!' She was yelling at me. And swearing. Jude never swears. This was bad. 'You don't have enough money to pay next month's rent so how the fuck are you able to afford that?'

'I just . . . I just wanted to cheer myself up,' I said weakly.

'Well, then you rent a fucking comedy, Cassie. You watch *Friends* on TV. You call Ali, you call me, call your mum, whatever. You don't spend two grand on some ridiculous fucking outfit.' I don't think I have ever heard Jude swear so much in such a short space of time. She marched across the room, picked up my laptop and plonked it down on the counter in front of me.

'Cancel it,' she said.

'What?'

'Cancel. It. Now.'

'No,' I said, 'I'm not cancelling it. You can't just order me around all the time, Jude. It's my money and I've decided to spend it on an outfit for this wedding. It's none of your business. You shouldn't be snooping around on my laptop anyway.'

'It's not your money, Cassie. You don't have any money, remember? It's the bank's money. And it *is* my business if we're going to get a sodding eviction notice next month.'

'I'm not cancelling it.'

'Fine, don't. I'm going to call the landlord this morning and give notice. I'm going to find myself somewhere else to live before we get thrown out onto the street.'

I cancelled the transaction. And I would never admit it to Jude, but I actually felt incredibly relieved as I was doing it.

9

Cassie Cavanagh *demands to know, what fresh hell is this?*

Just when you think you've hit rock bottom, a new low comes.

When Emily invited me to her wedding, I was delighted. It was going to be such a lovely weekend. I had pictured Dan and me driving up the night before the service in his Audi TT coupé, with the top down, a brightly printed scarf tied around my hair (in my imagination it was a very warm and sunny November). We would book a suite at the hotel, we would drink champagne and eat strawberries on the balcony (again, warm and sunny), we would have breakfast in bed, perhaps pop down to the spa for a shiatsu or a scrub before getting ready for the main event. I had not pictured myself having to take the train from London, or jammed into a carriage where there was standing room only (I stood) because there were engineering works on the line. I had not pictured staying in a grotty bed and breakfast two miles away from the reception venue. And I had certainly not pictured myself having to walk those two miles, in my nasty cheap high heels, because there is only one minicab firm in the entire bloody county and all their cars were already booked.

When I discovered that there were no cars available, I rang Ali, who was staying at Bramley House with the rest of the rich and posh.

'You have to come and get me!' I pleaded with her.

'I don't have my car,' she said. 'Sorry. I got a lift down with Sophie and Kate.' Sophie and Kate were the only other female traders on the Hamilton Churchill equities team.

'Oh. Well, maybe one of them could come and get me?'

'No, they can't, they've been drinking champagne since breakfast. Sorry.'

'Ali . . .' I started to say, but she'd already hung up.

She didn't sound very sorry. She sounded slightly irritated that I was bothering her. She was obviously still cross about the confrontation at my place, when I'd yelled at her and accused her of ganging up on me – with Jude of all people. There was nothing for it. I would have to walk.

Walking down country lanes in the Cotswolds is not a bit like walking in London. There are no pavements. There is tarmac and if you're lucky a bit of grass verge. If you're not lucky there are just hedgerows into which it is necessary to fling oneself when yet another sports car or SUV comes screaming around the corner.

I arrived at the hotel hot (despite the freezing temperatures outside), bothered, breathless and in quite a bit of pain (there's a reason people spend a fortune on shoes). I had just run up the steps and was about to nip into the loo to fix myself up when, to my horror, a large black Rolls-Royce decked out with white ribbons – unmistakably the bride's – pulled up. There was no time. I'd just have to go straight in. Picking bits of twig out of my hair, I flung my coat at the cloakroom assistant and slipped into the banqueting hall where the service was taking place, just seconds ahead of the bridesmaids.

I hid behind one of the enormous floral arrangements at the back of the room (rumour had it that the flowers for this bash cost upwards of fifteen grand. From my vantage point it looked like money well spent). Unfortunately, I could not see a single spare seat. I spotted Ali, about ten rows in, sitting between Sophie and Kate who were both wearing the sort of fascinators that Sarah Jessica Parker might reject for being over-the-top. She hadn't saved me a seat. Helplessly I scanned the room once more – the music was starting up, the bride was about to enter, there was not a moment to lose – there! Three or four rows in on the groom's side there was an empty seat right in the middle of the row.

I scuttled over and whispered at the gentleman on the end of the row, 'Would you mind terribly moving along a bit?'

'Yes, I would,' he replied loudly. 'People should arrive on time. Then they wouldn't have any trouble finding a seat.'

The people in front were turning around and looking. The bridesmaids were hovering in the doorway, waiting to make their entrance. I pushed past the man at the end of the row, past his wife, past the impeccable blondes next to her, and so on and so on. People tutted and sighed dramatically as I inconvenienced them. Eventually I got to the seat. As I sank down into it, breathing an enormous sigh of relief, I saw him. Dan was on the other side of the room, a few rows ahead. He was looking straight at me. For a second, our eyes met. The woman sitting next to him whispered something in his ear and he turned away.

The service was a long one. I wept as though I were the bride's mother, though her tears were unlikely to be quite so bitter. The woman sitting next to me handed me a Kleenex.

'I always cry at weddings,' she smiled at me. 'It's just so lovely to see two young people so in love.' I sobbed even harder. Eventually, after what seemed like three hours of vows, songs and sermons, we were allowed out. I made a beeline for the ladies loo.

I sized myself up in the mirror. Not good. I still had a few remaining bits of hedgerow in my hair and my face was shiny and flushed from the two-mile hike. As for the outfit . . . I was wearing a strapless gunmetal-grey satin dress which I'd found in H&M – when I'd tried it on in the shop I thought it looked simple and elegant. In the right light, if you squinted a little, it might just about pass for Calvin Klein. But now, in the ladies loos at Bramley House, standing in front of the full-length mirror, under unnecessarily harsh lighting, it just looked exactly what it was: cheap. Everyone would know. There I was, alone, in my cheap dress and scuffed shoes, and I had to go out and mingle with people wearing Chanel and Yves Saint Laurent, people wearing couture, for God's sake, people who arrived by helicopter or at the very least by Rolls-Royce.

I needed help. I needed a friend. Having done my best to fix my make-up, I went back to the party. There was still a throng of people surrounding the happy couple (she did look very good in her dress – but then who wouldn't look good in Vera Wang? – but I thought he looked a bit chinless) so I didn't even bother to try to get close enough to congratulate them – they had far more important people to speak to. I made my way through the crowd, keeping my head down, anxious to speak to Ali or at the very least to get some champagne down my throat before I had to deal with the likes of Nicholas, Christa or worse. I had almost made it – I could see Ali was just a few feet away from me, standing next to the bar – when disaster struck. Paul Fitzgerald, the odious hedge fund manager who had tried his best to humiliate me the night of the office party, lurched into my path.

'Hello there, love,' he said, breathing whisky at me.

He was swaying a little; he must have started the party early, just for a change. 'Dan not with you today?' Dan had come to my defence the last time I encountered this slug. Today there was no one to help.

'No, he's not with me,' I said, desperately trying to make my way past him.

'Oh, no, that's right, he's here with Tania, isn't he? Fantastic legs that Tania, they go all the way up. Must be difficult, splitting up, you know, with the two of you working together . . .' He laughed a nasty, snorting laugh. 'I do keep putting my foot in it, don't I? You don't work with him any more, do you? Where are you working these days?'

Abandoning any attempt to be polite I barged past Paul, shoving him into the gaggle of guests standing just behind him. Once again, there was much tutting and sighing. I finally arrived at the bar, grabbed a glass of champagne from the waiter and almost fell into Ali's arms.

'Oh, my God, I'm having a terrible day,' I moaned.

'There's a lot of it about,' she replied without looking at me.

'Why, what's up?'

'Oh, nothing much, just . . . stuff.' She was gazing into the crowd of guests, searching the room for someone. I noticed that the drink in her glass was clear and still, rather than champagne coloured and bubbly.

'You on the wagon?' I asked.

'I don't have to get completely pissed at every party I go to, do I?' she asked crossly. Finally, she was looking at me. Actually, she was looking me up and down. 'That dress isn't so bad,' she said, giving me a half-smile. She put down her drink. 'I'm just going to go and talk to Sophie. I'll catch up with you later.'

Well, that was weird. She was cold, distracted, unfriendly and – I sniffed her glass – she was drinking water. She'd driven up here with Sophie. She'd been sitting with Sophie during the service. And now she needed to talk to Sophie again? Feeling confused and upset, I grabbed a second glass of champagne and knocked it back in one. A gaggle of Hamilton Churchill women walked past, eyeing me with disdain. Oh, God. I couldn't just cower in the corner getting pissed. I had to get out there and mingle.

For about a half hour or so, I did quite well. I forced myself to go over and make small talk with Nicholas, who was surprisingly friendly to me.

'We miss you in the office, Cassie. Christa's terribly efficient but she doesn't anticipate my needs in quite the way you did,' he said, giving my arm a squeeze. I wondered whether he was drunk. Next up were Christa and Angela, the two who had shunned me in the street after the recent dog-walking debacle. They smiled at me stiffly.

'How *are* you, Cassie?' Christa asked. 'It's such a terribly difficult market out there at the moment, isn't it? Have you managed to find any work?'

'Oh, you know, this and that,' I said vaguely. She smiled sympathetically. I resisted the urge to punch her in the face. 'Actually, I'm thinking of taking some

125

time off,' I lied. 'Going travelling. Vietnam, maybe, or South America. London's so *grey* this time of year, isn't it? It's just so dull.'

'Sounds expensive. I didn't know you were independently wealthy, Cassie,' Angela smirked. I noticed that she had a piece of toilet paper stuck to the bottom of her shoe. That cheered me up.

'There's a lot about me you don't know, Angie. In fact, I'm sure there's a lot you don't know about a lot of things,' I said with a laugh. They stared at me, incredulous. I realised that I was feeling quite drunk. And that I was starting to enjoy myself. I moved on through the crowd, chatting amiably to those ex-colleagues who acknowledged my existence, and even managing to exchange a few words with the bride.

I was in the middle of telling Emily how lovely she looked when we were interrupted by a tall, dark-haired woman wearing what looked to me like Prada with a pair of Louboutins exactly like mine.

'Hi, babe,' the woman said, giving Emily a kiss on the cheek. 'Don't you look fabulous?' She turned to me and smiled. 'I don't think we've met. I'm Tania.' She held out a perfectly manicured hand. 'But then you probably knew that, didn't you?'

I didn't know what to do. I just stood there, smiling stupidly at her, desperately trying to think of something cutting or clever or at the very least vaguely amusing to say. Nothing came to me.

'You're walking dogs now, I hear?' she said. How the fuck did she know that? 'What's that like?'

'It's . . . uh . . .'

'That good, huh? Still, you obviously enjoy walking. Because you walked here, didn't you? I think we passed you on the way.'

This could not get worse. It just could not get worse. From nowhere, clutching two glasses of champagne, Dan appeared at her side. It had just got worse. He, at least, had the good grace to look ill at ease as he handed her a drink.

'Hello, Cassie,' he mumbled, looking at his shoes. 'You having a good time?'

He shifted awkwardly from one foot to another, looking excruciatingly uncomfortable.

I didn't say a word. Eventually, he looked up at me.

'Are you all right, Cassie?' he asked. He looked apologetic.

Tania slipped her hand into his.

'Come, darling,' she said, pulling him away from me. 'Let's go find someone fun to talk to.'

My champagne buzz well and truly killed, I retreated once more to the loo. Hiding in the cubicle, I wondered how in God's name he had fallen for her. How could he have chosen to be with someone so cruel? It was almost enough to make me feel sorry for him. It wasn't as though she had anything to fear from me: she was the one in the expensive dress and the great shoes. She was the one who had her man. What would make her want to stick the knife into another woman like that? The doors opened; people came and went. For the first time all day I felt safe. I wondered whether it would be possible to nip out, get a drink and come back to enjoy it without attracting attention. Probably not.

I heard the doors open again and the cut-glass tones of Christa Freeman and Angela Chenowith ringing out.

'God, she's full of shit, isn't she?' Christa was saying. 'All that crap about going travelling. As if. She's obviously broke. Did you hear she's walking dogs for a living these days!' They laughed.

'I know, my God, you'd have to be broke to come to a society wedding dressed like that. Hideous. I can't even believe she turned up at all. The only reason she got an invite was because she was seeing that trader. What's his name?'

'Dan something. Great-looking but a total shagger. He's slept with half the women in Canary Wharf.'

One of them pushed at the door of my cubicle. They fell silent.

'There's someone in here,' Angela hissed. There was shuffling, then giggling.

'Oh, Christ, I bet it's her!' There was more giggling and, eventually, the two of them left. I slipped off my shoes, rubbed my aching feet and did my best not to cry.

The good news was that I was on Ali's table for dinner. The bad news was that the rest of the table was made up of Hamilton traders who spent the entire time talking shop and ignoring me. And so much for it being a plus that I was sitting with Ali. She barely said a word to anyone, including me. She was behaving completely out of character – I couldn't believe it. After dinner I cornered her on the terrace where she was smoking a cigarette.

'Who did you tell about the dog walking?' I demanded to know. 'How is it that everybody seems to know about that? How is it that *Tania* knows about that?'

She sighed and flicked her half-smoked cigarette into the nearest plant pot.

'I don't know, Cassie, I might have mentioned it to someone at work. Is it really that important?'

'Yes, it bloody is, actually. Haven't I been humiliated enough? With the sacking and the Dan thing and the Tania thing?'

'Sorry,' she mumbled, looking over my shoulder.

'Who are you looking for?' I asked. 'What's going on? You've been weird all night. Whenever I come near you, you act like you would rather be somewhere else. You've barely said a word to me all night. What is this? Are you embarrassed to be seen with me now?'

'Jesus Christ, Cassie, not everything is about you! If you ever stopped moaning for just one second about how awful your life is you might actually notice that there are other things going on.'

'So what *is* going on? Why won't you tell me?'

'I really don't have time for this . . .'

'You don't have time? You don't have time? Why?

What's the hurry? Got to get back to Sophie and Kate, back to the important people?'

'Something like that,' she said, and walked away.

I went to the hotel reception and asked them to call me a cab. Mercifully, they could get one (it was only ten thirty, not many people would be leaving yet). Unable to face any more debilitating encounters I stood on the steps outside, shivering in the freezing night air, wishing I smoked. At least that would give me an excuse for standing out here.

I was just hopping into the minicab when my phone rang. It was Mum. And for the first time in ages, I was eager to talk to her. I am a very bad daughter.

'Hi, Mum,' I said, trying to sound cheery.

'Are you having a great time, love?'

'I am, it's been really lovely,' I lied.

'Oh, I am pleased. Where are you? I can't hear any music.'

'No, I'm standing outside,' I said. 'It's too loud to hear anything in there.' In the rear-view mirror I saw the driver raise his eyebrows.

'Well, I won't keep you – you must be freezing out there. I was round at Celia's today – she asked me to call you. She was going to give you a ring herself but she's ever so busy with the kids. Michael was at golf.'

Just for a change.

'In any case, she was wondering whether you could make it for lunch tomorrow. I mean, since you're out this way. It would be ever so good to see you. You could stay over with us if you like, get back to London on Monday.'

Well, it wasn't like I had a job to go to.

Sitting on the bright orange bedspread back in my room at the B&B I tried to form a mental list of the top five things I should be most depressed about:

1. Ali. Was our friendship really worth so little to her that she was going to dump me now that I was poor, unemployed and unglamorous? Or was it just now that she saw me for what I really am, a lower-middle-class nobody from Kettering, not the sophisticated City girl she'd met a couple of years ago?

2. Dan. I didn't want him to be at number two, I didn't want him to make the list at all, but I couldn't deny that seeing him at the wedding with her had been like a blade to the heart.

3. Joblessness. Four weeks had passed since I was made redundant and I hadn't had a flicker of interest from a serious employer.

4. Poverty. OK, maybe not poverty as such, but relative financial distress. It does not suit me.

5. The fact that I had to have lunch with my sister and her husband the following day.

10

Cassie Cavanagh *loves her mum*

The next morning I rose early and got the train from Chipping Campden to Banbury and from there to Kettering. Although I wasn't keen on the idea of lunch with Celia and Michael, for the first time in a long time I was actually looking forward to going home. It was the first time in a long time that I'd thought of my parents' house in Kettering as home. But for some reason, the presence of Jude the Judgemental perhaps, the flat in London was feeling a lot less welcoming these days.

I was looking forward to seeing my mum – I was in need of a little TLC – and also to having a conversation with my father. It struck me, on the train, that perhaps, if I asked them nicely, they might be able to help me out with a loan, just to tide me over for a few months. That way I could relax a bit about the job hunt, take time to refocus myself, to get in touch with what I really wanted to do. Perhaps I could go to a spa or a

133

retreat or something for a few days? That would definitely help. There was a good detox place I'd heard about somewhere in Oxfordshire. In fact, that would be ideal. I could get away, have a few days of completely healthy eating and no drinking, do a bit of yoga, have a massage . . . It would be just what I needed. Plus, if I could squeeze a bit of cash out of Dad I just might be able to get Jude off my back for a week or two.

And it wasn't as though I ran to them for money all the time. OK, when I was at college I had taken a couple of loans which were never fully repaid, but since I'd been working I hadn't borrowed any money at all. Unless of course you count the security deposit for the flat, but that was an emergency. (I had saved up for the security deposit myself but then that money ended up going towards the Dante kingsize bed from Heal's which was, after all, an essential. I couldn't very well sleep on a mattress on the floor, could I?) And they would get the security deposit back, eventually. Assuming we don't trash the place, which is unlikely – although with some of Jude's friends you never know. Perhaps I should suggest that the anti-capitalist lot get disinvited from our next party.

The key to getting money out of one's parents is, like so many things in life, about timing. Diving straight in is not to be advised. Money matters should wait until after lunch, when everyone's feeling sated and relaxed and has had three glasses of wine. In any case, if I asked Dad for money before lunch I could guarantee that someone would mention it over the dinner table and I could just imagine the reaction from Saint Celia and Miserly Michael who would never dream of hitting Dad or anyone else for a loan. Celia and Michael 'don't do credit', unless you count the mortgage.

'I don't trust anything that allows you to spend more than you earn,' Michael says.

Michael is living proof of the truth of the Wildean maxim that anyone who lives within their means suffers from a lack of imagination.

When I arrived at the house, around eleven thirty, Dad was out front in the garden, pruning something or other. Dad likes his gardening, although he's not a very imaginative planter. It's all pink and yellow roses, geraniums and begonias.

'Hello, darling,' he said when he saw me. 'You look tired. Rough night?'

'Not too bad,' I said, giving him a kiss.

'Well, you go on inside and have a cup of tea with your mother. I need to finish up out here.'

He always does this. Whenever I come home he makes himself scarce for about a half an hour or so, to let me and Mum chat. I've never worked out whether he does it because she tells him to, or simply because he can't stand to sit through the inevitable friends and boyfriends catch-up conversation we always seem to have when we get together.

Over a cup of tea at the kitchen table, Mum launched straight into it.

'So that Dan's history now, is he?' She did not seem distressed at the thought. Although she'd never met him, he'd gone down in everybody's estimation over the whole Dad's birthday affair. I nodded glumly.

'Are you OK, love?' she asked.

'I'm fine. I'll be fine,' I said, doing my best I'm-putting-a-brave-face-on-this face, aiming for sympathy as well as admiration for the fact that I was trying my best to cope under difficult circumstances.

'And work?'

'I've been applying for everything in sight, but it's an incredibly tough market at the moment. I have been doing part-time work though. Things are a little tight. I couldn't afford a new dress for the wedding, for example.' OK, that was a lie, but I honestly don't think a dress from H&M should count.

'Well, you've got lots of lovely things anyway, haven't you? Never known anyone with so many clothes. So, the wedding was fun, was it? Was Ali there? How is she these days?'

'Weird,' I said. 'I'm not sure what's going on with her. She's been acting really strangely lately.'

'Strange? How?' my mother asked, her face the picture of alarm. 'Do you think it might be drugs?' My parents, who don't smoke and who think that more than two glasses of wine a night constitutes binge drinking, are terrified by the very idea of illegal drugs. They firmly believe that a toke or two of marijuana will set you on a certain road to a lonely death in a bedsit with a needle sticking out of your arm.

'No, I do not think it's drugs, Mum. She's just been
... a bit distant. Quite unfriendly, actually.'

'Perhaps she's got man trouble? Does she have a
boyfriend at the moment?'

'No, I don't think so.' I wasn't about to tell Mum
about the married Frenchman, but she had a point. I
hadn't thought about that. So wrapped up in my own
Dan/Tania/bad dress drama that I hadn't even
thought about the Frenchman. Maybe he was at the
wedding? Maybe he was at the wedding with his wife?
God, that would have been awful for her, pure torture.
And I didn't even ask her about it. She was right, I *do*
think about myself all the time. I am a selfish cow.

Dad appeared at the back door, kicking the mud off
his shoes before coming into the house.

'Right. I'm going to wash my hands and then we'd
better get going. You know what Celia's like if we're
late.'

My twenty-seven-year-old sister hit middle age early.
I blame Michael. She was always a little uptight, a bit
of a control freak, but I'm sure she was more fun when
we were teenagers. She met Michael when she was
nineteen and they were married by the time she was
twenty-one. At twenty-two she had Tom, two years
later Rosie, and three years after that she had Monty.

Celia and I are very different. For one thing, she has
never worked. Well, she wouldn't say that. She'd say
she works harder than anyone else on the planet
because she has three children of five and under. She

137

may well be right. What I mean is, she's never had paid employment. She doesn't know what it's like to work in an office, to have colleagues, to receive a pay cheque. She went from school to Northampton college (where she did a catering course) but after she married they immediately started trying for a baby. Michael felt that the stress of working life would not be good for her while they were trying. She agreed.

She's never lived alone either. She went from my parents' house to a shared house at college to living with Michael. She says she can't think of anything worse than living by herself. I lived alone for two years when I first came to London and I loved it; I still miss it sometimes – being the only person authorised to touch the remote control, not being judged for spending entire days lying on the sofa in one's pyjamas reading *Vogue* and eating ice cream, never having to do anyone else's washing-up. Solitude has its compensations.

Celia missed out being twenty-something. If you ask me, she's already missed out being thirty-something, too, and pretty much fast-forwarded straight to her mid-to-late forties. She is incredibly grown up. I suppose you have to be once you become a parent. And while I know that Celia wouldn't swap her life for anyone's (and certainly not mine), I do feel a bit sorry for her. It doesn't seem as though she has a lot of fun.

As a result, she can be difficult. And annoying. Punctuality is one of her things – lateness is right up there with second-degree murder in terms of severity. Turn up at Celia's for dinner five minutes late and you can guarantee that this fact will be returned to, several times over the course of the evening, in a number of contexts. All manner of ills – from the slight under-seasoning of the soup to the crème brûlée's failure to set – will somehow be attributed to your lateness.

Fortunately, we arrived pretty much on time (she's not keen on people turning up early, either). I steeled myself for the inevitable barrage of I-told-you-sos that I was due from Michael.

'Cassie,' he said as he came down the steps of his house, trying to disentangle himself from Tom, who was attached to one leg, 'how are you? So, so sorry to hear about the job. But I did warn you. Didn't I? Didn't I?' He gave me a hug.

He is the father of your niece and nephews, I thought to myself. *You are not allowed to throttle him.*

'Yes, you warned me,' I said, smiling, but speaking through gritted teeth.

'So,' he slapped me on the back, 'how's the job hunt going? Slim pickings, I'll bet. You should maybe think of getting out of the big smoke, you know. Sounds counter-intuitive but smaller towns – like Kettering and Corby – may well turn out to be more resistant to recession than the Square Mile.'

'That's a good point,' I said. 'I might well think about that.' *Just as soon as hell freezes over.*

Celia was in the dining room, putting the finishing touches to her table setting.

'Hi, Cass,' she said when she saw me. 'How's the job hunt?' God, these people are obsessed.

'Slow,' I said. 'It's going very slowly.'

'That's a shame. Have you thought about looking for things somewhere around here? Because Michael was saying that we might not be as hard hit by the recession as you are in London.' Honestly, the woman would have almost nothing to say if she weren't able endlessly to parrot her husband's opinions. Good thing he has opinions on virtually every subject you care to mention.

Over lunch (a very good roast leg of lamb, cooked to perfection – there are some things Celia excels at), we were treated to a round-up of Michael's cases (conveyancing, conveyancing, one not particularly fruity divorce case, conveyancing) and, slightly more interestingly, a round-up of the kids' latest developmental milestones. Monty is now clearly saying Mama and Dada at appropriate times (for a long time he got them mixed up), Rosie has mastered the use not only of a spoon but also of a fork and Tom can tie his own shoelaces.

'A lot of kids don't do that until they're six,' Michael told me.

By the time we got to dessert (plum crumble with custard), Celia and Michael turned their attentions to me – specifically, to everything that was wrong about me.

'The thing is, Cassie, you have to learn to be a bit more sensible about things,' Celia said. 'Now that you have no job and no rich boyfriend, you're going to have to change your lifestyle.'

'Whatever happened with the boyfriend, anyway?' Michael asked. 'We never did get to meet him, did we?'

Oh, that's right, bring up Dad's birthday.

'He dumped her for another girl,' Celia said helpfully. Why oh why had I told her that?

'Still. You'll find someone else. You're looking well. Bit thin. Are you still going to that gym on the high street?'

'Yes, I still go.'

'You're still going there! I can't believe it. It was ever so expensive, wasn't it? How much was it again?'

'I don't know. Hundred quid a month, I think.'

'You don't know!' More incredulity, this time from Michael. 'That's where you're going wrong, Cassie. You need to keep on top of these things. You need to write down all your outgoings. Keep tabs on your expenditure. That way you won't end up living beyond your means.' Heaven forfend.

'Do you ever watch that programme, you know the one, *MoneySavers*? It's on ITV, I think it's on Wednesdays. You should watch that,' Celia said. 'They've got loads of good tips. They had a thing on last week about making gifts for your friends instead of buying them – you know, knitting scarves, crocheting a hat. That sort of thing.'

Last year I bought Ali a bracelet from Vivienne Westwood. I could imagine the look on her face if I presented her with a hat I had crocheted myself. Not wanting to be negative, I said, 'Oh, yes, I think I might have seen some of that. Jude Sky-Plussed it for me.'

'Sky Plus!'

Oh, God, why did I mention the Sky Plus?

'That's a bit of an extravagance when you don't have a job, isn't it?'

'I just haven't got round to cancelling it yet . . .'

Needless to say, that lunch was not ideal preparation for my loan discussion with Dad. I felt sure Celia had done it on purpose – she suspected I might ask for money and so she not very subtly demonstrated to my parents that I was still spending money on luxuries. She's a sneaky cow. Back at my parents' house I sat down on the sofa next to Dad, who was watching *From Russia with Love* on ITV for about the millionth time. I rested my head on his shoulder.

'You all right, Cass?' he asked. 'Sorry about that chap. Rotten thing to do.'

'Mmmm. I'll be OK. It's just that everything's happened all at once, you know. The job, Dan, worries about money . . .'

'You want to listen to your sister about that,' Dad said. God, I hated Celia sometimes. 'You have to be more careful about what you spend your money on.'

'I know, I will be more careful. I am being more careful. But it's still really tough, you know? London's such an expensive place.'

'Why don't you think about moving back up here then? Not back home with us, but back to Kettering. Rent would be much cheaper.'

This conversation was really not going the way I wanted it to.

'Well, perhaps if I was really struggling. But I've made a life for myself in London, now. All my friends are there.'

'Your family's here,' he countered.

Oh, for God's sake. I'd just have to come right out and ask.

'Dad, do you think there's any chance you might be able to lend me a bit of cash? Just to tide me over for a month or two, to help out with the rent, the bills, the essential stuff?' Probably best not to mention my idea of going to a retreat to get my head sorted. Dad sighed heavily and switched off the TV.

'Susan,' he called out to my mother who was in the kitchen making tea. 'You'd better come in here.' My mother appeared, carrying a tea tray. 'Cass has asked us for a loan,' Dad told her. 'I thought we should all talk about this together.'

My parents had anticipated the possibility that I might hit them for a bit of cash. They had discussed the matter at length and had decided that it was in my best interest to refuse.

'I can assure you that it's not in my best interest,' I protested. 'It's not in my best interest to be thrown out on the street by my landlord, is it?'

'Cassie, you're paying for an expensive gym and

143

using that Sky Plus thingamy. I don't think we're quite at the eviction stage yet, are we?' Dad said. 'You need to sort this out for yourself. You need to learn to live a bit more frugally. We're all having to do it. Everyone's having to tighten their belts. In any case, we don't have a lot to spare. Not now that we're building the conservatory.'

'What conservatory?'

'Out at the back,' Mum cut in. 'Off the kitchen. It's going to be lovely. A real sun trap.'

'We might grow tomatoes,' Dad said. Super. 'And there's the camper van . . .' he went on.

The what now? 'The camper van?'

'Oh, yes, didn't we tell you? Your mum and I are going in with Cee and Michael, buying a van so that we can go to some new places, you know, Devon and Cornwall, maybe to the Lakes. Been a while since we went anywhere other than Bournemouth.'

My parents, the last of the great explorers.

That night after dinner Dad went off to bed ('Early start tomorrow') while Mum and I stayed up talking in the kitchen.

'He won't change his mind, will he?' I asked. 'About the loan?'

'He won't and neither will I. Cassie, you know that you live a bit of an extravagant lifestyle. We understand you enjoy that, and that it's hard to give it all up, but times are hard and you're just going to have to prioritise. But I don't really want to talk about all the money malarkey – I'm sure you've had plenty of tips from Celia. I'm worried about other things. This business with Dan, for example. Are you really all right about that?'

I had the most cathartic cry I've had in a long time. Sitting there at the kitchen table with my mum's arm around my shoulders, I let it all out. How horribly he'd treated me, the way he'd been sneaking around behind my back, how mean everyone was to me at the wedding, how humiliated I had felt. I told her about how strange Ali had been, how unfriendly she was – I was really starting to worry that our friendship was in serious trouble, and I wasn't sure why. I hadn't intended to tell her all the gory details but once I started I just couldn't stop myself. By the time I got to the end of the whole sorry saga I was all cried out.

'Well,' my mother said, getting to her feet to put the kettle on yet again. 'I must say, I'm very glad he didn't come to your father's birthday party. You were quite right not to invite him. We wouldn't have liked him at all. And if you've any sense, Cass, you won't see him again. Sounds to me like you're very much better off without him. You're obviously much too good for him.'

'I am too good for him,' I agreed. 'That Tania cow can take all his crap from now on. She can put up with him ogling other woman right in front of her, she can deal with his mood swings and his ego and the Thursday-night trips to Spearmint Rhino.'

145

'To where, love?'

'It's just . . . a bar they all go to.'

I felt better already.

'So, we know you're better off without him,' Mum said. 'That's one less thing to be upset about. Far more important is this business with Ali. Boyfriends come and go, it's the girlfriends that count. I know she's upset you, but you need to talk to her about it – the sooner the better.'

She was right about that, too. Although I had tried to talk to Ali the night before, perhaps she would be more willing to confide in me if I wasn't so busy moaning about my own problems all the time. I was just going to have to be persistent.

'The other thing, Cass, is that you need to start focusing on what you want to do with your life,' Mum said. 'I won't ever regret being a full-time mum to you and Celia, but I can tell you that I wish I'd started teaching much earlier on in life. Doing something you actually care about, something that absorbs you, that you can commit to, that's invaluable. I know you enjoyed the last job – but that was mostly about the perks, wasn't it?' She knows me so well. 'Now you've got an opportunity to figure out what you really want. And if that means going back to college or something like that, then we would be prepared to help financially – and in any other way we can. So long as you are absolutely sure that it's what you want to do . . .'

'What about the conservatory and the camper van?' I asked.

She just smiled at me. 'We'd work something out.'

So all I had to do was figure out what I wanted to do with my life.

11

Cassie Cavanagh *wonders what she's done to deserve this*

Weeks to go until the money runs out: One
Weeks to go until my rent is due: Two

They were right. My parents were right. My sister, much as I hate to admit it, was right. I had to change my ways. When I got home, I logged onto my email account to see if I'd had any job offers (I had not) and then onto my bank account to get an update on the state of my finances. Not good. Really, not good. I was drifting into the red, next month's rent was due in two weeks' time and I had to make the payment on my credit card, too.

Cutbacks of the severest possible nature were going to have to be made. For as long as I was unemployed, for as long as this blasted recession lasted, I was going to have to stop living like a rich person. I sat down at the kitchen counter with a cup of (instant!) coffee and made a list of the luxuries I was going to have to cut out of my life.

1. Sky Plus – the thought of living without it filled me with horror (I would have to watch adverts again), but I figured it would be a double saving: first on the cost of the service and second because I'd be forced to stay in and watch my TV shows when they're on instead of going out all the time.
2. The gym – the park would have to do.
3. Massages; manicures and pedicures – home treatments only from now on.
4. Taking my shirts to the dry cleaner's – I would have to learn to iron.
5. Starbucks, Pret, etc. – must make own coffee, sandwiches, smoothies, etc.
6. Shoreditch House membership – the risk of bumping into Dan/Christa/Emily/the rest of the awful people from Hamilton Churchill was too high for me to be able to enjoy it any more anyway.
7. Champagne – nothing wrong with Prosecco. One bottle a week max.
8. Marks & Spencer's food – from now on all shopping to be done weekly, on the Internet, from Tesco.
9. Decleor face cream – the stuff from Superdrug is probably just as good.
10. Nights out – must start having people round for dinner instead.

Simple enough? Like hell. The thing you notice when you try to stop spending money is that the people who you usually give money to are extremely reluctant to let you stop giving them money. They plead and cajole, they coax and flatter, they seem to take everything so personally. It's rather like breaking up with somebody.

First off, Sky. I rang the customer service helpline and explained that I wished to cancel my subscription. Why did I want to discontinue Sky Plus? the man asked. Was it something they had done wrong? Was I aware of the advantageous features of Sky Plus? Was I aware that if I discontinued the service I would have to pay for a reconnection fee? That's right, once you've left us you can't just come waltzing back. Was there someone else? Was I being lured away to another provider? What exactly was that provider offering? They doubted very much that the other provider could offer the service that they did. No one could offer me the things that they had, no one would love me like they did. They seriously advised me to reconsider. Please, please stay. Eventually I told them that I had already cancelled the direct debit and hung up.

Next up, the gym. Having spent what seemed like an hour on the phone with the TV people, I decided that I would do my next bout of breaking up in person. The fit, tanned and extremely attractive young man on the reception desk in Holmes Place looked at me, aghast, disbelieving. Obviously, no one had ever broken up with him before. Let's face it, why would they?

'Are you sure?' he asked. 'You want to cancel your membership?'

I was sure. His expression changed, from disbelief to

disappointment with just a hint of disapproval. He looked me up and down, his eyes resting just a moment too long on my waist, which he clearly regarded to be insufficiently slender.

'Are you really sure you don't want to carry on exercising?' He didn't actually call me a fat cow, but he may as well have done. Breaking up with people really does bring out the worst in them. With a histrionic sigh, the receptionist called over a colleague (petite, blonde, lycra-clad) to explain to me in great detail the benefits of regular exercise. Attractive receptionist guy listened attentively, every now and again looking pointedly at her rock-hard abs before returning his gaze to her tits.

Excruciating, humiliating mission accomplished, I staggered home. There were no decent jobs to apply for, so I decided to make myself useful around the flat instead. I stripped the beds, collected towels and stuffed everything into the washing machine. Coming home to freshly laundered linens would put Jude in a good mood.

I rang Shoreditch House with a heavy heart. I had such good memories of the place: sitting by the pool, drinking gin and tonics with Ali on hot July afternoons, dinner by the fireplace on the rooftop with Dan, chaotically drunken ten-pin-bowling sessions with the traders from Hamilton . . . it was one break-up I really wasn't looking forward to.

'I'm afraid I'm going to have to cancel my membership.'

'What's the membership number?'

I gave it to him, steeling myself for the inevitable barrage of questions and attempts at persuasion.

'Ms Cavanagh?' he asked.

'Yes, that's me.'

'That's fine then, from next month your membership is terminated.' He hung up. Just like that! Just like that – it was like telling someone you wanted to end a relationship only for them to say, 'Fine, great. I never liked you that much anyway.'

I was still smarting from this rejection when I heard a loud and ominous rattling sound coming from the washing machine. There was a horrible grinding noise and a flashing red light appeared on the display. This did not look good. The grinding continued for a bit and then stopped. The light continued to flash. The machine fell silent. Oh, shit.

At the bottom of the bookshelf in the living room I found a copy of the Yellow Pages. It was from 1998. Why did we have an eleven-year-old Yellow Pages in our flat when we'd only lived here for a year? I found a local washing machine repair service on the Internet. Yes, they could come round, the call-out fee was £75 and they would then charge a further £66 an hour for labour (plus VAT). Parts would be extra. I rang another firm. No, they didn't have a call-out fee, no, they couldn't come round today. There was an opening on Thursday. But we have no sheets, no towels! Sorry, Thursday was the earliest they could do.

My problem, I reasoned, is that I always try and

spend my way out of trouble. That's what everyone keeps telling me. Whatever happens, I throw money at the problem. How about this time I try to sort things out myself, using just my own skill and ingenuity? After turning the house upside down looking for the washing machine manual, I eventually Googled the make and found it online. I clicked on the trouble-shooting section. Various problems were listed: the washing machine will not switch on, the wash cycle does not start, the washing machine leaks. Nowhere did it say: the washing machine starts, the wash cycle starts, the washing machine makes a weird grinding noise, a red flashing light comes on. It did say that if the orange indicator light (perhaps they were colour blind) started to flash rapidly I should try switching the machine off, unplugging it, waiting for a minute and then turning it back on again. They always say that though, don't they? Have you tried turning it off and then back on again?

It was worth a try. I marched back into the kitchen but didn't get as far as the machine: I skidded on a rapidly expanding pool of water accumulating on the tiles, slipped over and smacked my head on the counter.

This just wasn't funny any more.

I looked up the symptoms of concussion on the Internet: headaches (not yet), dizziness (no), nausea (not at the moment), vision disturbance (no), memory loss (no), irritability (yes), anxiety (yes), low mood (yes). Three out of eight, but my irritability, anxiety and low mood could possibly be explained by other factors. I decided I would live.

Back to the issue of the my non-functioning washing machine and the kitchen flood, which was about to become a living room flood. I needed to mop up the water. I needed towels. All the towels were in the washing machine. Crap. I dashed into Jude's room and grabbed an armful of the sarongs she has collected from her travels to Thailand and Vietnam and East Africa. I managed to form them into a sort of dam on the border between our open-plan kitchen and living room. It wouldn't hold for long. I needed to switch off the water. Where is the tap to turn the water off? Is it under the sink? I looked under the sink. Nope. The landlord would know. I scrolled through my phone, looking for the landlord's number. Why don't I have the landlord's number? Because Jude always deals with him. The dam is about to break. Crap, crap, crap. I would have to call Jude. First, I ran back to her room and grabbed the remaining sarongs to shore up the barrier. She was not going to be happy.

With mounting trepidation, I rang her number.

'Hi, Cassie,' she said curtly. We had barely spoken since the row over the dress for the wedding and despite my capitulation she was still pissed off with me.

'Jude, I've got a bit of a problem. I need to call the landlord. Do you have his number?'

'You can't pay next month's rent, can you? Christ, Cassie . . .'

'No, it's not that. It's not that. It's the washing machine. It's not working.'

'OK, have you called a repair service? Some of them don't charge a call-out fee.'

'Yes, I know, but they can't come until Thursday.' A trickle of water had made it over the barrier and onto the laminate flooring of the living room. With my phone wedged between my ear and my shoulder, I tried to pull the designer rugs out of harm's way.

'Well, Thursday's OK,' Jude was saying. 'We can wait until then, can't we? You could always go to the launderette if you need to wash stuff before then . . .'

'No, you don't understand! I've already started the wash. All our sheets and towels are in there . . . and the thing is . . . we need to do something urgently.'

'Why?' she asked nervously. 'What else is wrong?'

'It's leaking!' I wailed. 'There's water everywhere and I don't know what to do!'

'For God's sake, Cassie, why didn't you say that? Turn the water off!'

'I don't know how!'

'There's a tap next to the boiler, in the airing cupboard. Hurry!'

Crisis averted, I set about the clean-up. I wrung out the sodden sarongs and used them to mop up the rest of the water. They were in a fairly sorry state by the time I was finished, just in time for Jude to come crashing through the front door with Jake in tow. Oh, perfect.

'You couldn't have used something of yours, of course,' she said crossly, surveying the mass of filthy wet rags that her prized sarong collection had been reduced to.

'I'm sorry, I panicked and your room was closer.'

'Honestly, Cassie, how can you not know where to turn the bloody water off? You infuriate me sometimes.' She grabbed the armful of sarongs from me and stomped off to the bathroom to rinse them in clean water. Jake was crouching down in front of the washing machine, looking at the display.

'Lots of people don't know where the water in the house turns off,' he said, shifting the machine slightly so that he could take a look around the back. 'So what happened? Did it just stop midway?'

'It made a kind of grinding noise and then it stopped. And then there was water everywhere.'

'You didn't open the door, did you?'

'Of course I didn't! I'm not completely stupid.' He got to his feet and grinned at me.

'I know you're not stupid.' His smile faded and he stepped towards me, reaching out a hand as if to touch my face. More in surprise than anything else I flinched.

'No, hang on, it's just . . . you're bleeding. You've hurt yourself,' he said. He looked concerned. I told him I'd fallen and hit my head.

'I don't think it's serious,' I said.

'Let me take a look.' He pushed my hair back away from my face, leaning in to inspect the injury. He was standing very close to me. He smelt clean, like soap and water. Or perhaps that was just the laundry detergent. I could hear my heart thudding in my chest. Very gently, he slipped his hand under my chin and lifted my face to look at him.

'I think you'll pull through.' I had to admit he has a very sexy smile. Infuriatingly, I could feel myself blushing. I looked away. 'You should clean it up, though. Put some antiseptic on it,' he said.

'On what?' Jude asked, reappearing in the doorway, eyeing us suspiciously.

'Cassie slipped on the water, she fell and cut her head,' Jake said. I liked the way my name sounded when he said it.

'Oh, Cass,' Jude said, her brow furrowing with concern. 'I'm so sorry. Are you all right? I'm so sorry I yelled at you, you poor thing.' Jude can switch from strict schoolmarm to concerned parent in an instant. Taking my hand, she escorted me to the bathroom to clean up my cut. As she dabbed Savlon on my head, I noticed a small smile playing on her lips.

'What are you smiling at?' I asked. 'You think it's Karma, don't you, me cracking my skull open on the kitchen counter?'

'No,' she laughed, 'of course not. I was just wondering if I interrupted something, back then, in the kitchen? Between you and Jake?'

'I don't know what you mean,' I said, but I felt my stomach flip excitedly at the thought.

By the time we got back to the kitchen, Jake was on his knees on the floor, fiddling with something at the back of the washing machine. Apparently, the drum had not been unlocked correctly, which had caused the machine to vibrate excessively (or something) and because of the movement, the water inlet hose had become loose, allowing the machine to leak. It wouldn't take him long to fix it.

'That's really sweet of you, Jake,' Jude said, edging towards the front door. 'Is it OK if I leave you here? It's just I've got to be getting back to college.' She flashed me a wicked grin.

I made small talk while he fidgeted around at the back of the washing machine.

'So, you're doing cultural studies, are you?'

'Digital media,' he corrected me.

'Oh,' I said, trying to think of something intelligent to say, which was tricky since I didn't really know what the study of 'digital media' entailed.

'The course challenges technological determinism and over-optimistic visions of the technological future,' he said, deadpanning. I gulped. He started to laugh. 'It's all bollocks really. I'm just interested in photography and film and I like gadgets, so I thought it might be fun.' He got to his feet and slapped his hands together. 'There you go. That should work now.'

'Thank you,' I said. 'You're a life saver. Can I offer you a cup of tea?'

'I'd better be off, actually,' he said.

'OK then. Well, thanks again for helping.' I tried to

sound as breezy as possible. I didn't want to show that I was a little disappointed.

'Any time,' he said, putting on his coat. 'If you ever have a plumbing emergency, I am at your service.' I opened the front door for him to go. He just stood there, looking at me.

'What?' I asked. 'Changed your mind about the tea?'

'Do you like films?' he asked.

'Everyone likes films, don't they?'

'Yeah, OK. How about French films? It's just there's a thing on at the Ritzy, called *Entre les Murs*. It's supposed to be very good. I wondered if you fancied going one night?'

'Sounds lovely,' I said. A bit cultural for a first date, but I suppose it would give us something to talk about afterwards in case conversation dried up.

'Good. I'll call you, then.'

Yes, yes, yes!

That evening Jude came back from college laden with gifts: a Thai curry, a bottle of wine and a book called *Less is More! How to be Happy Without Spending Money.*

'What have I done to deserve all this?' I asked, delighted (with the takeout and the booze, in any case).

'I just thought you needed spoiling,' she said. 'I am sorry that you hurt yourself this morning . . .'

'Jude, it's nothing . . .'

'No, but it could have been much worse. And I've

been hard on you lately. I know. I think I'm just stressed with college stuff and missing Matt . . .'

For the second time in as many days I realised how selfish I could be. Just because Jude doesn't make a fuss about it doesn't mean that it isn't hard for her to spend nine months of the year away from the man she loves.

The two of us flicked through the book over dinner. It was written by someone called Araminta Foster who was clearly much too posh ever to have done a day's work, or indeed to worry about money, throughout her entire life. Most of it was ridiculous, a lot of guff about making jam and sewing skirts with elasticated waistbands. There were some useful things, though. The addresses of websites with cheap, organic beauty products, for example, or companies like ArmCandy that let you hire a statement handbag instead of buying one. Araminta also suggested clothes swapping parties.

'I love that idea,' I said to Jude. 'I was thinking I should have people round more, you know, entertain at home instead of going out, and I desperately need to revamp my wardrobe.' Jude rolled her eyes. As far as she's concerned I am the lovechild of Carrie Bradshaw and Imelda Marcos.

'No, I do, I really do. I need job interview outfits, something to wear for my date with Jake . . .'

'Oh, my God, he asked you out!' she shrieked excitedly, almost choking on her Pad Thai. 'I can't believe you didn't tell me!'

161

'Well, I'm telling you now. We're going to the cinema sometime next week.'

'Then we'll have to do the clothes swap party this weekend.'

12

Cassie Cavanagh *will never be a sushi chef*

When I signed up for those market research groups a few weeks back, I'd hoped that I would never actually have to attend them. But desperate times call for desperate measures. With time and money running out fast, I had no choice but to turn up at the nondescript building in Borough where, apparently, teams of marketers attempt to find out why we buy the mayonnaise we do in the quantities that we buy it.

I arrived dressed in some baggy jeans, a slightly grubby and oversized jumper and trainers. I had not bothered to wash my hair the day before, nor had I applied any make-up. I was, after all, supposed to be the thirty-something mother of two small children. A young woman holding a clipboard greeted me at the door. She was dressed in a blue skirt and pillarbox red jacket, and she looked like a British Airways stewardess.

'Hello,' she said, warmly shaking me by the hand, 'and you are?'

'Celia Wicks,' I replied.

'You've come all the way from Kettering, I see. We can give you travel expenses as well as the fifty pounds for attendance.'

Score.

'Your children not with you then?' she said, looking around anxiously, imagining perhaps that I'd left them on the pavement outside, tied to a lamppost.

'No, I'm afraid that Rosie, my youngest, had a bit of a cold, so I had to leave them at home with their dad. I hope that's OK?'

'Of course it is,' stewardess woman said, but I could tell she was disappointed.

She gave me a form to fill in, on which I entered my (i.e. Celia's) name, address and other details.

'You're thirty-four?' the stewardess asked, scrutinising me intently.

'That's right,' I lied.

'You have such lovely skin,' she said.

'That'll be all the mayonnaise,' I replied.

The testing itself was simple enough, though fairly revolting and no doubt hugely fattening. We had to eat various types of mayo and salad cream, occasionally neat but mostly smeared on either crudités or cheese biscuits, and say which ones we preferred and why. We had to express preferences for jars or bottles (squeezy or non-squeezy), whether or not we cared if our choice of mayonnaise was 'ethical'; and give our opinions on whether we thought mayonnaise was a healthy thing to be serving our children. I said I thought that it probably wasn't very healthy, but I gave it to them because they liked it. Stewardess woman looked very disappointed indeed.

With seventy quid in my pocket (they gave me twenty pounds for the train fare!) I was off to my next appointment: a group examining the World Outlook for Roll-On, Solid and Other Types of Underarm Deodorants Excluding Aerosol and Spray Types. Christ. And I thought my job was dull. Given a choice I think I'd rather walk dogs than ask people about how much Lynx they use in the morning. After answering questions about whether my brand kept me dry all day, how many reapplications I needed to make during the day and whether I felt my brand a) was reliable and b) reflected my busy and hectic lifestyle, I was sent on my way with another fifty quid in my pocket. Money for old rope, this.

Perhaps thrift wasn't so bad after all. I was really looking forward to the clothes swap party which I'd organised for Saturday night. In addition to Ali, I'd invited Kate and Sophie from Hamilton (they might be a pair of supercilious bitches but they're my size and have killer wardrobes), as well as a couple of girls from Fleet & Partners, the law firm I worked at before I went to Hamilton. Jude also invited five of her friends: we figured twelve was probably the maximum manageable number given the size of our flat.

I had done a thorough wardrobe cleanout. First to go was everything Dan ever gave me or which reminded me of him: this included the Marc Jacobs dress that I wore to the Hamilton Churchill party and which he thought looked so good on me, the Missoni scarf he bought me for Christmas and all the assorted tops and shoes and bags he'd lavished on me over the past year or so. I sighed. He really had been a very generous boyfriend. I did not include all the underwear he'd given me (his favoured gift but not really appropriate clothes swap attire), nor did I include the Louboutins, which remained hidden in their box at the back of my wardrobe. I just couldn't bring myself to part with them.

What my wardrobe needed, I had decided, was an edgier twist. All the stuff I used to wear to Hamilton was a bit corporate, so I ditched most of that, too. There were about four pairs of jeans which I never wore any more, half a dozen jumpers, the odd jacket . . . By the time I had finished deciding what I was going to be offering up for swaps, a mountain of clothes, shoes and bags had accumulated on my bed. My wardrobe was looking streamlined. Some might say sparse.

But this was a good thing, surely? My new life was all about change, and that included clothes and accessories. Plus, style gurus are always banging on about 'capsule wardrobes', and whenever you see one of those life coach programmes, they're endlessly berating their TV guinea pigs, demanding they chuck out their worldly possessions.

In true *Less is More!* spirit, Jude and I decided we

would ask everyone to bring a bottle to the party. I'd volunteered to organise the food, having nothing better to do all day. Not wanting the whole thing to seem too downmarket, I had decided that I would make sushi. At some point in my distant past someone had given me a home sushi-making kit, so on Saturday afternoon I rifled through our kitchen cupboards before eventually I found it. I was pleased to discover that inside the kit was a small, unopened bottle of sake. Just the thing to get me in the mood.

I thought I'd start out simple, with a little salmon nigiri. As per the instructions I had found on the Internet, I boiled up the shari rice, drained it and let it cool before grabbing a handful to shape into 'a long oval form'. The bottom was supposed to be flat, the top and sides more rounded in order to get the salmon to stay on top. Never mind flat on the bottom and rounded on the top, I couldn't get the rice to stick together at all. Bugger it. I ditched the first batch, had some more sake and started over.

The second batch worked a little better, and I did manage to form some respectable-looking rice bases. I had planned on doing fourteen, but it was laborious (and frankly, very boring) work, so I gave up after seven. Not everyone likes salmon anyway, do they? Next, I had to slice the fish into neat little rectangles. Or jagged, misshapen lumps, take your pick. These were to be glued to the rice with the help of a pea-sized serving of wasabi. I don't know if my wasabi was too watery or my pieces of fish too ungainly, but the salmon refused point blank to stay on top of the rice.

Damn. Nigiri is a deceptively simple-looking dish. I decided to move onto dragon rolls. I finished off the remains of the sake and got to work. It all started out rather well. I fried up my shrimp in the tempura mixture and they came out golden brown and delicious, exactly as they were supposed to be. I sliced the cucumber and peeled the avocado and got ready to do the assembly.

'Spread the rice on the nori sheet and flip it over the mat so that the rice is now facing upwards,' the instructions said. Huh?

'Lay the avocado and cucumber sticks you have precutted [sic] and line up some tempura shrimps and on top of that slice of eel.' Eel? Since when was there eel? Nobody had even mentioned eel until now. I laid out the avocado, cucumber and shrimp in a line.

'Roll it inside-out style,' the instructions said. Um, OK. I rolled up the nori sheet as best I could. Bits fell out from either end.

'Elegantly, cover the top of the roll with the layers of avocado.' What sodding layers of avocado? I'd used up the avocado. And there was nothing elegant going on here. The roll wouldn't stay rolled up, the stuffing (I'm sure that's not what you're supposed to call it) kept falling out . . . it was a total bloody disaster.

This just couldn't happen. Here I was, trying to show how together I was, trying to prove to Jude that I could cope, trying to prove to Kate and Sophie that my life was going swimmingly, trying to prove to Ali that I wasn't a total basket case, and now look at me. It was quarter to six, the guests were due here in just over two hours, the kitchen was a mess of soggy rice and greyish green wasabi paste, topped off with random bits of fish, and I hadn't even started tidying up the living room. There was nothing for it. I dialled Tsunami, the very expensive sushi restaurant around the corner.

'You have to help me!' I wailed at the man who answered the phone. 'I need twelve California rolls, twelve vegetarian California rolls, twelve salmon nigiri, twelve prawn nigiri, six salmon and six tuna sashimi and I need them now. I mean, within two hours. I could come and collect?'

'We don't usually do takeaways, miss,' the man said. 'We do cater parties, but we would need some notice for that.'

'What if I paid extra?' I asked, scarcely believing the words were coming out of my mouth even as I said them.

There was a long pause.

'There are twelve people at your party, I take it?'

'That's right.'

'We can put together a mixed platter for twelve. It will cost one hundred and sixty pounds.'

'Done.' I gave him my credit card details, trying as hard as I could not to think about how self-defeating all this was. I wished I had some sake left.

I tore through the flat, scooping the assorted sushi

mess into a bin bag and taking it to the bins outside (you never know, someone might notice it in the bin in the kitchen). I speed-tidied the living room, grabbing armfuls of trainers, laptops, iPods, magazines and other assorted junk and dumping them on Jude's bed. Realising that I smelt strongly of fish and ginger, I hopped into the shower and was just in the middle of washing my hair when the doorbell rang. Crap.

Wrapped in a tiny towel (where have all my enormous White Company bath sheets gone?), I buzzed up the delivery men from Tsunami. There were three of them, all bearing platters covered in the most exquisite-looking Japanese delicacies. Perfect. Absolutely perfect. I laid them out on the kitchen counter. Way too perfect. Even if I decanted everything from the Tsunami-branded platters, it was going to be completely obvious to everyone that I hadn't made these. Shit.

I grabbed a bunch of plates from the kitchen cupboard and began the process of laboriously transferring the rice-and-fish constructions from the platters to our plates, while at the same time squidging them in an effort to make them look less perfect. I took a fork and mashed a few of them a bit, and with a sharp knife I managed to unpick some of the nori roll in order to make everything look less professional. I heard keys rattle in the door. Jude was home. Bugger.

I grabbed the platters from the kitchen counter and sprinted to my bedroom, losing my towel on the way. I slammed the door and flung the platters under the bed.

'Cassie?' I heard her call out. 'Is everything all right?' She was coming down the hallway. I grabbed a robe and flung it around me. She knocked softly on the door.

'Come in,' I trilled, as casually as I could.

'It's weird, I could have sworn I just saw you run through the living room naked,' she said. 'You weren't preparing the food with no clothes on, were you? Because that would be unhygienic. And quite disturbing.'

I laughed heartily.

'You need your eyes tested, Jude. I was in my robe. And I wasn't making anything. Everything was ready ages ago. I was just . . . checking.'

'Well, it looks very good. I am impressed. I was expecting the kitchen to look like a bomb had hit it.'

Phew.

By eight thirty, half the guests had arrived. Well, Jude's guests had arrived, anyway. They were all gathered around the kitchen counter, trying to find the bits of vegetarian sushi.

'What's this one got in it, Cassie?' people kept asking. *I don't know, I didn't bloody make it.*

'Oh, that's avocado and cucumber,' I said, sounding less than confident.

'What's the pink stuff?'

'That's . . . the sauce.'

I'd ordered one hundred and sixty pounds' worth of sushi and most of it wasn't getting eaten because all of

Jude's friends are bloody vegetarians and none of my friends had turned up. Or should I say my 'friends'. I'd emailed Ali about this thing when we thought about it on Wednesday and she'd sent back a message saying:

Bit late notice but sounds like fun. Will rope in Kate and Soph. See you then x.

The 'rope in' part of the message annoyed me. It was as if I'd asked them to do something arduous or inconvenient. I'd invited them round for drinks, for God's sake.

In any case, the non-appearance of Ali, Kate and Sophie as well as my other former work colleagues was inconvenient not just for sushi reasons. I had been expecting a bottle or three of Laurent Perrier Rosé to get the party started. Jude's friends had all brought variations on a Jacob's Creek Rioja. Rioja? Really? With sushi? I had mentioned to Jude that I was planning a Japanese menu. Perhaps she hadn't told them.

But worse than that, far, far worse, were the clothes. When Jude announced that we were going to get started (it was after nine and despite my increasingly frantic texts there had been no news from Ali or anyone else), I began to get a glimpse of my prospective new wardrobe. Much of it – the best of it – came from Topshop. Some of it was handmade. There was tie-dye, there was crochet, there were old pairs of leggings, there were endless nasty, stretched, holey T-shirts which I would feel embarrassed donating to a charity shop, let alone offering as realistic swap material to my friends.

Oh. God. I *had* to get out of here, and I had to get out of here with *my* clothes. I was sitting cross-legged on the living room floor with my back to the hallway (the escape route to my bedroom), sipping a glass of warm red wine. My clothes, the clothes which I had intended to offer up for swaps, were in a pile next to me. Slowly, surreptitiously, I tried to push my pile behind my back while at the same time inching backwards on my arse towards the door. I was just about starting to think that I might be able to shove my clothes into the hallway, taking them out of eyesight and out of reach, then spill some red wine to create a diversion and leg it into the room with my stuff, when Tilly, one of Jude's trustafarian mates, said, 'Oh, gosh, look at these,' pulling a pair of True Religion jeans from the pile behind me. 'God, there's a load more stuff here!'

They descended like jackals on a half-eaten zebra carcass, delightedly snatching up the delicious tidbits which I had hoped to save from their grasp. Who cared that a couple of hours ago I was happy to be rid of all this stuff? That was before I knew that all I'd be getting to replace it would be a bunch of tasteless student tat not fit to clean the house in.

Jude and friends had decamped to the pub, crowing over newly acquired designer items. I remained behind.

'I'm feeling a bit tired,' I said, clutching the one decent item I had managed to scavenge from Jude's mates, a slightly gothic but quite sexy black dress from All Saints. Not much good for wearing to job interviews, but I had to come away with something.

'I'm not surprised after all the work you've put into this, Cass,' Jude said. 'It's just such a shame Ali and the others couldn't make it.'

As she left I cursed her and her bright ideas. Dog walking, clothes swaps . . . it was all her fault. I could have sold all my old stuff on eBay. But oh no, I had to listen to Jude and now, here I was, a hundred and sixty quid out of pocket, half a wardrobe down, left with enough uneaten sushi to feed the five thousand.

Annoyed as I was, that wasn't what was really bothering me. What hurt me – if I'm honest, what broke my heart – is that Ali hadn't shown up. Not only had she not shown up, she hadn't even called to say she wasn't coming, to explain why, to apologise. She hadn't even returned the calls I made earlier in the evening asking her where she was. I was starting to realise what was going on: she had dumped me. Ali had dumped me.

How had I not recognised the signs earlier? I've seen her dump men enough times before. First, there's the slight cooling of the relationship as she puts some distance between them. Then she starts to look elsewhere, in an obvious way. Her targets are often completely unsuitable people (in this instance Kate and Sophie). She gets irritable in the man's presence, snaps at him for no reason. Then, if the poor sod hasn't already got the message, she just snubs him. Doesn't turn up when she's supposed to and doesn't take his calls. It was official. I had been dumped three times in the space of two months: first by my employer, then by my boyfriend and now by my best friend. And this hurt most of all.

13

Cassie Cavanagh *is injured*

Hours to go until the date with Jake: 28
Number of pounds in my bank account: -£1,789
Available bank balance: £11
Credit left on my card: £18.88
Weeks until the rent is due: One

Dog walking continued, out of sheer necessity. After I'd taken Susie and Stanley out (she's the only one he'll walk with without biting), I went to see Mrs Bromell to pick up payment. As she handed over the cash, she said, 'Would you mind popping over to see Mrs Mellor at some point this week, dear?' Mrs Mellor is the owner of Thierry and Theo, the skittish greyhounds.

'Of course,' I said, a little nervously. 'Is something wrong?'

'I don't think so,' she said. 'I think she may just have a favour to ask of you.'

Well, as long as it was a paid favour, I didn't care.

Dog walking over the past week had earned me the princely sum of £70 – not enough to cover half the damned Tsunami sushi bill. Jude had very sweetly offered to give me a bit of cash for the party.

'After all,' she said, 'you did all the work and you didn't seem to take many clothes.' She handed me a tenner.

Money wasn't the only thing playing on my mind. The date with Jake was coming up and I was unaccountably nervous. So nervous I had spent the past three days reading Jude's *Guardian* from cover to cover. I was sure he was the sort of person who would have opinions on world events and I didn't want to come across as a complete idiot. After all, we had only met twice: the first time I had been lying on the bathroom floor, the second I was recovering from a mild concussion following a flood in the kitchen. Come to think of it, why did this man want to go out with me?

No use obsessing over it, the point was that he did. He did want to go out with me – and he wanted to go out with me tomorrow. I was starting to panic: I had nothing to wear and I was looking, shall we say, a little unkempt. Yes, I know it was only a first date, but there is an unwritten law somewhere that if you go out with a man without sufficient depilating you are guaranteed to be removing your clothes in his company at some point in the evening.

The long and short of it was that I was in need of a wax. I rang Body & Soul. The full leg and Brazilian cost

£120. I literally could not afford it. I consulted *Less is More!*. There was an entire section on beauty therapies, including home sugar-waxing. I rang Jude to make sure that she was not planning on coming home until that evening. She wasn't. I double-locked the door, putting the chain on as well (just in case) and got down to business.

'Waxing at home need not be a painful or messy experience,' the book said cheerily. *'In fact, you can recreate the atmosphere in some of the world's best spas in the comfort of your own bathroom.'* What a load of unmitigated bullshit, I thought, skipping through the rest of the blurb until I reached the actual recipe.

All I needed, the book said, was a cup of sugar, two tablespoons of water and two tablespoons of lemon juice, as well a saucepan, butter knife and some cotton or linen scraps cut into strips. The book recommended old sheets. I rummaged around in the airing cupboard and found some pillow cases that looked as though they had seen better days. Those would do.

In the kitchen I boiled up the sugar, water and lemon juice in one of Jude's copper-bottomed saucepans. According to the book, I had to simmer the mixture over a medium heat for five to eight minutes while stirring CONSTANTLY until it became slightly frothy. After ten minutes or so my arm was starting to ache and there was not a lot of froth going on. I turned the heat up and stirred vigorously. My phone buzzed on the counter opposite. It was Ali calling. Not like her to be calling in the middle of the morning on a

179

weekday; not like her to be calling at all these days. I picked up.

'Hello, stranger,' I said.

'Hi, Cass.' She sounded forlorn and distant. There was an odd echo, as though she were calling me from a church.

'Where are you?' I asked.

'In the loo at work,' she replied. There was a sharp inhale on the other end of the line. She was smoking. Smoking in the loos at Hamilton in the middle of the morning with the markets open? All was not well.

'Look, I'm really sorry about Saturday,' she said. 'I've been having a total bitch of a time at work and the thought of having to spend an evening with Jude and the hippies as well as Kate and Sophie was just too fucking much for me.'

'So you thought you'd just ignore me, did you? You could have called me, Ali. You could at least have replied to my texts.'

'I know, I'm really sorry. To be honest with you I went to bed at about six thirty and I turned off my phone.' A likely story.

'You were with that guy, weren't you? You blew me off to see your married man.'

'I didn't, Cassie. I swear, I've just been feeling . . . Oh, whatever. How'd the clothes go anyway?'

'Total disaster,' I said. 'Because you and the Hamilton girls didn't turn up, I ended up with a load of tasteless crap from Jude's mates while they took all my good stuff. So cheers for that.'

She sighed. 'Look, I've said I'm sorry . . .'

'And I had to shell out loads of cash for food because the stuff I'd made didn't work out . . .' I realised that I was doing it again – moaning about myself when there was clearly something going on with her. Suppressing my disappointment with her, I asked, 'Ali, why aren't you on the floor? You're in the loos, smoking – don't deny it, I can hear you – this isn't like you.'

'Shit, there's someone coming. Hang on . . .' There were some scuffling noises, the pffft of a lit cigarette hitting water, then she was back on the line, whispering, 'I can't talk now. Gotta go.'

Feeling more than a little irritated by her half-hearted apologies (I was sure that she'd been with that French guy; there was no way Ali would gone to bed at six thirty on a Saturday unless there was someone else going to bed with her), I realised that there was an unpleasant stench emanating from the kitchen. Oh, fuck, the sugar wax

The mixture had boiled down to a nasty brownish-black treacle which was now smoking ominously. I grabbed it off the heat, and chucked it in the sink, yanking open windows as I did in an attempt to stop the smoke alarm going off. Too late. Still, at least I knew the alarm worked. After fighting with it for a minute or two, answering the door to my irate upstairs neighbour, Mr Poole, apologising profusely to Mr Poole and finally, when Mr Poole refused to accept my apologies telling Mr Poole to sod off, I got back to the home waxing.

I grabbed another saucepan from the cupboard and started boiling up my mixture again. I managed to get to the frothy stage, checked whether there were any granules left (there weren't) and decanted it into a ceramic bowl. The book instructed me to put the mixture into the fridge for AT LEAST fifteen minutes before I used it.

My phone buzzed again. It was Mrs Bromell, asking if I'd be able to take Paddington out this afternoon. He had a vet's appointment at three and they really wanted him to go out first. It meant I'd be a bit pushed for time, but I really couldn't afford to turn the work down. I stuck the sugar wax in the freezer for a couple of minutes. That ought to do it. Then, standing in the kitchen dressed in a bra and nothing else, I got to work. Get the worst over first, I thought, slathering some wax at the top of my inner thigh.

I screamed. I howled, I hopped around in agony. Too hot, it was too bloody hot! Hoping the people in the apartment block backing onto ours couldn't see me, I clambered up onto the counter and splashed the scalded area with cold water. There was a banging on the door.

'Could you *please* keep the noise down in there?' It was Mr Poole from upstairs. 'I am *trying* to work here.' Jude and I have never been able to figure out exactly what it is Mr Poole does and I was not in the mood to find out.

'Oh, will you just piss off!' I yelled at the top of my voice. There was a stunned silence from the other side of the door.

'Well, I must say . . .' I heard him mutter before he stomped off upstairs.

Oh God oh God. What the hell should I do? It was agony. I couldn't bring myself to pull the strip of linen off, convinced that if I did it would take three layers of skin with it. What to do? Araminta, the stupid bloody *Less is More!* woman did not give advice on how to deal with third-degree burns as a result of home sugar waxing, so I called NHS Direct.

In between bouts of barely stifled laughter, the woman on the other end of the line told me that I needed to get to Accident & Emergency as soon as possible. Would I be justified in calling an ambulance? I asked her. No, she didn't think so.

'If you can't face public transport, get a minicab, love.'

Economy drive or no economy drive, there was no way I was going to get on the tube in that state. I rang our local car service, pulled on some tracksuit bottoms using extreme care, donned a long coat and trainers and made my way gingerly down the stairs to the cab. I lowered myself onto the back seat and we set off towards St Thomas's. The taxi cost £9. I handed over a tenner and waited for my change. Sighing dramatically, the driver handed back my pound. Now marked as a non-tipper, I was going to have to change minicab firms.

In A&E, I explained my situation in hushed tones to the woman on the reception desk. She kept a straight face throughout and even managed to sound sympathetic.

'That must be very painful,' she said. 'I'll do my best to get someone to see you as soon as possible.'

Unable to sit down with any comfort, I stood by the window of the waiting room and, ignoring the prominent *'No Mobile Phones'* signs, rang Mrs Bromell to cancel Paddington. She sounded pained. Not as pained as I was. Then, in dire need of some hand-holding, I rang Jude. There was no answer from her phone. I looked at my watch. It was after four thirty. The market had closed. I rang Ali. She was still in the office, but she took the call.

'Where are you?' she asked. 'Sounds like you're in a train station. Are you going somewhere?'

I told her the whole sorry tale. When she had stopped crying with laughter, she said,

'God bless you, Cassandra Cavanagh, that is the funniest thing – the only funny thing, in fact – that I have heard in about a month.'

'Very pleased I could be of service,' I grumbled, but it was lovely to hear her laugh like that again.

'Stay put,' she said. Not that I had much choice. 'I'll be there as soon as I can.'

A minute later, a nurse came to call me through to the treatment area.

The nurse, a jovial South African lady called Josephine with a dazzling smile and enormous bosom, instructed me to slip off my clothes, put on a robe, and lie down on the bed in the cubicle. The doctor would be with me in a second. When he arrived, I knew for sure. Events of the past few weeks had given me the

184

strong suspicion that God hated me, but I couldn't be certain. Now I knew. There in front of me stood Dr Dragovic, a six-foot-four Serb, all dark hair and smouldering eyes, St Thomas's answer to Luka Kovač off *ER*. (Dr Dragovic probably wouldn't welcome the comparison – I had a feeling the Serbs and the Croats didn't like each other that much – but it was true.)

Dr Dragovic read my notes. He read them again. He looked up at me. I smiled stupidly. He went back to his notes.

'OK, Miss Cavanagh,' he said in his delightfully brooding accent, 'I'm just going to take a look here.'

Oh, sweet Jesus, he's lifting up my robe.

'Right, I see,' he said, examining the area with a frown. I could no longer bear to look at him. I just lay back with my eyes closed, feeling my face turn puce.

'I think there is some quite bad scalding there . . . And we will of course have to remove the . . . the material in order to treat . . .' He stood up straight and I yanked the robe back down to my knees. He smiled, revealing a gold tooth which for some inexplicable reason made him even sexier. 'It won't be too bad. We just need to get the material off without damaging your skin. Don't worry too much.'

He disappeared for a few minutes and returned with Josephine who now bore a range of unguents and something that looked like a heat pack that you'd put on a swollen ankle.

'We need to soften the wax a bit, then we can remove it and treat the burn,' Dr Dragovic explained kindly.

'But first I will give you something so that you cannot feel it so much.' Oh, thank God. Drugs. Unfortunately, all he gave me was a local anaesthetic which meant him inspecting my unwaxed upper thighs once again. I swore under my breath that if I ever came across Araminta Foster I would make her feel my wrath.

Fortunately, the procedure was relatively painless. There was a nasty red welt on my upper thigh which they covered with antiseptics and a bandage, and I was under strict instructions not to get the burn wet for three days.

'No showers?' I asked, incredulous.

'No showers,' Josephine replied firmly. 'In three days you must come back and we'll change the dressing and make sure everything's OK.' She smiled sweetly at me. 'Next time, I would go to the beauty salon. I know a good one in Chingford if you'd like a recommendation.'

By the time I was finished, Ali had arrived. She was standing outside the A&E waiting room, smoking a cigarette. She started to laugh as soon as she saw me.

'Oh, you poor thing,' she giggled, giving me a hug. 'That must have been a special experience.'

'You have no idea,' I replied. 'You should have seen the doctor. Luka Kovač, only better.'

'Jeez, can we go back in? Perhaps if I stub my cigarette out on my arm I'll get to meet him.'

Ali bundled me into a cab and the two of us headed over to her flat near Angel. She was renting the most fabulous, canal-side warehouse conversion (complete with roof terrace, hot tub and Porsche kitchen) which she'd snapped up last year just after getting her bonus.

'Don't think I'm going to be here much longer,' she said miserably as we took the lift to the fifth floor.'

'Worried about work?' I asked.

'It's not so much that . . .' she said.

We were barely through the door when she broke down in tears.

'Oh, Cassie,' she blubbed at me, collapsing in a heap on the sheepskin rug in the entrance hall, 'I can't believe what a mess I've made of everything.'

I couldn't believe what I was seeing. Ali, stone-cold sober, totally losing the plot? It just didn't happen. She was the strongest, most in-control woman I'd ever met; she was one of the most macho of traders at Hamilton, feared at poker games because she never, ever gave anything away.

'What is it?' I asked, kneeling down to put my arms around her. 'What on earth's happened?'

She continued to blub but didn't say anything.

'Can I get you a drink?' I asked. 'Vodka? Wine?'

'Nooo!' she wailed, and blubbed even harder.

When she'd finally stopped crying and I managed to move her from the floor to the sofa, she asked for a cup of tea. As I handed it to her, she said, 'I'm pregnant.' I almost dropped the scalding tea in her lap, the bluntness of her announcement caught me so by surprise. This entire time I had imagined that there was either something up with the Frenchman or

187

something up at work. Never for a moment did I think . . . And at that moment I cast my mind back to the wedding, to the way she reacted when I asked her why she wasn't drinking. God, I could be stupid sometimes.

'I take it this is the Frenchman's?' I asked, handing her a Kleenex.

She blew her nose loudly, nodding at the same time.

'He's been a total shit about everything. Doesn't want to know about it and doesn't want anything to do with me any more. He's gone scampering back to wifey, his tail between his legs. God, it's such a fucking cliché! Do you know what the first thing he asked me was?' I shook my head. '"Are you sure it's mine?"'

'Jesus, what's the French for wanker?' I asked.

'I know! And the thing is, it *is* his. I know it is. There hasn't been anyone else for ages . . .' she tailed off. 'I didn't tell anyone about it, but I'd been sleeping with him on and off for most of last year.'

'Ali! I can't believe you didn't tell me . . .'

'I know. It was just – I knew that the whole thing was stupid – he was married and everything, so it was never going to go anywhere. But I wanted it to. I liked him, Cass. I really liked him.'

'And now? Do you love him? Are you in love with him?'

'I was,' she said sadly. 'At least I thought I was. Funny how quickly you can go from being madly in love with someone to planning what track's going to be playing when you dance on their grave.' She put down her cup of tea and lit a cigarette. 'Help yourself to a real drink, by the way. Just because I'm on the wagon doesn't mean you have to be.'

'Ali . . .' I said nervously. 'You're not drinking but you are smoking? What does this mean? What are you planning to do?'

'I'm not smoking a lot,' she said guiltily, stubbing it out in the ashtray in front of her.

'So . . . you're going to have the baby?' I was astounded. I do love Ali, I love her to bits, but she's about the least maternal person I know.

'I think so,' she said softly, without looking at me. I gave her a hug.

We talked for hours, me knocking back Chianti, her drinking endless cups of tea. I told her she ought to switch to herbal. She told me to fuck off. I suggested she at least stop smoking; she said she was down to just five a day, and was planning weaning herself off them over the next few weeks. I looked sceptical.

'I will, Jesus, I promise. God, it's not like I'm not prepared for my sacrifices. This will be the end of my career, you know. I'll be mummy-tracked. If this were a good market I might be shoved into corporate finance. But today? I'll be incredibly lucky to keep my job. If I were a bookie I'd be giving odds of around twelve to one against.' She smiled ruefully. 'Still, I tell you what. If I am on my way out I'm going to use the remaining weeks and months I have at work to lose Jean-Luc all the money I've made him over the past year.'

Later on, with the help of a little Dutch courage, I asked her why she'd decided to keep it.

'Why, when you know it's going to be the end of your career, when the father doesn't want to know, when you're only twenty-seven . . . Why are you going to have the baby? Not that I think it's a bad thing, I don't,' I added hastily. 'I'm just . . . surprised, that's all. You've never talked about wanting kids.'

'Never thought I wanted them,' she replied. 'I mean, not even five or six years down the line, even if I were married and settled – which is, let's face it, unlikely – even then, I didn't picture myself with kids. And I have no problem with abortion. I can't really explain it. It's just that now that he or she is here, I don't want him or her to not be here. Does that make sense?'

After that much wine, combined with some seriously strong painkillers, not a lot made sense. I certainly didn't. Unable to persuade me to go to bed in the spare room, Ali laid me down on the sofa and covered me with a blanket before disappearing off to bed.

The next morning she woke me with coffee. Groggily accepting the mug, I pulled myself upright. My upper thigh hurt like hell. My head was almost as bad.

'Christ, Ali,' I groaned. 'What time is it?'

'Just after nine.' Maybe it was just because I knew, maybe it was because she hadn't had a drink in weeks, but she looked fabulous, a peachy glow illuminating her complexion.

'Why aren't you at work?'

'Took a sickie,' she said with a grin. I don't think Ali has ever taken a sickie in her life. 'If I'm going to get fired or sidelined anyway, I don't see the point in working like a dog for those bastards.'

'Talking of dogs,' I moaned, 'I have to get back to Clapham. I have a ten thirty with a pair of dachshunds.'

I was very glad that the only dogs on my schedule that day were the smaller ones. It was a freezing day, a bone-chilling wind blowing in from the north, not a ray of sunshine to be felt. The Common wasn't too muddy, thankfully, but there were treacherous patches of ice on the pavements and I didn't fancy getting yanked left and right by some of the more powerful hounds on my rota. Particularly not with my injury, which was still very painful, industrial-strength Codeine tablets notwithstanding.

After the dachshunds there was a series of other small, yappy, annoying little creatures and it wasn't until after lunchtime that I got home. I collapsed on the sofa with a (home-made) tuna sandwich and flicked on the TV. Nothing on. That's what happens when you get rid of satellite TV. I checked my emails for job news.

Hallelujah! There was a message from a temp agency saying they needed someone to work Monday to Friday next week in a 'mid-sized City investment bank'. Could I come in for an interview? Real work! I thought, ecstatic. I fired off an email saying I would be very happy to attend the interview on Friday morning. Then it struck me: I'd given away most of my City suits at the fated clothes swap. What the hell was I going to

191

wear? Then another thought struck me: Friday was two days away. I was under strict instructions not to shower for three days. I'd cross that bridge when I came to it.

I skipped into my bedroom (as best I could under the circumstances), feeling as though a weight had been lifted from my shoulders. This was it – this was the break I'd been waiting for. All I needed was to get my foot in the door. Then I could dazzle them all with how marvellously efficient, friendly and presentable I was, I would fetch the coffee, I would stay late in the office, I would go that all-important extra mile. I would make myself indispensable. And by the end of next week, I thought to myself, I could have a real job!

I was right in the middle of trawling through my wardrobe for something decent to wear to the interview when I realised I was having a sense of déjà vu. Looking through the wardrobe for something to wear . . . I had done this recently . . . very recently. Oh, shit. Jake. In less than five hours' time I was supposed to be standing in the foyer of the Ritzy cinema wearing something casual-yet-sexy, preferably with my hair washed and blow-dried. I looked at myself in the mirror. Oh, God. There was no way I could get away with this. I had to cancel.

He picked up on the third ring.

'Hey. How's the washing machine?' he asked when he answered. 'No more floods? No more severe head injuries?'

I laughed weakly.

'No, no, everything's OK. It's just . . . I'm really sorry to do this to you at such late notice, but I was wondering whether we could reschedule?'

Silence on the other end of the line.

'The thing is . . .' I really ought to have written something down before I made this call. Lying, I've found, is usually the best idea in these sorts of circumstances. 'The thing is that I've just been offered a job interview – it's tomorrow morning and I really need to focus, you know? I need to think about what I'm going to say and it would be a good idea to get an early night. I don't think I'll be able to relax if we go out this evening. I won't be any fun. Could we do it another night?'

'Course we can,' he said. 'That's great news on the job interview. Good luck with it. Give me a ring when you're done, let me know how it went and we can set something else up.'

'That would be brilliant, Jake, thank you so much.'

Crisis averted.

I returned to the job at hand, which was to find an outfit for an interview and, assuming that I would get the job, trying to find a way of mixing and matching things so that I didn't look as though I was wearing the same clothes all week. I was still in a frenzy of outfit consideration when Jude came home.

'You'll never guess!' I yelled excitedly to her, running out into the hallway in a skirt and bra.

'You're thinking of becoming a stripper?' she ventured.

193

'I've got an interview! It's just for a temp job, but I think it could lead onto something permanent.' Actually the temp agency had suggested no such thing, but it never hurt to be upbeat.

'Brilliant news, Cass. Do you think that warrants opening a bottle of champagne?' I said yes, of course, and we settled down on the sofa with our glasses.

'So when's the interview?' she asked me.

'Friday,' I said. 'Friday morning.'

Thursday passed fairly uneventfully in a blur of dog leads and job applications – two things I was hoping to be able to leave behind for good in a few days' time. It wasn't until the evening that things went downhill. Jake phoned at around six.

'How'd the interview go?' he asked, his tone flat.

'It was fine . . . OK, you know.' There was a long silence. I knew that something was up.

'You know what, Cassie? I don't know why you cancelled last night and right now I honestly don't care. I find all this game playing unbearable. You obviously are better suited to rich City boys who treat you like shit.'

He hung up, leaving me standing in the kitchen with the phone to my ear, red-faced and crushed.

I wasn't sure how he knew that I'd lied, but I had my suspicions, which were duly confirmed when Jude got home.

'Did you talk to Jake at all today?' I asked her.

'Yeah. We had a bit of a weird conversation actually.

He was asking what time your interview was, and I said it wasn't until tomorrow, and he was really insistent that it must be today . . . Anyway. I did eventually convince him that it was tomorrow morning, and then he just went all moody and silent and walked off. What's that about?'

I admitted that I'd lied to him about the interview.

'Cassie! You idiot. You could at least have told me that so we could have had our stories straight. In any case, you could have told him the truth. He's a lovely guy, he's not like—'

'Dan? No, I'm sure he isn't, but how could I have told him the truth, Jude? What was I going to say? "The thing is, Jake, I can't go out with you tonight because I can't have a shower and wash my hair. Why can't I do that? Well, thinking that there was a slight chance that we might have sex on our first date, and being too broke to go to a salon to get waxed, I decided to attempt a bikini wax at home by myself and ended up giving myself second-degree burns on my inner thigh."' Jude started to giggle. 'You see? Sometimes, truth-telling really is out of the question.'

The only good news of the week was that the interview with the temp agency went well. I had five whole days of real work set up: five days in which I would put on a suit and heels and wedge myself onto the tube with the rest of London (oh, how I'd missed that), five days in which I would eat sandwiches from Pret A Manger and drink coffee from Starbucks with the rest of London, five days in which I would not have to be dragged around the freezing, muddy Common with five dogs attached to my arm, five days in which I would not have enough time to sit around the flat, moping about how rubbish my life is. I was going back to the City. I was going back to work.

14

Cassie Cavanagh *is still laughing at Christa*

Bank balance: -£1,877.30
Weeks to go until the money runs out: One, possibly two. Unless I get very prompt payment for this temping job.

Monday
I couldn't believe how excited I was to start my new (temp) job. I'd hardly slept the night before, I was like a five-year-old on Christmas Eve. I woke up at six, leapt out of bed as though stung and began preparing myself for the day ahead. I nipped downstairs to the newsagents and bought not just the *Guardian*, but the *FT*, too. I washed and blow-dried my hair, put on the very best of the suits I had left (dark grey wool from Max Mara, very fitted, very elegant, very grown up) and a pair of high – though not so high as to look frivolous and flighty – red heels. I didn't have to be at the offices of Simmons & Blaythe until nine, but I set

off early at quarter to eight anyway. I was leaving nothing to chance. This was the best opportunity I'd had in ages.

Simmons & Blaythe is another London investment bank. It's much smaller than Hamilton Churchill, and I quite liked the idea of working for them because they specialised in corporate finance rather than trading, so that would make for a somewhat less fraught atmosphere in the office. On the downside, corporate finance people worked every hour God sent – no market hours to follow – and I wasn't quite sure how that would apply to personal assistants. I had read through all their corporate blurb and they seemed like pretty good employers – they even featured on *The Times* list of the best places in the UK to work, which is pretty unusual for a financial services firm. And although they were small they had offices in Hong Kong, Frankfurt and New York, so there might be opportunities to go abroad, if I could move up the ladder a little. Assuming, of course, that I lasted more than a week.

Simmons & Blaythe's London offices were in Canary Wharf, like Hamilton Churchill's, although they were situated in the less prestigious Number 25 Canada Square. Still, I had to recreate the journey that I used to enjoy so much, and even the unpleasant bits (the Northern Line, the Waterloo & City Line) brought back pangs of nostalgia. For once, everything ran smoothly. Trains arrived as I descended to the platform and parted immediately after I had got on, there were no long, inexplicable delays in the middles of tunnels, there were no signal failures, no people taken ill on trains, no bodies on the tracks. It was one of those days when you wonder why everyone whines so much about working in London.

To get to Number 25, I had to walk past Number 1, my old stomping ground. Despite the sun barely breaking through grey clouds, I donned my sunglasses, just in case I bumped into anyone I knew and wanted to avoid. I had passed the main entrance and was just breathing a sigh of relief, believing I had snuck past unscathed when she appeared, walking in the opposite direction. Christa Freeman, dressed in a short (unnecessarily short, I thought) black skirt and jacket and waiting-list-only snakeskin heels from Miu Miu. She was striding towards me, her head held high, a trace of a smile on her lips. Bugger. She'd seen me. I steeled myself for an onslaught of patronising remarks. And then it happened. It was a glorious moment. Everything seemed to go into slow motion. As Christa stepped onto a grid covering the guttering outside the building, her stiletto heel slipped into the grate. She stumbled slightly, her smug little smile disappeared from her face. She righted herself just in time but as she pulled her heel out of the grid there was a loud and satisfying snap. One of the heels on her £400 shoes had just disappeared, quite literally, down the drain.

I didn't collapse into hysterical laughter. I didn't even break stride. I just kept on going, calling out,

'Morning, Christa,' as I swept regally past her. When I glanced back over my shoulder I could see her hopping around on one foot, trying to keep her balance while peering desperately into the grate in an attempt to recover her heel, all the while revealing a good deal more of her stockings than I'm sure she intended. Maybe God doesn't hate me that much after all. Or perhaps he just hates Christa Freeman too.

After an exceptionally good start to the morning, my day just got better. My boss for the week was Ms Stella Conrad-Pickles (a woman!), who was tall and thin and terrifyingly elegant but turned out to be lovely. She did not bark orders at me, she said please and thank you and smiled when she did so. Astoundingly, she even offered to drop in at Starbucks and buy *me* a coffee on the way back from her lunch. Extraordinary! Nicholas would sooner have taken out an eyeball with a fork.

The Simmons & Blaythe offices were much more civilised than Hamilton's. People didn't tend to scream at each other across the open-plan floor; some of them acknowledged the presence of the assistants – even temp assistants like me – occasionally with a smile. And the other PA in my section, an Australian girl called Becky, was a world away from Christa. She didn't exactly greet me with a hug, but she showed me where everything was and how everything worked, she took me to the canteen at lunchtime and overall she seemed perfectly pleasant. By five o'clock (which was when Stella told me I could go, despite the fact that I was supposed to work until six), I was convinced: this was the job for me. I just had to convince them of that fact, too. God, I love the City.

Wednesday

I hate the City. Everyone is shallow and consumerist, they're obsessed with money and cars and clothes and things. Things, things, things. The men are pigs and the women know that unless they fit in with the boys they'll be harassed to within an inch of their lives, so most of them ending up being pigs, too.

Tuesday went well, almost as well as Monday, but on Wednesday I was a little bit late getting in. Stella, who'd got stuck in traffic on the M25 on her way in from Tunbridge Wells, was also late – but she was late for a meeting with the board of directors, so it was an altogether more serious matter. She came haring into the office, threw her coat and bag at me (much in the style of Meryl Streep in *The Devil Wears Prada*) and hissed, 'Where's my Chai latte?'

'I thought I'd wait until you got in before I got it,' I explained nervously. 'I didn't want it to get cold.'

'There's a microwave in the kitchen, you moron,' she snapped. A bit taken aback, I offered to go and get her one straight away.

'Well, it's too late *now*, isn't it?' she said witheringly, looking me up and down as she did so. I was wearing black trousers and a rather bobbly black jumper, my hair scraped back into a ponytail. I'd overslept a bit and hadn't had the time to put the usual thought and effort into my appearance. After Stella had disappeared into her meeting, Becky came over to my desk.

'Stella prefers it if we wear jackets or shirts, not jumpers,' she said. 'She thinks it looks more professional.' She said this without a smile. She obviously didn't approve of my outfit either.

At the canteen at lunchtime I felt as though I was in one of those awful scenes from a US high school drama where the new kid walks around aimlessly while everyone else makes it quite clear that they don't want him or her at their table. It wasn't quite that bad – since most people didn't know me they just ignored me – but when I spotted Becky, sitting with a couple of other girls in the corner, I could tell from the look on her face that she didn't want me to join them. It was odd. We seemed to have got on fine on Monday. She obviously *really* disapproved of my jumper. Too bad. Since I was already approaching their table and couldn't see anywhere else to sit, I just smiled cheerfully and asked, 'Mind if I sit down?'

'Course not,' Becky said, without looking at me. She introduced me to the two blonde girls at the table who also said hello without really looking at me. I don't recall their names.

'So anyway,' Blonde 1 was saying, 'Sebastian wants to go to St Barts for New Year, but I'm like, God, really? Again? I'm so bored with the Caribbean.'

'Oh, God, yah,' Blonde 2 agreed. 'Fregate Island, you know, in the Seychelles. That is like, totally the place now. It was on the Forbes list of the most

202

expensive hotels in the world.'

'Oh, my God! Really? That sounds amazing.'

It sounds amazing? All you know about it is that it's really expensive. Why is that amazing?

'Yah, you should tell him that's where you want to go. If he won't take you I'm sure Charles would be happy to step in.' They all cackled for a bit. I was having a hard time matching Becky with these two insufferable poshos. Why did they tolerate the Aussie?

'Or you should get a villa on Necker,' Becky said. 'My dad took the whole family there for Christmas last year.' Oh, OK, Daddy has money.

'I know,' Blonde 1 said, 'I did think about that. But Sebastian keeps going on about the recession, about how he can't count on a bonus this year, blah blah blah. Well, I'm counting on his bonus, so if he doesn't bloody well get one . . .' They all cackled again. I smiled weakly and regretted the decision not to go and sit by myself in the corner with the paper.

I thought back to my days at Hamilton, sitting sipping champagne with Ali and the other traders in the Beluga Bar after work. Is this what we sounded like? My God, Ali and I can talk about shoes and boys, we like nice restaurants and good hotels, but I don't think we ever talked solely about things based on what they cost, or ranked people solely on the basis of how much they earn.

After a painful half-hour lunch, I returned to the office to find Stella flicking through the papers on my desk.

'Cassie! There you are,' she said, beaming at me. 'Really good work on the PowerPoint presentation! This looks great!' So, this morning I was a moron, this afternoon I am a genius. OK. 'Listen, pop into my office for a bit, I'd like to have a chat.'

Oh, my God, I thought, she's going to ask me to stay on. She's going to offer me a job! Thank God for my PowerPoint skills.

'Have a seat,' she said, wafting her hand in the direction of one of the leather chairs facing her enormous desk. I sat down. 'As you know,' she said, 'you're here to replace Ellie, who's had malaria, poor darling.'

'Oh, how awful,' I said.

'Yah, terrible. For her honeymoon – she married a fabulous American, can't remember his name now, anyway – for their honeymoon, they went to Kenya,' she pronounced it Keenyaah, 'and the poor girl got malaria despite taking the pills that the government tell you to. Doesn't surprise me really, this government's so useless. Get everything wrong, don't they? Can't wait till Dishy Dave takes over! Ha ha. Anyway, turns out that the bout she had is not as awful as they'd thought and she's actually feeling much better, so she's going to be coming in tomorrow.' My heart sank. 'So, awfully sorry, Cassie, but that's it for you and me! Still. Been lovely to have you in. Do hope you enjoyed it.'

As I left her office, Becky was passing.

'Oh, Becky,' Stella called out. 'Did you hear the good news? Ellie's back tomorrow.'

204

'That's great, Stella.'

'I know. God, hasn't it been just awful without her?'

As I wandered through Canary Wharf on my way back to the DLR I passed half a dozen bars, full to bursting point with City boys, a sea of men in suits, drinking and shouting, talking over one another, flashing expensive watches, talking about expensive cars, betting on anything from who could down a pint the fastest to which one of them was mostly like to get that blonde with the long legs into bed that night. I made my way through the throng of smokers, braying about their latest deals, talking to the guy in front of them but always keeping an eye out for someone more interesting, someone more worthwhile speaking to.

It struck me that I didn't miss this at all. I missed the perks. I missed the good salary. I missed hanging out with Ali after work, drinking cocktails. And thanks to the Frenchman, those days were over – for now at least – in any case. I didn't miss the rest of it. The rest of it was awful. And, as far as I was concerned, boring. I was never interested in how the markets work, how the traders make their money. I didn't care what a derivative was or whether Bank X merged with Bank Y and what the implications of that would be. My mother was right. Mothers usually are. I had to get myself a job in a field that I was at least vaguely interested in.

On the tube on the way home, squeezed into the carriage between overweight City boys in need of some anti-perspirant, I made a mental list. Top six fields in which I would like to work, in one capacity or another, in descending order:

1. Fashion
2. Food or booze (catering, events, running my own organic food company, etc.)
3. Media (preferably glossy magazines or TV)
4. Interior design
5. Public relations
6. Showbiz (a girl can dream, can't she?)

At home, I went back to the now all-too-familiar recruitment websites on which I spent my days. Nothing in fashion or interior design. Plenty in food, but you needed relevant experience. Ditto media. There were some interesting jobs in public relations, although I suspected that they would probably also go to more experienced people. Reed Recruitment don't have a showbiz section.

15

Cassie Cavanagh *is on the breadline*

Bank Balance: -£1,755
Overdraft limit: £1,800
Expected arrival date of payment for temp job: unknown

I was starting to think that I was destined to dog walk for the rest of my days when fate intervened, oddly enough as a direct result of dog walking. Mrs Bromell had told me a few days previously that Mrs Mellor, owner of Thierry and Theo, wanted to speak with me. I had never met Mrs Mellor – she worked, so I usually just returned the dogs to the grumpy housekeeper or the au pair.

I turned up on Mrs Mellor's doorstep fully expecting either to be castigated for some transgression or another, or simply to be sacked. Once upon a time, in the not-too-distant past, I used to be a glass-half-full type of girl, but the past couple of months had persuaded me that whether the glass was half-full or half-empty, the milk was bound to be sour.

The door flew open almost the second I took my finger off the doorbell.

'Hello!' the woman who had opened the door said, beaming at me. 'You must be Cassie.' She didn't look like a Mrs Mellor at all. She was quite exotic looking, with long, black hair, piercing green eyes and a somewhat left-field – though still elegant – choice in clothes. 'Come inside, come inside,' she said, ushering me into the elegant hallway. I noticed that she had a bit of an accent, something European, Spanish maybe, or Italian. I hadn't noticed it before. I took off my parka while she fussed over the dogs.

'Go on through to the living room, have a seat,' she said. 'I'll be with you in a minute.'

She disappeared with the dogs in tow, leaving me perched incongruously on the edge of her beautiful white leather Corbusier sofa which I was convinced I was going to get dirty. She reappeared a little while later clutching two glasses.

'Do you like sherry?' she asked, then she laughed. 'I know, it sounds like an old lady's drink, but this is good stuff, it's amontillado, it's really very nice.'

'Sounds lovely.' She handed me a glass and I took a sip. It was delicious – dry, smooth and chilled. 'This is a lovely place, Mrs Mellor,' I said, wondering what on earth I was doing here. She laughed again.

'Mrs Mellor! It sounds so awful, doesn't it? As though I am married to a fat Tory MP. Call me Gabriella.'

Over two glasses of sherry, Gabriella told me that

she was half Spanish, half Italian. She was the manager of an art gallery on Great Titchfield Street and was married to an Englishman she'd met when she was running a bar in a ski resort in Pragelato, in the Italian Alps.

'You have been there?' she asked me.

'I haven't, I'm afraid.'

'You must go, it's wonderful. You ski? I thought you City types were always off skiing. You did used to work in the City, didn't you?'

'That's right. I was made redundant a couple of months ago. Cutbacks, you know.'

'I know. It's terrible. My husband works for a bank – commercial not investment – but even for them it is very bad at the moment. But this, what you are doing now, walking dogs, that is just . . . for a little while?'

'Hopefully,' I said a bit sheepishly. 'I've been looking for other things, but I haven't found much yet.'

'Well. You must come round for drinks on Saturday. I am having a party, there will be lots and lots of people there who work in all sorts of different fields. Interesting people.'

'Um . . .' I didn't know what to say. 'OK. That would be . . . very nice.'

'You think I am strange, asking you for drinks when I don't even know you!' she laughed. 'It's just . . . I would like to have some young people there. We are all so old. I have children, but they are too young. Eleven and nine. I am just trying to bring down the average age, you see?

And I think you do a good job with my lovely dogs, and I feel bad that I haven't made the time to get to know you. So there you go. No ulterior motives.'

Gabriella was, without a doubt, the nicest and most interesting person I'd met in ages. The fact that she had been so warm and welcoming meant that I turned up at the drinks party on Saturday with my glass half-full and my guard down. I had not been fretting about who would be there or what they would be wearing, I'd just been imagining myself chatting away happily to cool, arty yet wonderfully friendly people all night. So I was somewhat taken aback when almost the first person I encountered at the party was none other than Nicholas Hawksworth.

'Hello there!' he said, clearly just as surprised to see me as I was him. 'How *are* you?' He kissed me on both cheeks. Surely he couldn't be drunk already, it wasn't yet eight o'clock. 'What a surprise! How do you know Bill and Gabs?'

Oh, God, this was the point at which I had to admit that I was part of the hired help, along with the au pair and the gardener. I wondered whether they were invited, too?

'Actually, I haven't met Bill,' I said. 'I . . . um . . . I know Gabriella a bit . . .' I tailed off.

'How did you meet? At her gallery?'

'No, um . . . I haven't been to her gallery yet.' I took a deep breath. 'I walk the dogs,' I said, slightly louder than I had intended to. 'That's what I do these days. I'm walking dogs.' There, I said it.

'Good for you,' Nicholas said. 'Tough market out there now. Got to roll up your sleeves and just get on with it, haven't you? Good for you, Cassie.' I was just trying to get over the weirdness of Nicholas being so nice to me when Gabriella appeared at his elbow.

'So glad you could make it, Cassie, you look lovely. I see you've met Nick?'

'We used to work together, Gabs, would you believe it?'

Work *together*? Not exactly the way I'd have put it. Not exactly the way I imagined he'd have put it either.

'Fantastic secretary, Cassie was. When the firm made her redundant it was like they'd cut off my right arm.' He patted me on the back heartily. Forget drunk, was he on drugs?

When Gabriella threaded her arm through mine and escorted me away to meet some of the other guests, I was mightily relieved. Nicholas was being so nice it was starting to scare me. I met Gabriella's husband, Bill, a tall and distinguished-looking man in an immaculately cut blue suit, and Gabriella's 'oldest and dearest friend', Milena, a voluptuous Bulgarian who ran her own catering company. I was relieved (and touched) to be introduced as Gabriella's 'new friend, Cassie' rather than 'Thierry and Theo's new dog walker, Cassie'.

'Cassie used to work in the City, but she is looking for new opportunities, yes?' Gabriella said.

'That's right, I'm just . . . between jobs at the moment.'

'What did you do in the City?' Bill asked.

'Oh, I was just a PA.'

'Not *just* a PA,' Gabriella cut in. 'She worked for Nick Hawksworth and he says she was fantastic.'

'Christ, coming from Nick that's high praise indeed. Nick's one of my oldest friends but I can think of few things worse than having to work for him,' Bill said with a grin. 'I bet you've got some stories to tell.'

'Not at all,' I lied, 'he was a great boss.'

They all laughed heartily.

'Discretion, you see,' Milena said. 'This is what you want in an assistant. You must call me,' she said to me, giving me her business card. 'My company must be one of the only ones in the UK that is expanding at the moment. I am not taking on anyone full-time right now, but we often have need for people to come in, just from time to time, you know? Ring me on Monday.'

This was turning from a good into a great party.

The guests were an eclectic mix, media types and entrepreneurs rubbing shoulders with bankers and artists. Fortunately, Nicholas aside, I didn't spot any of the Hamilton Churchill crowd. I was chatting to Gabriella and Milena, who were commenting on the fact that, judging by the quality of the champagne people bring to parties, it would appear that the artists were making more money than the bankers these days. And so the conversation turned, as it so often does now, to the state of the economy. There was, unsurprisingly, a certain amount of gloating from the more arty guests at the party that the bankers were 'finally getting their comeuppance'.

'Sorry, Bill, sorry, Nick, but you boys have had it too good for too long,' a man with a goatee and Red or Dead glasses said. 'The bonuses you people earn for gambling with other people's money are ridiculous. The whole culture of the City needs to change.'

'Absolutely,' his wife agreed. 'It really is difficult to feel sorry for all those boys in two thousand pound suits driving their Maseratis home after they've been laid off.'

'But it's not just boys in two thousand pound suits who drive Maseratis,' I piped up. Everyone turned to look at me. 'I worked in the City – I was an assistant on a trading floor. I earned a modest salary, I certainly didn't earn a bonus, and I lost my job a couple of months ago. I'm still out of work. It's not only the City boys in their flash cars who are feeling the pain, you know.' There was a moment of awkward silence. 'I'm just saying . . .' I mumbled.

'Too right,' Nicholas chipped in, relieved that the focus had been taken off him and his alleged fat-cattery.

'Aren't you angry, then?' the woman asked. 'With your bosses, with the way the whole system works?'

'Well, obviously a lot of mistakes have been made,' I said, 'but it's actually fairly difficult to apportion blame, isn't it? You can blame the government, you can blame the regulators, you can call the bankers greedy, certainly, but you also have to remember that it was part of their job description to make money for

213

their masters as fast as they could. One theory holds that it's all the fault of Ronald Reagan and Margaret Thatcher.'

They looked at me curiously.

'Well, they were the ones who pushed for a massive expansion of home ownership in the UK and the States – mortgage companies were under a lot of pressure to extend lending, and they began to start lending to people who couldn't necessarily afford to repay the loans. You can argue that all the trouble started with the mortgage market.'

Even as I was saying this I was surprising myself. I really *had* been paying attention to the newspapers lately. Even so I clearly wasn't half as surprised as Nicholas, who was regarding me, open-mouthed, but definitely with greater respect than he had done before.

'Well said, Cassie,' Bill said. 'It's very easy to oversimplify these things, isn't it?'

By ten o'clock the party was winding down and I decided to make my exit while things were still going well. I kissed Gabriella and Bill goodbye, thanking them for a lovely evening, and had almost made it out the front door when I felt a hand on my shoulder.

'Not so fast, young lady,' Nicholas slurred at me, a lascivious grin on his face.

Oh, Christ, I thought, he isn't going to make a pass, is he?

Fortunately, he was not.

'Friend of mine just started up a wine business,' he

said, thrusting a card into my hand. 'He's looking for someone to answer the phones, do the office admin, that sort of thing. Pay wouldn't be top-notch, but you never know. Give him a call. Might be fun. Keep you in high heels, or whatever.' Some things never change.

16

Cassie Cavanagh *is making a comeback*

I rang Milena on Monday morning.

'Of course I remember you,' she said when I introduced myself. 'And what perfect timing you have! Tom, our office manager, has just phoned me up telling me he has food poisoning – I think that is English code for hangover, no? – and I desperately need someone to come in and answer the phones for me. Could you come?'

'Right now?'

'Right now.'

By eleven o'clock I was sitting behind a desk in the rather chaotic offices of Appetite, Milena's catering company, feeling completely overdressed. The pain of the jumper-wearing incident at Simmons & Blaythe still fresh in my mind, that morning I'd put on my sharpest suit. How was I to know that here in unfashionable Southwark, separated from the City only by the River Thames but feeling worlds apart,

217

jeans and trainers seemed to be the accepted uniform? But if I felt self-conscious at first, I didn't have a lot of time to think about it. The day sped by, a blur of orders were taken, invoices issued, payments made to suppliers and coffee fetched for superiors. It was seven o'clock by the time I left the office and I realised that that was the first time all day I had looked at my watch.

'We may need you again tomorrow,' Milena said to me, 'depends how much Tom had to drink over the weekend. Would you be free again?'

I worked for Milena for three days. The money I earned, combined with the latest dog walking dues and the money I'd got from the few days' temping at Simmons & Blaythe meant that I could just about cover the month's rent, though there was precious little left over. Looked like my family and friends would be getting home-made Christmas presents this year. I was sure that *Less is More!* would have plenty of handy hints. Baked Christmas tree decorations, anyone?

'What would you think if I gave you a jar of home-made marmalade for Christmas?' I asked Ali when she rang me that evening.

'I'd probably throw it at you,' she replied. 'Mind you, you could buy me a Prada handbag right now and it wouldn't cheer me up.'

'You not feeling so good?'

'I feel horrible. Allegedly the morning sickness, which ought to be called all-day-every-day sickness, is supposed to go away around now, but it's not showing any signs of letting up. I spend more time in the loos puking than I do at my desk these days. People are starting to talk.'

'You haven't let on yet?'

'No, I think they just think I've developed a drug habit. Can't be bulimia, obviously, given how fat I am.'

'Is there anything I can do? Maybe we could get together over the weekend, watch DVDs, stuff our faces with pickles and ice cream or whatever it is you pregnant ladies crave? I can get fat with you.'

'That sounds like a plan, Cass. But I was actually going to ask you another favour.'

'Anything.'

'Would you come to the doctor with me tomorrow? It's the scan.'

I met Ali outside the Royal Free Hospital the following morning. I held her hair back for her while she threw up into a bin in the car park. That done, we went in for the appointment, which was over in no time at all. The technician smeared gel on her tummy, and then pointed to a blob on the screen which she claimed was the baby.

'There,' she said, 'you can make out the head . . . and oh, there's the arm.' I was amazed to see that tears were running down Ali's face. It must be the hormones, I thought. She's never usually this sappy.

'Can you see it, Cass?' she asked.

'Yes . . . it's lovely,' I lied, peering at the monitor trying desperately to make out what it was I was supposed to be looking at. Afterwards we ordered prints (one for her, one for me) and then went for a cup of tea in a café down the road. Ali gazed lovingly at the picture.

'It's like an alien,' she said with a smile.

'Mmm,' I murmured, still not quite sure I was actually looking at the right blob. 'A parasitic, puke-inducing alien. Adorable.'

'No going back now,' she said, squeezing my hand. 'God, I'm going to have to tell them at work soon. That's not something I'm looking forward to. Nicholas is not going to be impressed.'

'You never know,' I said. 'After all, he's a father. And sometimes I think he's not as bad as he likes to make out.'

She looked at me quizzically, sipping her tea. 'You're defending Nicholas? Have you been drinking?'

I told her about the party, about how Nicholas had given me a contact for a possible job.

'And?'

'And I haven't rung them yet.'

'Cassie!'

'Well, I feel a bit weird cold-calling people asking for jobs. Particularly as Nicholas was quite pissed when he gave me this guy's card. He probably forgot all about it, so I'll just be ringing this guy up out of the blue.'

'Doesn't matter, you can't ignore opportunities like this,' Ali said, waving at the waitress to bring over another muffin. 'Even if Nicholas didn't tell him about you, it doesn't matter. You can sweet talk him into giving you an interview. You could charm snakes when you're in the mood, Cassie.'

Back at home I decided to bite the bullet. I fished the business card out of my purse and dialled the number.

'Yes?' a man's voice snapped at the other end of the line. For a millisecond I toyed with the idea of putting the phone down.

'Is that Rupert Forsythe?' I asked nervously.

'Speaking.'

'My name is Cassie Cavanagh,' I started out. 'I was given your number—'

'Cassie!' he boomed at me. 'Nick said you were going to ring. How are you today?'

'I'm . . . uh . . . very well, thank you . . .'

'When can you come in and see us?' he asked.

'Whenever is convenient for you,' I replied.

'Why don't you meet me tomorrow morning at Tapas Brindisa? Do you know it? Spanish place in Borough Market. Just round the corner from our offices. See you there at ten?'

I never thought I'd hear myself say it, but thank God for Nicholas Hawksworth.

The following day I turned up at Brindisa clad in jeans and a dark green Paul & Joe coat (two seasons old but still fabulous). I realised that I had no idea what Rupert Forsythe looked like. I hovered in the doorway, slightly panicked, realising that I had left his card at home and would not be able to ring him on his mobile. Damn. The café was busy, packed with what looked like a mixture of market traders getting a quick caffeine fix and creative types taking their sweet time over their lattes. Did any of them look like a Rupert Forsythe? I was just about to call home in the hopes of catching Jude before she left and getting her to search for the number when a very tanned forty-something man approached me, holding out his hand.

'Cassie?' he ventured. Thank God.

He ushered me to a table at the back of the café where he was sitting with a younger, equally tanned man who turned out to be his brother and business partner, Oliver ('Call me Olly'). They were posh, jovial and somewhat excitable – like a pair of pedigree Labrador puppies.

'We're terribly excited about the new venture,' Rupert said, shifting around in his seat and spilling coffee onto his trousers. 'Difficult market to start things going, but we think we've nailed the business model.' They asked me about my background and I handed them a CV which Olly scanned briefly before handing it back to me.

'Oh, that's for you,' I said.

'No need, no need,' Rupert said. 'Nick's told us awfully good things about you. And to be perfectly honest with you, we're in a bit of a jam. Last girl we got in was bloody useless. Do you think you could start next week? Three-month trial, four hundred quid a week. Not great, I know, but it's the best I can do at the moment. If it all works out, we can renegotiate in a few months' time. What do you say?'

I was stunned. I'd only been here five minutes and they had already offered me a job. I hadn't had to answer a single question yet, unless you count whether I'd prefer a latte or an espresso. When I eventually regained the power of speech, I said, 'I say yes! That would be fantastic. Thank you so much.' The money was not particularly good, but who cared? Working for a wine company for minimum wage would be better than dragging a pack of hounds around Clapham Common in December for seven pounds an hour. I would be working for a wine company! There would be tastings and free booze and – oh, my God, the excitement, the glamour – trips to check out vineyards in exotic locales.

'Excellent!' Rupert said, and he and his brother took turns in shaking me warmly by the hand.

'I think that calls for a celebration, don't you?' Olly asked. 'Fancy a sneaky glass of Villa Anita? Lovely stuff.'

'It's a bit early for me,' I said, glancing nervously at my watch. It was ten thirty in the morning.

'Nonsense!' Rupert said and ordered three glasses of wine.

This was going to be a fantastic job.

Rupert and Olly sent me on my way with a folder full of bumf on the company as well as a brief job description typed up on a sheet of A4 which appeared to have been written by either a dyslexic or a very poor

223

typist. I counted three spelling errors in the first paragraph. They certainly were in need of a secretary. The official title of the post was *'office administrator'*: I would be *'responsible for maintaining the smooth running of the office, including managment* [sic] *of administration, office supplies, maintenance, invoicing and reciepting* [sic] *payments, IT support systems and recruitment'*. I would need to be able to *'work independantly* [sic] *and take responsibility for a wide variety of tasks'* etc. etc. In other words, I would have to do a bit of everything.

On the tube on the way home I read through the company information.

Vintage Organics was set up in October 2008 by Rupert and Oliver Forsythe with the aim of bringing the finest in organically grown wines from across the globe to the British consumer. Our staff have travelled the world to select the best wines made from the finest grapes. We have visited vineyards in France, Italy, Spain, Portugal, California, New Zealand, South Africa, Argentina and Chile; buying only from environmentally and socially responsible producers.

The Forsythe brothers have wine in their blood. Their maternal grandfather, Nicolas Leroy, is the proprietor of Chateau Saint Chinian in the Corbiere region of the Languedoc. He is a pioneer of organic wine production in France and is renowned as one of the region's finest viticulteurs. 'My fondest memories of childhood are of holidays spent at the chateau with my grandfather, playing hide-and-seek among the vines with my brother, helping with the harvest and being allowed to taste a drop of the new wines when they were ready to drink,' Rupert Forsythe says.

Having spent the first part of his career working in the City, Rupert decided that he wanted to return to his wine-making roots. 'Although both Olly and I have always had a passion for wine, it has taken us many years to realise that wine for us is more than a simple pleasure, it is a calling.'

Rupert Forsythe has an impressive business pedigree: he has worked in the corporate finance departments of some of the world's largest financial institutions, including Barclays, HSBC, Grant & Waters and Hamilton Churchill.

Oliver Forsythe trained as a solicitor before joining the Civil Service, where he worked in the Department of Agriculture, Fisheries and Foods. He is the Liberal Democrats' parliamentary candidate for the Borough of Kensington and Chelsea.

The more I found out about the firm, and about the brothers Forsythe, the more excited I became. Rupert had told me that, at present, they had a staff of just six people: himself and Oliver, Melanie, who covered marketing, Peter and Fabio who took care of research and purchasing and Aidan who dealt with all the IT. The fact that it was such a small team boded well: opportunities to rise up through the ranks – and to break out of the assistant mould – were far more likely to present themselves in a team of seven than in a team of seven hundred.

I arrived back at the flat ready to open the bottle of Moët which I'd bought to replace Jude's offering.

Drinking before midday is not something I usually do, but since I'd already started, it seemed reasonable enough to carry on. In any case, that day I felt as though I'd been given a reprieve; I'd been flat on my back, strapped to the gurney, waiting for the lethal injection and at five minutes to midnight the Governor had called. A bit melodramatic, perhaps, but I was days away from defaulting on my many debts. In any case, I burst through the front door, yelling, 'Jude! Crack out the champagne! I'm no longer unemployed!'

Silence. That's odd. She doesn't go into college on Fridays. The door hadn't been double-locked so I was pretty sure she was in.

'Jude!' I called out again. 'Where are you? You're not in bed, are you? It's nearly twelve o'clock, for God's sake.' I gave her door a perfunctory knock before pushing it open. Then I closed it again. Very quickly.

'Shit. Sorry. Sorry, sorry, sorry,' I called through the door. I could hear some muffled giggling from the other side. 'Hi, Matt,' I said. 'Good to see you again.' I'd been so wrapped up in thoughts of my job interview I'd completely forgotten Matt was arriving today.

Several hours later (to be fair to them they hadn't seen each other in months), the happy couple emerged.

'Sorry about the interruption,' I said, feeling myself blush as I said it.

'Did you interrupt?' Matt asked with a grin. 'I didn't

notice.' He came over and gave me a kiss. He looked very tanned and very tired.

'How was Sierra Leone?' I asked.

'Good. Bit grim in parts, but basically promising. Darfur, on the other hand . . .' he passed his hand over his eyes and shrugged, '. . . doesn't bear thinking about.'

Jude was hopping about from one foot to the other, clearly desperate to say something but not wanting to interrupt.

'So?' she asked. 'What happened? You were yelling earlier – I couldn't really hear what you were saying . . .'

'The earth was moving,' Matt said.

'Of course it was . . . So? Was it good yelling or bad yelling?'

'It was good yelling. Very good yelling.'

Over a glass of champagne or three, we decided that we'd all go out to dinner to celebrate Matt's (temporary) return to the UK and my new job.

'I'll get this one,' Jude said. 'You can repay the favour once you're a successful wine entrepreneur.'

The three of us headed into town to the Anchor & Hope in Waterloo. As usual, the place was packed to the rafters, but Jude, who used to work behind the bar, managed to get us a table straight away.

'For three?' the waitress asked us.

'Four, please,' Jude said.

'Three,' I corrected her.

'No, four,' she said with a smile.

'Awww – you invited Ali! That's so sweet of you,

Jude,' I said, squeezing her arm. The waitress escorted us through the pub to a table at the back and took our drinks orders. 'You know Ali isn't drinking at the moment,' I told Jude and Matt. 'She's just . . . being healthy. Don't make a big deal out of it, OK?' The pregnancy was still not common knowledge.

'OK,' they chirruped in unison, grinning at me.

'What?' I asked them. 'I know you've just spent eight hours shagging but do you have to look quite so pleased with yourselves? You're starting to make me feel ill.' The waitress brought over a bottle of red. She was just pouring me a glass when I saw him, pushing through the crowd, walking towards us.

'Jesus Christ, Jude!' I hissed at her. 'You invited Jake? Do you not recall that he isn't speaking to me?' There was no time for her to reply, he was already upon us, he was standing right next to the table. He was tall. He was incredibly tall. Had he always been that tall? He bent down to give me a kiss on the cheek.

'Congratulations on the new job, Cassie,' he said with a smile. He was wearing jeans and a white Fred Perry shirt underneath his jacket. He looked fantastic. Why the hell hadn't I gone on that date?

'Hey, you,' Jude said, getting up to give him a kiss, 'let me introduce you – this is Matt, Matt – Jake.' The boys shook hands.

'Great to finally meet you at last,' Jake said, sitting down next to me. Under the table, he gave my leg an affectionate squeeze. I nearly fainted. 'You feeling better?' he asked.

'I'm fine,' I said. *Oh, Christ, what did Jude tell him?*

'Sorry I gave you a hard time last time we spoke,' he said. 'I was just disappointed that I didn't get to go out with you.'

After a brief toast to Matt's safe return and my new career, Jude started quizzing Jake about what he'd been up to.

'Haven't seen you in college all week,' she said. 'Have you been working, or just skiving?'

'Working, of course. I've been getting ready for the college exhibition most of the week, although today I had a proper job. Actual paid employment.'

'Who for?' Jude asked, popping an olive into her mouth.

'Women's magazine,' he said, casually. '*InStyle*. I was shooting a spread for them.'

'Bloody hell!' Jude said. 'That's brilliant.' I was pretty sure she had never read *InStyle* in her life, but you always can count on Jude to be enthusiastic.

'So,' Matt said with a smile, 'you've been hanging out with models all day? And I thought I'd had a good afternoon.'

'Models in their underwear, actually,' Jake replied. 'It was a lingerie shoot.'

'You lucky bastard,' Matt said, clinking Jake's glass with his own. Jude rolled her eyes. I didn't say anything, but I felt a familiar twinge in my gut. I recognised it as the feeling I used to get when I watched Dan flirt with other women. I was jealous. I was horribly, painfully jealous of the fact that Jake had just spent the entire day in the company of a group of very beautiful, half-naked women. And I hardly even knew this man. How ridiculous am I?

Dinner was a long and relaxed affair, so relaxed that Matt was starting to nod off by the end.

'I think I'd better take him home,' Jude said, ruffling his hair. 'He's getting old – can't handle these late nights any more.'

'Excuse me,' Matt protested. 'I had a seven-hour flight, getting in to Heathrow at six o'clock in this morning and then had to spend the entire day in bed keeping you happy . . .'

'Oh, you *had* to, did you? Don't recall any protests . . .'

'How about you two?' Matt asked. 'You ready to call it a night?'

'I don't think I am, actually,' Jake said. 'How about you, Cassie? You fancy staying for another?'

They were stacking chairs on tables by the time Jake and I left. I toyed with the idea of inviting him back to the flat for a nightcap, but by a Herculean effort of will power managed to stop myself. I had a really good feeling about him – it would be idiotic to rush into things at this point. Anticipation is ninety per cent of the pleasure, I reminded myself as he hailed me a cab. As the taxi pulled up next to us, Jake slipped his arm around my waist and pulled me close to him, giving me a long, lustful, delicious kiss goodnight.

'I'm visiting my little brother in Manchester this

weekend – he's at university there – but I'll be back on Tuesday. Can I see you next week?'

'That would be lovely,' I said, reluctantly disentangling myself from his arms. 'Just give me a call.'

I hopped into the cab and sank back into the seat, grinning like an idiot.

'Good night, love?' the cabby asked me.

'Heavenly,' I sighed.

Just then, my phone buzzed. *You have one message from Jake*, the display read. I clicked on the text message icon.

Models, schmodels. You are without doubt the most beautiful girl I've seen all day xxx

17

Cassie Cavanagh *is overqualified*

On Sunday evening I had a call from Rupert. After a moment of brief panic (were they going to cancel the job offer?) I discovered that in fact he was just ringing to ask me to come in a bit early on Monday.

'We've got some potential investors coming round in the afternoon, so I was hoping we could get an early start. Eight o'clock OK with you?'

I arrived at Vintage Organics' offices at ten to eight. For a girl who was used to working on the forty-second floor of Number 1 Canada Square, the VO headquarters came as a bit of a shock. They were situated on the third floor of a dingy walk-up a couple of alleyways back from the Thames and they consisted of three rooms. In the main office, which could not have been more than ten feet by fifteen, there were four desks: one each for Melanie, Peter, Fabio and Aidan. Leading off the main office on the left-hand side was a small meeting room and to the right was another office in which Rupert and Olly had their desks.

'We haven't actually found you a space quite yet,' Rupert said apologetically.

I managed to find a chair to sling my coat over and was given brief introductions to the rest of the team and then asked to get coffee.

'Do you prefer Starbucks or Nero?' I asked Rupert.

He looked aghast.

'Oh, we don't go out for coffee. Got to keep an eye on the cost base. There's a kettle over there in the corner.' There it sat, on top of a mini-fridge in which I found some decidedly iffy milk. I nipped down to the newsagent to get a fresh pint.

'One of your duties, I think, Cassie,' Rupert said. 'To ensure we always have fresh milk in the fridge.'

The second task of the day was to sort and distribute the post. After that, I just sat around for a bit, on my chair in the corner of the room. Without so much as a computer screen to gaze at, no Internet to surf or solitaire to play, the morning passed slowly. I had expected Rupert, Olly, or someone else to give me a more detailed run-through of how everything worked and what I would be expected to do day to day, but everyone, apart from me, seemed frantically busy. Peter (fluent in German and Spanish) and Fabio (fluent in French and Italian) were constantly babbling away on the phone to suppliers. Aidan was fixing a problem with the office network and Melanie was negotiating prices for a full-page advertisement in *Decanter*. No one had time to show me the ropes.

Around midday, Rupert popped his head round the door and summoned me into his office.

'Sorry everything's a bit disorganised today,' he said. 'We'll get you properly sorted tomorrow. Now, as I mentioned last night, we've got some potential investors coming in this afternoon, and for some reason or other it doesn't look to me as though the meeting room was cleaned this weekend. The management of this building leaves a bit to be desired, I'm afraid. In any case, I spoke to one of the maintenance guys and he's given me a key to the closet on the fifth floor where they keep the cleaning stuff. Would you pop up there, get the vacuum cleaner and give the place a once-over? Not just the meeting room, the whole place actually? We do want to make a good impression.'

This, I thought, as I lugged the vacuum cleaner (which appeared to be older than I was) down the stairs, was not what I signed up for. I can be the coffee maker, the milk monitor and the post sorter – these are not things I've dreamed of becoming, but I don't mind taking on those roles in the short term. But what I am most certainly not is a cleaning lady. It was humiliating. Rupert and Olly had disappeared out for lunch but the others were all still in the office, beavering away at their desks, making calls and typing furiously. And there I was trying to hoover around their feet, clear away their dirty mugs, empty their bins. Utterly humiliating.

I had just returned the surprisingly heavy vacuum

cleaner to its closet on the fifth floor when Rupert and the investors – two middle-aged men in grey suits – arrived in the office. They gave the place the once-over; they looked less than impressed. I didn't blame them. If I were Rupert I would conduct business meetings elsewhere. This dive hardly gave the impression of a thriving and vibrant company.

'Would anyone like coffee?' I asked, taking the investors' coats. I wasn't sure what I was going to do with them, but it seemed like the thing to do.

'Lovely, Cassie. We'll be in the meeting room.'

The investors left after about half an hour. Rupert and Olly retreated to their office looking fairly glum. A couple of hours later, we were all called to a staff meeting. The five of us trooped into the bosses' office and arranged ourselves against the wall, as though lining up to be shot. The atmosphere was sombre.

'No dice, I'm afraid, chaps,' Rupert said. 'They're looking for an operation that is at a more . . . advanced stage of development.'

There were a few moments of uncomfortable silence before Rupert spoke again.

'Don't worry about it, guys. We've got some more people coming in a couple of weeks. We're fairly sure we can raise the level of finance we need to keep us in business . . . oh, at least for the next few months.' There was some nervous laughter among the group. I didn't know what to do. Was he joking? The look on Olly's face didn't suggest that he was. Oh God, what had I got myself into? Had I just boarded a sinking ship?

On my second day at Vintage I arrived early, armed with my laptop. I was pleased to find that Aidan was already in the office.

'Morning,' he called out without looking up at me. I plonked a latte down in front of him. That got his attention.

'You want something, don't you?' he asked.

'Well, I was hoping you might be able to get me linked into the rest of the office computers,' I said, whipping my laptop out of the stripy Paul Smith case Ali gave me for my birthday. 'At least that way I might be able to make a useful contribution.'

He grinned at me, raising the latte to his lips. 'Far as I'm concerned you've already made a useful contribution today.' He took a sip. 'Of course I can get you networked in. Since you're here early I can give you a quick tutorial on how everything works.'

By the time everyone else had arrived in the office, I was installed in the meeting room with a passable knowledge of how the VO ordering system worked. Not that I was to need it that day. Instead, I was dispatched to deliver urgent mail to a number of London addresses – Rupert thought couriers were an unnecessary expense – so I spent most of the day on the underground.

Days three and four in the office passed in much the same fashion, with everyone else apparently incredibly busy while I carried out menial tasks. I revolutionised the chaotic filing system, first colour coding different sections (pink for purchasing, green for research, blue for bills), then arranging the documents within those sections chronologically. Then I changed my mind and arranged them alphabetically. I rearranged furniture. I bought a map of the world into which I stuck pins to illustrate the vineyards from which Vintage Organics gets its wines. I tidied up other people's desks while they were out at lunch.

It was really starting to get me down. Staring out of the office window I caught sight of a tall blonde girl walking a poodle and felt a sharp pang of regret. I missed them. I actually missed my hounds. I missed Thierry and Theo. After months out of work I had been looking forward to a challenge, something I could get my teeth into, and here I was, feeling more useless and insignificant than I had ever felt at Hamilton Churchill.

Perhaps it was because my self-esteem was pretty low at this point that I turned up to my first official date feeling ridiculously nervous. I had changed outfits fourteen times (a record, even for me), eventually deciding to go relatively low-key: jeans, heels and the Vivienne Westwood top I'd bought the day Dan dumped me. I was already out the door and halfway down the street when I decided that might be a bad omen. I retuned home and changed for the fifteenth time: different jeans, different heels and a top that had no Dan connotations whatsoever.

As a result of all the changing, I arrived at the bar on

the top floor of the Tate Modern twenty minutes late. Jake was sitting by the window, an untouched drink in front of him, checking his watch. Oh, crap, he was going to be annoyed about my lateness now. As soon as he saw me, he leapt to his feet, bumping the table and spilling beer everywhere. He then spent ages mopping it up with paper serviettes before eventually giving me a quick peck on the cheek.

'Hi, Cassie,' he said, not quite meeting my eye. 'You look nice.'

'Thanks,' I said. We both stood there awkwardly for a moment.

'I'll get you a drink,' he said, bumping into the table yet again as he moved past me towards the bar. I mopped up the beer while he got me a cocktail. So far, so disastrous.

Desperate to avoid any awkward silences, I launched into a ten-minute diatribe about how disappointing my job was the moment he returned to the table. Jake gulped his beer. I knocked back my cocktail. We ordered a couple more. I realised that I had barely paused for breath since I arrived.

'God, I'm sorry,' I said eventually. 'I'm being rubbish company. I promise to stop whingeing about work.'

'And I promise to stop spilling beer all over the place,' he said. We both laughed. He leaned over the table and slipped his hand into mine. 'You're not being rubbish company at all. Feel free to moan all you like. It does sound like your employers are a bit disorganised.'

'They are,' I agreed, 'and the thing is, I'm actually concerned that they're not particularly good business-men! It sounds ridiculous – Rupert was a corporate financier, for God's sake, he should know what investors are after – but the whole thing just looks amateurish. I mean, I'm sure the business model is great, but the first impression that investors get when they come to that office is awful. They really need an extreme makeover on that place if they want to get anyone to put any money into the business.'

'Have you told them that?'

'No – I can't. Not only am I the new girl, but I'm the nobody. The dogsbody. The coffee-making milk monitor.'

He laughed. 'Your boss is an approachable guy, isn't he?' I nodded. 'So you should speak to him. State your case. I bet he'd be prepared to listen. He'll probably be impressed that you're taking the initiative.' He reached over and pushed my hair away from my face. 'You shouldn't sell yourself short.'

We didn't talk about work after that. Well, not my work anyway. His work was much more interesting. Technically, Jake was still a student – he had six months to go of his digital media course at Goldsmiths – but he was spending around half his time working as a photographer.

'Any more fashion shoots?' I asked him.

'Not this week. The *InStyle* shoot was fun, but fashion isn't actually what I'm interested in. I'd much rather do reportage photography, you know, real world stuff.'

'Are you saying fashion isn't the real world? Sacrilege.'

'Don't get me wrong – I wouldn't turn down more shoots if they offered them to me. And not just because I get to spend the day hanging out with hot naked girls,' he grinned. 'The money's really good.'

'What about paparazzi-type stuff? Not interested in hanging around outside Chinawhites in the hopes of getting a few pics of Big Brother contestants and glamour models?'

He pulled a face. 'Definitely not. I'd be hopeless at that anyway – I wouldn't recognise a Big Brother contestant if they slapped me in the face. I don't watch that crap.'

I remembered how Dan used to have Big Brother on all the time, even when he wasn't really watching it, just as background. I think he had it on just in case one of the girls took their tops off. Sitting there with Jake – gorgeous, interesting, intelligent Jake – I suddenly couldn't remember a single good thing about Dan. What was it I had liked about him so much? It couldn't just have been the fact that he was good-looking and bought me stuff. Surely it couldn't have been that. I'm not *that* shallow.

'What are you thinking about?' Jake asked. 'You're staring into the middle distance there. Am I boring you?'

'Not at all,' I said, leaning in to give him a kiss. 'I'm having a brilliant time.'

We talked about his family: his parents were English

241

but lived in Wales. His father had been a journalist on *The Times*, now he taught journalism at Cardiff University; his mother was a curator at the National Museum. He had one sister (older, a sculptor) and one brother (younger, studying engineering in Manchester). They all sounded terrifyingly interesting. I dreaded the inevitable 'And what about your family?' question.

'What about your family?' he asked, right on cue. 'Any brothers or sisters?'

'One older sister, Celia.'

'What does she do?'

'She's a mum.'

'Really?' he sounded genuinely interested. 'You're an aunt? You don't look like an aunt. You're much too young and beautiful.' I rolled my eyes at him. 'Seriously, how many kids?'

'Three. Tom's five, Rosie's three and Monty is ... oh, about nine months now. They're all really gorgeous actually. Well, I would say that, wouldn't I? But they are.'

'You and your sister get on well?'

'Not really. Well ... I don't know. We're very different. There's a lot about her that annoys me – and vice versa – but I do admire her sometimes. She's incredibly grown up. Very sorted.'

'I'd like to meet her,' he said. And he meant it. And I realised that I wouldn't mind introducing Jake to my family at all. I wouldn't be embarrassed. OK, so his family sounded much more interesting than mine, but

I just knew that he wouldn't care about that. He'd be kind and polite and interested and he'd chat to my dad about gardening.

In the taxi on the way home (alone, I was still being a good girl, taking it slow), I made a mental list of things I like about Jake:

His hands. He has long, delicate fingers, a pianist's hands.

The way he gesticulates wildly when he's explaining something.

He laughs all the time.

He makes me laugh all the time.

He has perfect skin.

He's kind.

When I'm with him, I'm feel like I'm a better version of myself.

I took Jake's advice. When I got to work on Monday, I knocked on Rupert's office door.

'Brought you a coffee,' I said, putting it down on his desk.

'Oh, thank you, Cassie. When you're done with the post will you do the invoicing? There's a list of customers here who need statements sent out.'

'Of course,' I said, taking the list. 'But I was wondering whether I could have a brief word first?'

'By all means. Sit down. Is everything all right?' He leaned forward, placing his elbows on the desk and pressing his fingertips together. 'I know you haven't had the ideal introduction to the company. Things have been a bit chaotic – as soon as things calm down a bit we'll be able to discuss your role more thoroughly.'

'No, no – it's fine. Everything's fine. I was just thinking . . . I was wondering . . . it's about the office. Basically, I was wondering whether you would allow me to give it a bit of a makeover. I just think that investors might be getting the wrong impression when they come here.'

Rupert frowned. 'It's not that bad . . .' he said, casting an eye over the office. He looked almost hurt.

'Not that bad, no,' I said hastily, 'but it's not that great either. I just don't think the place looks . . . well, it's not slick. We don't look like a professional outfit.'

There was a moment of silence. I wondered whether I had gone too far. Had I just called him unprofessional?

'I can see where you're coming from, Cassie,' he said, nodding sagely. 'Presentation *is* important. But we just don't have the budget for a fancy office just yet . . .'

'I'm not saying fancy . . .'

'No, no, let me finish. You're used to working for very rich investment banks – or investment banks that used to be very rich, anyway – which have gleaming, steel and glass corporate headquarters with gyms in the basement and coffee shops in the foyer. We're a long, long way from that.' He got to his feet and began to pace the short distance from his desk to the window and back again. 'Eventually, yes, I would like to get this place spruced up. But we have more pressing issues to deal with just now. And I can assure you that when investors take a look at the business plan, they will know that we're a professional outfit.'

Oh, God, I had gone too far. I'd pissed him off. I slunk out of the office and into the meeting room, where I got back to sorting through the post.

I stayed late that evening, re-ordering the office filing system for the umpteenth time. It didn't really need doing, but I thought that perhaps by staying late and showing willing I might make up for that morning's faux pas. Rupert had barely spoken to me all day. He hadn't been rude, but he had certainly not been his usual garrulous self.

When everyone else had gone home, I took a good look around. I examined the blinds over the windows, once white, now a nicotine yellow. They had probably been there for so long, they *were* remnants of a time when you could still smoke in offices. Behind the blinds the windows were grimy. The office furniture was cheap, tired and unmatched: it looked as thought it had been recovered from a skip. The carpets were a dirty beige, worn thin in patches. The entire place looked as though it hadn't been redecorated since the early 1980s. In the corner of the meeting room, I pulled up a bit of carpet. There was parquet tiling underneath. Good, solid oak parquet tiling. And someone had stuck a nasty beige carpet on top of it.

I started to calculate what it would take – in terms of money and time – to give the place a facelift. All I needed, I reasoned, was to replace the ugly office furniture, pull up the carpet, get new blinds, reorganise a bit, and give everything a really good clean. It could probably be done in a weekend. And it really wouldn't cost that much.

I flipped open my laptop and started to do a bit of research. I figured out that I could get a completely new set of passable – and matching – office furniture for a couple of thousand pounds and new blinds for a couple of hundred. If you tossed in a few nice desk lamps and pulled the carpets up the place would look pretty damn presentable. And it wouldn't take long either. I really thought Rupert was being short-sighted about the whole thing.

A sentiment I expressed when Ali rang me a moment or two later to tell me that she had discovered the meaning of life: peach yoghurt and sardine sandwiches.

'Ugh,' I replied.

'Honestly,' she mumbled, her mouth clearly full of the foul mixture, 'I can't stop eating them.' She agreed with me about the whole office thing. 'You're totally right. Investors are going to be put off straight away if it looks like an unprofessional outfit. You should do something about it. Particularly if it's only going to cost a few grand.'

'If I had a few grand, I might just go ahead and do it anyway,' I said, pulling down one of the filthy blinds. 'I could do the work myself and I reckon it wouldn't take longer than a weekend.'

Ali laughed. 'But you wouldn't really do that,

would you? Go against what the boss says?'

'I would if I had the money,' I said. 'After all, what have I got to lose? It's only a three-month stint anyway, and the way things are going round here, the company might well not be here in three months.'

I could hear Ali chewing on the other end of the line.

'Shall I call you back later?' I asked. 'You sound . . . busy.'

'I'm thinking!' she protested. 'I'm just . . . thinking about it. How about if I lend you the cash, you do the makeover, and if they like it, they repay you and you repay me?'

'No, Ali, you can't do that – I can't risk your money.'

'Why not? I'm a trader. I like risk. You should go for it. Stick everything on one of my credit cards and then pay me back as and when . . .'

'You may like risk, but you also like a return, Al. I know you.'

'The return is your brilliant career,' she said. 'It's an investment in you.' She can be very sweet sometimes. 'Anyway, I'll lend you the money, but I won't be coming in to do the DIY. You know that's not my thing. Get Jude to help out with that – she's good at that sort of crap. And that new boyfriend of yours . . .'

'He's not my boyfriend.'

'Yet.'

'Yet.You're an angel, Al. I owe you one.'

'I'll remember that when it comes to drawing up the babysitting rota, I can promise you.'

Armed with Ali's credit card details I ordered seven

ergonomic desks and chairs, a new meeting room table, two new filing cabinets and a set of chic red and white blinds which matched the Vintage Organics company logo perfectly. They would be delivered on Saturday afternoon, the furniture company assured me. The window cleaner could come on Saturday morning.

At home, I told Jude about my plan. She listened in silence, fidgeting manically with her worry beads all the time.

'This is either a brilliant idea or it's the worst idea you've ever had,' she said nervously. 'I can't make up my mind.'

'Me neither. But I've done it now – the stuff's all ordered so it's too late to turn back. Can you help me?'

'Course I will. Matt's off on Thursday so I was just going to be spending the weekend moping around the flat anyway. Shall we rope Jake in, too?'

'I think we should.'

I left the office at six on Friday night as usual, but I didn't return home. Instead, I rendezvoused with Jake and Jude in a bar around the corner. They were both dressed all in black. Jake had brought a balaclava.

'Just in case,' he said. 'This is a covert op, after all.'

After a quick sharpener or two we headed back to the office. As expected, there was no one there – the employees were all long gone and Rupert and Olly, who usually work until nine or ten, had both been given the three line whip to attend some family gathering, so the were gone too. The door was locked, the lights were off. The three of us tiptoed into the office, locking the door behind us. I turned on the lights.

'God, it is horrible,' Jude whispered.

'I know. When does the van get here?' I whispered at Jake.

'Eight,' he replied, in a completely normal voice.

'Shhhhh,' Jude and I both hissed at him.

'Why? There's no one around, the building's deserted.'

He was right, but this was the part of the plan that was making me most nervous. Jake had arranged for a friend of his to bring a van round so that we could get rid of all the old furniture and pull up the carpets before the new stuff arrived the following day. To anyone who saw us doing this, under cover of darkness on a Friday evening, it might well look as though we were just stealing. Technically, I supposed, we were actually stealing, since we were removing company property from the premises without permission. Jake's friend, Stan, was going to take the furniture and store it in his garage, so it could be returned should Rupert and Olly veto the whole plan, so it wasn't really theft as such. It wasn't as though we were going to sell the stuff. Still, the whole thing was making me very jittery.

I took all the papers out of the nasty metal filing cabinets while Jude set about moving the rest of the stuff into the corridor and Jake began the laborious task of carting it down three flights of stairs.

'Bet this isn't the second date you had in mind,' I said to him.

'Not exactly, no,' he said with a laugh. 'Perhaps next time we could do something just the two of us? Maybe something that doesn't involve back-breaking manual labour?'

Fortunately Stan showed up a bit early and was able to give us a hand. By nine o'clock we'd cleared the place, and no one had so much as given us a sideways glance.

'You've just got to act like you're authorised to do whatever you're doing,' Jake assured me. 'Trust me, I spend my life barging into places I'm not supposed to be in order to get a picture. If you just act like you own the place no one will ask you any questions.'

We stayed in the office until eleven thirty, pulling up carpets and taking down blinds. The parquet tiling underneath was actually in pretty good shape. All it would need was a buff and a polish and it would look pretty good.

'The walls are kind of bare, though,' Jude commented. 'It would be good to have some nice art up there.'

'Yeah, but nice art you really can't buy on the cheap,' I said, 'and I'm not putting up crappy posters. We'll just have to deal with the basics this weekend.'

The following morning, Jude and I got up early to go into the office. We had to stop off at Gabriella's on the way to borrow her special floor buffer – apparently an essential household item when you have dogs and children – and at Sainsbury's to stock up on cleaning products. By the time we got to Borough, Jake was already sitting on the steps outside drinking a coffee. At his side were three large canvases.

'Thought you might like to borrow these,' he said, turning one of them around. It was a photograph of a vineyard at dawn, the mist just rising off the vines. It was beautiful. 'I took some shots when I was on holiday in the South of France last year. They're a bit postcard-esque, but they're not bad. I got them printed up onto canvas a while back. I was thinking of selling them. What do you think?'

'They're gorgeous,' I said to him, carefully turning the other canvases around. One was taken in late afternoon, with the sun turning the leaves a reddish-gold, the other was a shot of a chateau and the vineyards surrounding it. 'Probably not one of our chateaux, but frankly, who cares? They're stunning.'

By the end of the weekend the place was transformed. The floors were polished to a shine, the new blinds were hung and behind them were windows you could actually see through. The new furniture, while hardly top quality, all matched, which gave the place a feel of professional uniformity. And Jake's photographs were absolutely perfect. We hung one in the meeting room and one in Rupert's office, but the largest was reserved for the wall opposite the main entrance: it was the first thing that you saw when you came into the room and it set the perfect tone.

For a few moments after we'd finished, we all just stood there, admiring our handiwork.

'It's like a completely new place,' Jude said. 'They have to like it. They just *have* to. If they don't, they've got no bloody taste and no sense either.'

'Too right,' Jake agreed, slipping his hand into mine. Not for the first time the contrast between Dan and Jake was thrown into sharp focus – the idea of Dan giving up a weekend to help me redecorate my employers' office was nothing short of laughable. And Jake had not only helped, he'd actually managed to make the weekend fun.

It did look better, infinitely better, but I was still terrified. After all, I had suggested a makeover to Rupert and he had specifically vetoed it.

'I'm not going to get any sleep tonight,' I said.

'You will if we get you pissed enough,' Jake replied, and we all repaired to the pub.

18

Cassie Cavanagh *may have a future in interior design*

I wasn't sure whether I should go into work early, so that I could be there to start explaining as soon as they all turned up, or whether I should turn up late – give them all the time to soak in their new surroundings, to process the change, to let off some steam if needs be. I wasn't just worried about Rupert and Olly. I was worried about the other staff members, too. After all, they barely knew me, I'd only just turned up, and here I was reorganising everything, going through all their desks, removing their things and placing those things in new desks. I wondered whether that was a huge invasion of privacy. I suspected that it probably was.

In the end, I decided that I would go in a little late. I dawdled on the way, stopping at the Deli Delivery place across the road from the office for a cup of coffee (£1.50 as opposed to £2.35 at Starbucks – and they remember my name).

'Morning, Cassie,' Andrei, the cheerful Russian behind the counter greeted me. 'Usual?' As Andrei made my latte I checked my phone. I already had three text messages, though all from my accomplices.

How pleased/pissed off are they? Ali asked.

Fingers crossed, Cass. Sure they'll love it, Jude said.

Good luck, gorgeous. If they don't appreciate you, tell them to stick it, was Jake's advice. I tended to agree with him. I'd done my best, with the good of the company uppermost in my thoughts and if they didn't like it, sod them. All the same, it might be an idea to sweeten them up a bit, too.

'Actually, Andrei,' I said, 'could you do seven lattes? And I'll take some of those pastries, too.'

Laden with beverages and baked goods, I made my way slowly up the stairs, my heart thumping in my chest, my hands starting to shake. I pushed the door open. They were all there, all six of them, standing in the main office, looking around, expressions of bewilderment on their faces.

'Has someone got a fairy godmother?' Melanie was asking.

Fabio was clapping Olly on the back.

'What a great surprise!' he was saying. 'Eees so much better than before.'

Rupert and Olly were regarding each other in utter confusion. I coughed to attract attention to my presence and put the tray of coffees and bag of pastries down on the nearest desk, the one I had allocated to myself. Everyone turned to look at me.

'Morning!' I said cheerfully. 'Would anyone like coffee?'

No one said anything for a minute. Then Aidan came across to me.

'Don't mind if I do,' he said, grabbing a latte and a pain au chocolat. The others began to converge around the table.

'Hang on, hang on a minute,' Rupert said. 'This is your doing, I take it?'

'That's right,' I said, trying to sound as confident as possible, 'I thought—'

'In my office,' he said coldly. 'Now.'

Rupert sat down at his new desk. Olly followed us into the office and closed the door behind us.

'This is not going to work out, I'm afraid,' Rupert said. I tried to say something but he held up his hand, silencing me. 'I understand why you did this – it all looks very good – but I explicitly told you to leave the presentation issue. You cannot simply take matters into your own hands like that.' His voice was low, but his face was turning from its usual mahogany to an angry puce. 'Leaving aside the issue of you going through everyone's desks to transfer their personal things, you simply disobeyed me. And you've been here for two weeks! I'm sorry. Take your things now, and be on your way.'

I couldn't say that I wasn't prepared for that, because I had been. I had hoped that he would look past the fact that I'd done the complete opposite of what he'd asked me to do and just appreciate the good work that I'd done, but I knew that there was a risk I'd get the sack. I'd gambled and lost. But even though I had known the risks, this still felt like a punch in the gut. I'd tried so hard. It just felt unfair. I wasn't simply upset, I realised, I was also quite angry.

'I'm sorry,' was all I said, my voice trembling a little. I didn't see much point in explaining. My motives were pretty obvious. I was heading for the door when Olly stepped out in front of me.

'Hang on a sec,' he said. 'Could you just wait outside, Cassie? Just for one minute?'

I went back into the main office. The others stopped munching on their pastries and turned to look at me.

'You are completely insane,' Melanie said, grinning at me. 'This is brilliant! I can't believe you did it. Did you do this all by yourself?'

'I had some help,' I said.

'What are they going to do?' Peter asked. 'Is Rupert throwing a hissy fit?'

'I've been sacked,' I said glumly.

'That's ridiculous!' Melanie said, placing her hands on her hips. 'OK, it was kind of an unorthodox way to go about things, but this place looks great. Plus you can actually find things in the filing system.' The others nodded enthusiastically.

'Good croissants, by the way,' Peter said. 'I think we should make this a Monday morning tradition. We could take it in turns to buy if those tight gits aren't prepared to shell out . . .'

At that moment, Olly opened the office door. He

glared at Peter. I wasn't sure whether he'd heard the 'tight gits' remark, but it looked as though he might have done.

'Would you come back in please, Cassie?' he asked. I followed him into the office, carrying a latte each for my masters in the hopes that it might appease them.

'You like to do things your own way, don't you?' Rupert said, accepting the latte from me. 'In a way, I rather like that . . .'

'We wouldn't like you to take matters into your own hands like this again,' Olly said, 'but in this case, we're going to let it slide . . .'

'Provided, that is, that this turns out to be a reasonable investment,' Rupert went on.

'Ah, you see, that's the beauty of it,' I said, breathing an enormous inward sigh of relief. 'This is my gamble. I decided, foolishly perhaps, to take a risk: I thought I would invest in doing an office makeover. If the investors who are coming tomorrow agree to put some money into the business, then I win and Vintage covers the cost – which,' I said hurriedly, 'was actually very reasonable. If they decide not to invest, I take the hit.' Or Ali takes the hit, anyway, at least in the short term.

'Although if the investors sign up tomorrow it will probably have absolutely nothing to do with the way our office looks, Cassie,' Rupert said.

'True, but at least they won't be put off from the moment they step into the office,' I pointed out.

Rupert harrumphed. Olly started to laugh.

'What's so funny?' Rupert asked his brother.

'The look on your face when you got here this morning. It was hilarious.'

Rupert started to laugh too. 'For a moment, I thought I was having some sort of episode. It was just such a shock to walk in here expecting to see one thing and finding something completely different.'

'Something better?' I asked hopefully.

'Much better,' he agreed. 'Go on, you go and get on with the post and the invoicing. And put together a statement of what you spent on this place, with the receipts attached.'

The following day I turned up for work almost more nervous than I had done on Monday. The next round of potential investors were visiting. Unless they gave us the nod, my finances would be taking a major hit. I spent the morning drinking so much coffee that by the time the men in suits were due to arrive I had developed a tremor in my left hand and was having palpitations.

The men in suits turned out not to be men in suits. Instead there were two preppy thirty-something blokes in jeans and rugby shirts accompanied by a very attractive, slightly older woman in a brightly printed Diane Von Furstenburg wrap dress and sky-high heels. I liked the look of them immediately.

'What a wonderful picture,' was the first thing the woman said as I showed her into the office. She was looking at Jake's photo on the opposite wall. 'Where did you find it?'

'The photographer's a good friend,' said Rupert,

who had just appeared at my elbow. He winked at me. 'Would you run out for coffees, Cass?'

The meeting lasted over an hour. I took this as a good sign – the last one had barely lasted twenty minutes. Eventually, Rupert stuck his head around the door and summoned me over.

'There are a couple of bottles of champagne in the fridge. Would you open them for us, Cassie?' he said, grinning like a Cheshire cat. 'And then could you ask everyone to join us in the meeting room for a quick celebratory drink? Yourself included, of course.'

The investors, venture capitalists from a small but successful private equity company, had agreed to pay half a million pounds for a slice of stock (how much was not disclosed to the rest of us) in the company. Whatever the percentage they had purchased, Rupert and Olly seemed to think that they had negotiated a very good deal. We toasted our new partners and the future success of the business. Once the investors had gone, Olly raised a glass to me.

'To Cassie, our new assistant-slash-interior decorator, without whom we might not have done such a fantastic deal.' Rupert rolled his eyes dramatically, but he raised his glass anyway.

Life at Vintage Organics became a lot more hectic – and the learning curve a great deal steeper – once the cash injection had been received. With some money in the bank the firm could afford to seek out new suppliers in order to broaden its range: Peter and Fabio were dispatched to Spain and Italy respectively to carry out in-the-field research. I was required to take on quite a bit of their workload, which involved dealing with suppliers, arranging meetings with possible new suppliers, endless correspondence negotiating prices and discounts on orders and a huge amount of desk research. I actually started to look forward to making the coffee and sorting the post as at least it gave me a chance to do something which wasn't incredibly mentally taxing.

I found myself working long hours – eight in the morning until seven at night was not uncommon – with half an hour for lunch if I was lucky. I even had to go into the office on Saturdays to catch up with admin that I hadn't been able to get finished in the week. I was still required to run all over town delivering urgent post, I was still asked to do the more boring, assistant-type jobs like picking up dry cleaning, managing Rupert's diary and booking flights and hotels for Peter and Fabio, but I was also getting more and more involved in the real running of the business – and I was loving every minute of it.

The downside, of course, was that I was completely exhausted. I'd make it home by eight thirty, hastily cook myself something to eat and crash out on the sofa. My social life had died a very sudden death – I was just too tired to go out in the evenings. Jake and I spoke almost every night, but every time he asked whether I felt like doing something, I turned him down. After a couple of weeks of this, he sent me a text, saying, *If you've changed your mind, just say so.* I rang him straight away.

'Changed my mind about what?' I asked.

'About me.' He sounded a bit sulky.

'I haven't, Jake, I'm just absolutely exhausted. I know it sounds ridiculous, but honestly, I'd be no fun if we did go out. I'm just feeling wiped out.'

'Well, why don't you come round to my place tomorrow then? I'll cook, we can watch a DVD. Nothing strenuous, I promise.'

'That sounds perfect. Around eightish OK? I'll bring the wine.'

At seven fifty the following evening I was still at work, on the phone with an irate customer who had not received an order due to be delivered that afternoon. All my attempts at appeasing him – offers of discounts, vouchers, money back – were doing no good whatsoever; he had ordered the wine because he was having a drinks party that very evening. His guests had arrived and he was going to run out of booze in about an hour's time thanks to our incompetence. I rang the delivery company. They couldn't explain what exactly had gone wrong, but the two cases due to be delivered to Mr Richard Eames of 12 Gowan Avenue, Fulham SW6 were still sitting in their dispatch office. I suggested they deliver them straight away.

'We don't do deliveries after seven,' came the reply.

I argued with, pleaded with and cajoled the delivery man for the best part of fifteen minutes, to no avail. There was nothing for it. I would have to do it myself.

I worked out that if I could borrow Ali's car, I could get to the delivery company in Wandsworth by around eight thirty (traffic permitting), and then across to Mr Eames's place by nine.

The first hitch was that Ali's car was not available – it was in the garage for a service. The obvious thing to do would, of course, be to call a cab, but since Rupert didn't even allow us to pay for couriered mail, I wasn't entirely sure I could count on getting the cost reimbursed. And I was wary of spending without permission given the whole office makeover affair. Starting to get desperate, I was pondering the logistics of trying to transport a case of wine across south London on public transport when I noticed Andrei, the Deli Delivery man across the road, shutting up shop. Andrei the Deli Delivery man has a Deli Delivery bicycle, a bicycle which has a little trailer attached to the back in which he stashes his Deli goods for delivery.

I ran downstairs.

'Andrei!' I yelled at him across the traffic. 'I need to borrow your bicycle.'

I hurried across the road, narrowly avoiding getting flattened by a taxi. 'It's an emergency,' I panted. Andrei peered at me suspiciously.

'Are you all right?' he asked. 'Are you hurt? Do you need to go to hospital?'

'Not that sort of emergency. It's a work emergency. I need to deliver a case of wine to south London by nine o'clock.'

There followed a short period of haggling over what the cost of borrowing his bicycle should be. We settled on one bottle of Vintage Organics claret and another of Pinot Grigio.

'My wife likes it,' he explained, as though requesting Pinot Grigio was something to be ashamed of.

The deal done, I hopped onto the bike, which proved heavier and more difficult to manoeuvre than I'd expected, and started pedalling south.

Halfway there I remembered that I was, at this very moment, supposed to be at Jake's having dinner. I pulled over onto the pavement (thankful to have a quick rest) and dialled his number.

'You're not going to believe where I am at the moment,' I panted at him when he answered.

'Well, I take it since you're phoning me that you're not currently standing on my doorstep.'

'I'm not, I'm really sorry—'

'You're not coming?' he interrupted tersely just as I was about to launch into a witty and amusing explanation of my current predicament.

'I'm really, really sorry, Jake. It's a work crisis—'

'Fine. See you when I see you then,' he said and hung up.

Oh, bugger. I got back on the bike and resumed pedalling.

The good news was that, amazingly enough, I managed to make it to the delivery company and across to Mr Eames's place by nine fifteen. I arrived, hot, sweaty and dishevelled, with his two cases of wine and half a case of champagne by way of an apology for the inconvenience. He was not just mollified, he seemed absolutely delighted, if slightly alarmed by my appearance.

'You're the girl I spoke to on the phone?' he asked as I lugged the second case of wine up the steps to his front door.

'That's right,' I huffed. 'I'm really sorry, but there was some sort of cock-up at our delivery company.' I wondered whether cock-up constituted bad language. 'So sorry for the inconvenience.'

'Well. I must say I didn't expect you to come here personally. Thanks very much. It really is very good of you.'

'All part of the service,' I said, smiling sweetly. *Never mind the fact that you probably just got me dumped*, I thought. *Just so long as your party goes well.*

By the time I'd cycled, slowly and wearily, back to Borough, where I chained the bicycle to the railings outside the Deli Delivery shop, and taken the tube back home it was after eleven. I sent Jake a text apologising once again and then went to bed. I fell asleep almost instantly. I dreamed that I was at the office, trying to compile an order for a client, but even though I had found all the right wines to fill the case there always seemed to be one missing.

There were no messages on my phone when I woke the next morning. I left for work with a heavy heart, the first time I'd felt that way in ages. I slouched into the office feeling miserable, trying to think of ways I could make it up to him. All the ideas I had come up with by the time I reached the office involved copious quantities of champagne and very expensive lingerie, neither of which I could really afford right now. Plus, I had the feeling that the sort of tricks that worked on Dan might not be so successful with Jake. I might have to be more creative in future. I consulted *Less is More!*, which sadly didn't have a chapter on cheap and innovative ways to placate an irate boyfriend. I supposed I could volunteer to go to the Polish film festival at the South Bank. Dark, moody, impenetrable, subtitled films might be my idea of hell, but he'd enjoy it.

As I pushed open the door to the office, Rupert greeted me like some sort of conquering heroine.

'There she is!' he boomed, spreading his arms wide as though he was about to hug me. 'The woman of the hour!' I smiled nervously at him. 'I just had a call from Richard Eames who tells me that you personally delivered two cases of wine to him last night. Is that right?'

I explained what had happened, and that I'd thought it was probably best to go the extra mile (and donate the extra champagne) rather than lose a customer.

'I looked through his orders and he's been a pretty good customer since we opened, so I thought it was worth it.'

'Abso-bloody-lutely!' Rupert beamed at me. 'That's

excellent work, Cassie. Exactly the kind of thing we need. Well done. Now I'm just going to go and bollock the delivery people. They do that again and we're going to have to find someone else to take care of the orders.'

I felt a warm glow envelop me, a feeling I had never had before. I realised with a shock that it was job satisfaction.

It was just after six when Rupert called me into his office.

'I think it's time your weekend started, young lady. You must have been worked very late last night. Take a bottle of champagne out of the fridge and go and enjoy yourself. You've really earned it this week.'

Excellent, I thought. I'll nip home, change into something a little less comfortable and then turn up at Jake's unannounced, brandishing a bottle of champagne. Hopefully that should go some way to putting me back into his good books. I was just heading off to the tube when my phone rang. It was Ali.

'Cass,' she said, her voice sounding oddly strained. 'Can you come round?'

Perfect timing. 'What's up? Is something wrong?' There was an odd wailing on the other end of the line. Oh, Christ, something *is* wrong. Oh, shit. She'd been for her twenty-week scan. 'What is it, Ali? Is it the baby?'

'Yes!' she sobbed. Oh, God. This was awful. This was too awful. She'd lost it.

'Oh, God. What's happened? Have you miscarried, Ali?' I asked softly.

'No!' she wailed even louder. 'I just can't do this. It's insane! I can't have a bloody baby. What was I thinking? What the bloody hell was I thinking?'

I sighed. Jake was going to have to wait. As my mother had told me, girlfriends come first. Particularly pregnant, hysterical girlfriends.

I did a noticeable double-take when Ali opened the door. My beautiful, tall, blonde friend, usually so perfectly groomed, looked a state. She was washed out and pale, racoon-eyed from all the crying, her hair scraped back from her face. She was dressed in a grey, holey T-shirt, a pair of boxer shorts and Ugg boots.

'Do you know how much I weigh?' she howled at me as I opened the door. 'Eleven stone. Eleven fucking stone. I can't believe this. It's horrible.' Given that Ali is five foot nine, eleven stone is actually not that bad at all. But since she's used to being closer to a slender and toned ten stone, her distress was understandable. 'Eleven fucking stone and I've still got twenty weeks to go. I'm going to be an elephant by the time this bloody thing is out of me.'

'Don't call it a bloody thing,' I said. 'You'll feel guilty when you meet him or her. And eleven stone is not fat, Ali. In any case, you should just bloody enjoy it. It's the only time in your life you're allowed to be fat without being treated like crap by everyone.'

'Easy for you to say, you skinny cow. And why have you brought champagne? You know I can't drink. You're just torturing me, aren't you?'

I explained about the champagne.

267

'Have you quit smoking?' I asked her.

'Yes. I've quit smoking. I've also quit drinking, quit eating sushi, quit running, quit dancing, quit everything. Pregnancy's rubbish. You can't do anything fun. Except have sex, of course, but then no one wants to have sex with me looking like this. This is why people have husbands, isn't it? They *have* to have sex with you when you're pregnant.'

'Ali, I've no doubt that there are still plenty of men in the world who'd be very happy to sleep with you if you asked nicely,' I said, giving her a hug. 'But what's brought all this on?' I asked. 'You seemed fine when we spoke the other day. You were talking about getting that ludicrously expensive buggy – you seemed really excited about everything.'

'That was before,' she sniffed.

'Before what?'

'Before I knew it was a boy!' she wailed, and burst into tears again.

I made her a cup of tea and opened the champagne.

'I thought you weren't going to find out the sex?'

'I changed my mind at the last minute.'

'Boys aren't that bad.'

'They're horrible. They're difficult and badly behaved. They're interested in tedious things like sports . . . Oh, Jesus. I'm going to have to take him to football matches, aren't I?'

'Not necessarily,' I replied. 'You never know, he might turn out to be gay.'

'We can but hope.'

'He'll be lovely, Al. Can you imagine how good-looking he'll be – tall and gorgeous, just like you, only with a bit of exotic, ne'er-do-well Frenchman thrown in?'

'He is going to be a heartbreaker,' she admitted. I clinked my glass with her mug.

'He's going to be amazing.'

We sat on the sofa in front of the fire, talking names.

'Seth,' I suggested. 'Or Nate.'

'Too American.'

'Jean-Marc? Olivier?'

'He's definitely not having a French name,' she said. 'Oh, give us a glass of that, will you? I can't stand sitting here drinking bloody herbal tea all the time.' I poured her a small glass of champagne. It was organic, after all. How much harm could it do? 'He rang today,' she said.

'Who rang today? The Frenchman?'

'Mmm.' She was looking away from me, but I could tell she was starting to cry again.

'So that's what this is all about.' I put my arm around her shoulders. 'What did he say?'

'Well, I told the powers that be at Hamilton Churchill that I'm pregnant. I was going to try to keep it quiet for a bit longer, but I was getting tired of all the remarks about me getting fat. Anyway, someone at work obviously told him that I was pregnant. Still pregnant, I mean.'

'You hadn't told him you were keeping it? I mean, keeping him.'

269

'No. Why should I? He made it perfectly clear that he wanted nothing to do with me or the baby as soon as I told him about it. I think he just assumed I'd have an abortion, and I never disabused him of the notion.'

'So what did he say?'

'He was furious. He said that he expected to be kept informed about what was happening with *his* child.'

'What a wanker. What a total wanker. What did you say?'

'I told him to fuck off. The last time we talked about it he didn't even acknowledge that it was *his* child, so as far as I'm concerned it has bugger all to do with him.'

'Too right,' I said, finishing the last of the champagne. 'What do you think of Joe?' she asked.

'After your dad? I think it's lovely. Joe Vaughn the second. It's perfect. Have you told your dad, by the way?' Ali was an only child, the apple of her father's eye and his only family now.

'Not yet. I think in some ways he'll be pleased – he'll be a such a brilliant granddad – it's just the part about getting knocked up by a married Frenchman who dumped me the second he found out about the child he's not going to be turning cartwheels over.' She sighed and handed me her glass. She'd only had two sips. 'I'm going to go and see him next weekend.'

'Do you want me to come along, for moral support?'

'That would be brilliant, Cass.'

I was going to go straight home after I left Ali's, but somehow, half an hour later, I found myself standing on Jake's doorstep with a six-pack of cider I'd bought from the off-licence. Not my usual taste, but Jake loves the stuff. The bottle of champagne had put me in an excellent mood and I was utterly convinced he'd be thrilled to see me. I rang the doorbell. There was no answer. I rang again. Still nothing. I rang a third time. Someone yanked the door open violently. A middle-aged, female someone, wearing a dressing gown.

'What on earth is it?' she demanded.

'Does . . . Jake live here?' I asked, slightly confused.

'Who? Do you know what time it is?' She glared at the six-pack of cider in my hand. 'Are you drunk?'

'Little bit, actually. I think I may have rung the wrong doorbell. Don't suppose you know if there's a Jake in the building, do you?'

'Flat C,' she replied with a murderous glare, slamming the door in my face.

I rang the doorbell again. The door was yanked open a second time.

'That's B!' the woman yelled at me. 'For God's sake, can't you read?'

'It's very dark out here,' I mumbled, squinting at the buzzer. That champagne really had gone to my head. The woman pressed the correct doorbell for me. I heard a door open upstairs.

'Jake!' the woman called out. 'Would you come down here? There's some drunk girl here to see you, she keeps ringing my doorbell.'

Jake leaned over the handrail on the stairs.

'Sorry, Mrs Blackburn. Would you send her up?'

I climbed the stairs, swaying ever so slightly as I did, wondering if in fact this might have been a bad idea.

'I believe I may have upset your neighbour,' I announced, holding up the cans of cider as a peace offering. He didn't look impressed, but he took the cider from me.

'Come on in,' he said.

Jake had a one-bedroom flat on the third floor of a converted Victorian house near Chalk Farm tube. Cat-swinging was out of the question, but it made up in character what it lacked in size, with an original working fireplace in the living room and a little balcony at the back looking out across manicured lawns towards Primrose Hill. The walls were covered with his photographs, the furniture all looked as though it had come from second-hand shops. There was a reassuring lack of anything that looked remotely as though it might have come from IKEA.

'I'm sorry I cancelled on you last night,' I said, collapsing onto his battered red leather sofa.

'That's OK,' he said. 'Do you want one of these? Because I have a feeling you may have had enough.'

'Mmmm . . .' I replied. The sofa really was very comfortable. I stretched out a bit, leaning my head on the armrest.

And then I must have fallen asleep, because the next thing I knew it was three thirty in the morning and I was still on the sofa, covered in a blanket. A pillow had been placed under my head. Oh, God. The memory of the encounter with his downstairs neighbour came flooding back to me. Oh, God, oh, God. Had I really turned up at his place, drunk and disorderly, and then passed out on his sofa? Why oh why, Cassie? As quietly as I could, I got up, folded up the blanket and searched around for my handbag, which was tricky given that I'd no idea where I put it, and it was pitch dark in the room. Eventually, as my eyes adjusted to the darkness, I spotted it, over in the corner. In my eagerness to retrieve it, I didn't notice the magazine rack next to the sofa, over which I tripped. I reached out to steady myself, grabbed onto something in the darkness and brought a standard lamp crashing down on top of me as I fell. Shit.

A figure loomed above me in the darkness.

'What on earth are you doing?' Jake asked.

'I was trying to go home . . .' I said weakly, as he pulled the lamp off me. 'I'm so sorry, Jake. I'll just get out of your way now.'

He pulled me to my feet.

'Don't be silly,' he laughed, wrapping his arms around me. 'I don't want you out of my way. I want you in my way. It's the middle of the night. Stay.'

'Really, I should go . . .' I started to say, but he shut me up with a kiss. So I stayed.

19

Cassie Cavanagh *loves Paris in the winter*

Ten days before Christmas, the Cavanagh clan (including Celia, Mike and the kids) descended on London for their Christmas shopping trip. They do this every year, and every year I tell them not to. They insist on coming up two Saturdays before Christmas (the final Saturday is always spent wrapping and preparing food) and they insist on going to Oxford Street which, at this time of year, bears a striking resemblance to the ninth circle of hell. I have tried telling them they'd be better off coming in November, but Celia insists that the kids want to see the lights. Actually, I think she likes leaving it so late because it then gives her ample opportunity to moan about how horrible London is.

'I don't know how you can stand it, Cassie. Dirty, busy, everyone's so rude. I honestly don't see why anyone would want to live here,' she announced as they arrived en masse, exhausted and fractious, for dinner at my flat on the Saturday evening.

I had been stressing about this dining all day. Usually when they came to London we would all go out somewhere, but I'd decided this year to prove that I could do the domestic goddess thing just as well as Celia could. And just to dial up the stress a little further, I'd invited Jake along. It was a little early in our relationship for meet-the-family, but since my drunken appearance at his flat things had been going so well between us. We'd barely spent a night apart. Plus, to be perfectly honest, I wanted to show him off.

I consulted *Less is More!* for ideas on cheap dinner parties. There was a long section on 'freegans', people who scavenge for food in supermarket dustbins. Tempting as it might be to serve my sister something I'd found in a dumpster, I discounted the idea on the grounds that I'd rather die than be caught fishing things out of bins, and decided instead to go for the low-cost menu option: a wholesome and warming French onion soup followed by slow-cooked lamb.

The cooking had gone surprisingly well. I had only managed to scald myself twice, which is pretty good going for me, and I had succeeded in manoeuvring the furniture in our living room so that there would be space for six adults to eat, with the kids sitting at the counter. I was showered, spruced up and ready for anything by the time my family arrived.

Well, almost anything. I kept my cool when Celia launched straight into her diatribe about how horrible London is. I grinned and bore her criticisms of the flat ('Not very practical for dinner parties, is it? Don't know how you cope without a proper dining room'). Somehow I managed. But I started to lose my temper when she expressed exasperation that I had not prepared a separate meal for the kids. 'French onion soup? For a three-year-old? Honestly, Cassie, you just don't *think*, do you?

Celia was saved from having a drink dumped in her lap by my doorbell. Jake had arrived. And he was perfect. He chatted to my dad about gardening. He (remarkably convincingly) feigned interest in Mike's golf handicap. He had a lengthy conversation with my mother about the problems facing teachers today. And he charmed Celia, not so much by saying anything to her, but by spending half an hour playing hide-and-seek with Tom and Rosie, and apparently enjoying it.

Over dinner, my parents announced with great excitement that they were planning a caravanning trip to the Lake District.

'In December?' I asked.

'No, we're not going until March,' Mum said, 'but we just thought we'd mention it. There's a lot of preparation goes into these things.' Despite myself, I cringed. Anyone would have thought they were going trekking in the Himalayas.

'I love the Lake District,' Jake said. 'I took some great pictures there last summer.'

'You and Cassie should join us,' Mum said.

'Not sure caravanning's really Cassie's cup of tea,' my sister chirped up. 'She's more the five-star-hotel type, aren't you, Cass?'

Everyone laughed, including Jake. I got up to clear away the plates.

'Actually,' Jake said, 'I was thinking of going a bit farther afield next year, after my course ends. I did a trip to East Africa a couple of years ago, which I really enjoyed. I'm thinking of West Africa next – Senegal, perhaps, or the Ivory Coast.'

'Not much in the way of five-star hotels there, I shouldn't imagine,' Celia said with a sly little smile.

'Oh, I'm sure Cassie's capable of roughing it,' Jake replied, as he got up to give me a hand with the dishes. Although Celia was annoying me, it struck me in that moment that she knew me a little better than Jake did. Roughing it, particularly in a tropical country with an abundance of large insects, was not my idea of a great time.

Later, as my parents pored over the images on Jake's digital camera, Celia joined me in the kitchen to make coffee.

'Well, Mum and Dad are smitten with him,' she said.

'That's good, because I am too.'

'He is very nice. Although I wouldn't necessarily have put you two together. I mean, he doesn't really seem like your type? All that talk about dropping everything to run off to dangerous places, I can't really see you doing anything like that.'

I slammed the cafetière down on the counter, slightly harder than I'd intended to.

'Celia, I don't have go everywhere he goes,' I snapped. 'There are plenty of couples who don't do everything together. We're not all like you and Mike. Just look at Jude – she and Matt spend months apart, and they're just fine.'

Celia retreated, wounded, to the living room. I immediately felt guilty. She did have a point. I also felt a little guilty about using Jude as my example. She was not 'just fine' all the months that Matt was away; I remembered quite clearly her watching news reports from foreign countries with mounting alarm. I knew it had been hard for her. I also knew that she'd been able to cope with it because:

a) they shared the same ideals, and

b) Jude knew Matt was the one.

Much as I adored him, I wasn't entirely sure I could say the same about Jake.

For all my irritation with Celia, the evening was a success. My parents adored Jake and they were delighted with my attempts at domesticity, as well as my enthusiasm for my new job. And my job did have many fringe benefits. One of the myriad advantages of working for a wine company was that it made gift giving fairly simple. Everyone I knew (everyone over the age of eighteen, anyway) got Vintage Organics vouchers for Christmas. The kids were a little more challenging, but shopping for them was the most enjoyable retail experience I'd had in a long while. Tom got a drum kit (it was expensive, but the look on Celia's face when he unwrapped it was priceless), Rosie got a bright pink tricycle and Monty got a Thomas the Tank Engine.

I spent Christmas Eve at Mum and Dad's, Christmas Day at Celia's and Boxing Day with Ali and her dad back in London. As she had predicted, although he was initially absolutely furious about the fact that she'd got herself 'into trouble' with 'some bloody frog', he was also incredibly excited about the prospect of becoming a grandfather.

New Year's Eve, ordinarily spent in a champagne blur with City pals, was looking set to be a non-event this year. Everyone else had made alternative arrangements. Including Jake.

'I'm really sorry, Cass,' he said, 'but I'm going to be in Manchester with my brother. We organised it a while ago – he and a bunch of his mates are going clubbing and they invited me along – he'd be really disappointed if I backed out now.' I was completely gutted, but determined not to show it.

'That's fine, Jake. It's absolutely fine,' I said, breezily. 'I'll spend New Year with Ali and Jude.' I didn't tell him that Ali was going to be in the Maldives (her last opportunity for a real holiday before the baby came) and that Jude was going to be in Edinburgh with Matt (who was paying one of his flying visits to the UK) and a group of their friends. I didn't want to make him feel bad.

'Are you sure?'

'Of course,' I said, wondering whether spending New Year alone in my flat would be preferable to spending it with Celia and Michael, which was really my only other option this late in the day.

I decided that it would be a) a bit sad and b) not very kind to do nothing in preference to accepting my sister's invitation, so on the thirtieth I packed some things and headed off to King's Cross to get the train. Jake rang just as I was leaving the house.

'You off to the station now?' he asked.

'Yeah,' I said, not terribly enthusiastically. 'Celia's picking me up at the other end.' I'd had to admit to him that I was spending New Year with my sister since Jude had told him she was out of London and Ali had announced her Maldives plans on Facebook.

'Don't sound so glum,' he said. 'I'm sure it'll be fun.'

'I'm sure it'll be a hoot. I'll give you a call when I get there, OK? Have a lovely time,' I said, congratulating myself on being such an incredibly sweet and easy-going girlfriend.

Killing time while waiting for the train, I had just purchased a couple of magazines for the journey and was heading over to Starbucks to pick up a latte when someone grabbed me from behind. I shrieked and flung my elbow back, whacking my assailant in the face.

'Bloody hell, Cassie!' Jake yelped, clutching his bleeding nose.

'Oh, my God! Oh, my God! I'm so sorry,' I said, fishing around in my bag for something to stem the blood flow. 'What the hell are you doing sneaking up on me like that? Oh, God, have I broken it?'

'I don't think so,' he said, dabbing at it gingerly. 'Christ, remind me never to piss you off.'

'Are you all right, miss?' A member of the British Transport Police had appeared at my elbow. 'Is this man bothering you?' I looked around – we'd attracted quite a crowd of onlookers.

'No, I'm fine. It was a misunderstanding. This is my boyfriend,' I explained. The policeman looked sceptical. 'Honestly, he *is* my boyfriend. I didn't actually mean to hit him like that. I mean, I meant to hit him, only I didn't know it was him. If you see what I mean.' The policeman looked confused, but apparently satisfied that Jake was under no immediate threat from this deranged woman, he let us go.

Having stopped the bleeding, Jake grabbed my hand.

'Come on,' he said, 'we've got a train to catch!'

'Have we?' I asked, confused. 'I can't go to Manchester with you, Jake, I've promised Celia I'll go to her place.'

'I've spoken to Celia,' he said, dragging me along. 'It's all sorted.'

'We're going to the wrong way, Jake. The trains to Manchester go from the other end of the station.'

'So they do, but we're not going to Manchester,' he replied with a grin. I looked up. We were heading towards the Eurostar terminal.

Please tell me we're not going to Brussels.

We were not going to Brussels. On the train, over coffee and croque monsieurs, Jake told me he'd booked the trip the day after I surprised him at his flat.

'You know, the day after the night you wrecked my living room,' he said with a charmingly coy smile. He'd spoken to Jude and Ali, confirming that I hadn't made plans with either of them, and arranged for Jude to deliver my passport to him before she left for Edinburgh. He'd also rung my sister to let her in on the plan.

He'd booked us a room at L'Hôtel, on the rue des Beaux-Arts on the Left Bank.

'It's where Oscar Wilde breathed his last,' Jake told me cheerfully. Our room – thankfully not the one where poor Oscar checked out – was lavishly decorated in deep reds and gold, with an enormous green and gold mural depicting peacocks above the bed. The whole place was dark and opulent and smacked of decadence. Outside it was beautiful and sunny, albeit freezing cold, and we spent hours wandering along the Seine, occasionally popping into brasseries to drink café au lait or red wine we climbed the hill to the Sacre Coeur, we visited the Musée d'Orsay and the Musée Rodin, we ate at La Coupole, we spent hours and hours in bed. It was almost perfect (I say almost because I wasn't allowed to go shopping – Jude had made Jake promise). It was the best New Year I'd ever had.

20

Cassie Cavanagh *feels very grown up*

By early March, New Year's Eve was a distant memory; it seemed like a different life. Since 3 January, the day I'd got back to work, I'd been under constant pressure. The initial cash injection we received in early December had been followed by another from a second group of investors in January, and the company was expanding its operations at breakneck speed. This was great news, of course, although it did have its drawbacks.

Peter and Fabio were almost never in the office, and Rupert and Olly decided to take a three-week trip to Australia and New Zealand to meet with potential new suppliers out there. With four of the VO's seven employees out of the office for long stretches, those of us who remained were left with a crushing workload. I was having to take on more and more of the day-to-day running of the business and had less time to do the more tedious, menial tasks – but since there was no one else to do them, it simply meant I was working longer and longer hours.

February had passed in a blur, the only highlight being Valentine's Day, spent with Jake, a chilly picnic of wine and chocolates on Primrose Hill which was so much more romantic than the wallet-bustingly expensive dinner I'd had at Nobu with Dan last Valentine's Day. And, unlike Dan, Jake didn't send an ostentatious show of red roses on the day itself. He sent me irises the day before and bought me an orchid the day after.

'*Everyone* gets flowers on Valentine's Day,' he explained. 'You're special.'

Outside work I spent almost every spare minute I had either with Jake or with Ali, whose state of mind seemed to be in a constant state of vacillation, from near-hysterical excitement to sheer terror. She was now just nine weeks away from her due date and had decided all of a sudden that there was no way she could stay in her smart, child-unfriendly apartment.

'I have to buy a house,' she announced over breakfast at Shoreditch House, where she still had her membership. 'I can't stay in my flat. It's totally impractical for a child. He'll fall off the balcony into the canal. I have to move. And I only have two months in which to do it.'

'You do realise, Ali, that once the baby is born it will be quite some time before he's moving about on his own? They don't start crawling till they're about eight or nine months old. And even then he's highly unlikely to be able to fling himself over the balcony.'

'You never know,' she said, tucking into her second helping of pancakes with blueberry compote. 'In any case, I'm going to have to move sometime. It'll be easier now than once he gets here, won't it?' I wasn't sure that house hunting when seven months' pregnant was likely to be easy, but once Ali gets an idea into her head she's unlikely to be deterred. 'In any case, I might not be working for a while after I have the baby, and that's going to make it more difficult to get a mortgage, isn't it? In any case, I was thinking of ringing round some agents this afternoon, just to see what's available.'

'I can help out if you like,' I said, although I wasn't sure when I was going to be able to help out, since I seemed to spend almost every waking hour at the office. 'I could come along to viewings with you, that sort of thing.'

Three days later, she rang me at the office.

'I've found a house!' she said excitedly.

'Bloody hell, that was quick.'

'I know, and it's absolutely perfect. I really, really want it.'

'How much?' I asked.

'I don't know.'

'What do you mean, you don't know?'

'It's up for auction next Friday. The guide price is two hundred and fifty grand, but that doesn't necessarily mean anything. I'm off to see a broker now, to get a mortgage agreed in principle. And I'm going to take a look at it this evening.'

'You mean you haven't actually seen it yet?'

'No, but I can just tell it's going to be perfect. Can you come with me tonight? It's on St Mark's Road. A stone's throw from Notting Hill! Viewings start at six.'

St Mark's Road was a stone's throw from the dodgy end of Notting Hill, otherwise known as Ladbroke Grove. But I could see why Ali liked the place. It was a little Victorian house with three bedrooms and a garden out back. The interior was gorgeous: dark hardwood floors, sash windows, a brand new kitchen and a master bedroom in the converted loft which had enormous skylights in the roof.

'I know we're in a crummy market,' I said to Ali as we tiptoed around the place, trying not to bump into other viewers, nor to convey to them any excitement or enthusiasm about the place whatsoever, 'but why is this place selling at auction? You would have thought it would go quite easily through an agent.'

'It's a repossession, apparently,' Ali whispered back. 'The guy who did it up was a property developer who took on too many houses, spent a fortune doing them up and then couldn't get rid of them quickly enough. If it goes for anything like the guide price it'll be an absolute bloody steal.'

Later, over steaks at Black & Blue on Kensington Church Street I asked the obvious question.

'Say it doesn't go for anything like the guide price. Say it goes for considerably more. Can you afford a three hundred grand property if you're not going to be working, Ali?'

She chewed a mouthful of ribeye thoughtfully.

'Not really. It depends how long I'm out of work for, I suppose. It isn't absolutely guaranteed that Hamilton will sack me. Nicholas has actually been making quite encouraging noises since I told him I was pregnant – I think since there are so few women or ethnic minorities at the firm he reckons that having a single mother on the trading floor will be good for the company's social responsibility rating. I don't know. I'm not even sure I'm going to want to work as a trader once the baby comes.' She sighed. 'I have got enough for a fairly sizeable deposit – I had three years of good bonuses before last year, which was obviously rubbish, and I haven't spent a great deal of the money. All I did was buy a car, rent the flat and go on a couple of holidays. What would be really helpful would be if I could get someone to move in with me.'

'Got your eye on anyone?' I asked with a smile.

'What, like a man? In this state? Are you joking? I weigh more than half the forwards on the England rugby team, for God's sake.' It was true that she was starting to look fairly hefty. 'No, what I need is a nice young Eastern European who'll double as a lodger and babysitter.'

When I eventually arrived home that night, Jude was sitting on the sofa, talking on the phone and weeping. My first thought was that someone had died. But when she looked up at me, she seemed to be smiling and weeping. I was confused. She put the phone down, leapt to her feet and flung her arms around me.

'He's asked me to marry him!' she sobbed, squeezing me so hard I thought she might break a rib. 'Matt's asked me to marry him!'

'He asked you over the phone? That's not terribly romantic.'

'Yes, it is,' she replied. 'He's in Somalia, you see, and his car was shot at by rebels when he was driving from one of the refugee camps back to Mogadishu, and he thought he was going to die and all he could think,' she sobbed, 'all he could think was that he was never going to see me again and he just couldn't bear it. So as soon as he got back into town he got hold of a satellite phone and he rang me.'

'God, that is romantic,' I said. I was welling up too.

'Do we have any booze in the house?'

'No, but the offie's open for another . . . twelve minutes.' I kicked off my heels, slipped on my trainers and sprinted all the way.

I dragged myself into work the next day, my head aching and the rest of my body protesting at the lack of sleep. Jude and I had sat up drinking and chatting until three in the morning, planning the engagement party she was going to have when Matt returned from Somalia in a couple of weeks' time. A triple-shot latte clutched in my right hand and a copy of *Decanter* magazine in my left, I staggered into the office to be greeted by Rupert and Olly, beaming at me as though they'd just won the lottery.

'How are you this morning, Cassie?' Rupert boomed.

'I'm very well, thanks,' I lied.

'Lovely morning, isn't it?' Olly asked. Was it just me, or were they speaking unnecessarily loudly?

'Do you know what day it is?' Rupert asked.

'Umm. Your birthday?' I ventured.

'It's the end of your trial! Your three months are up!'

'I hope you're not about to tell me that my services are no longer required,' I said. They both laughed heartily. And loudly.

'Course not! We've got your permanent contract all drawn up. Thought we'd take you out to breakfast to celebrate.'

They took me to Roast above Borough Market where I tucked into an extremely welcome smoked streaky bacon and fried egg butty accompanied by a glass of champagne (hair of the dog). Rupert laid the contract down on the table in front of me.

'The money's still not fantastic, Cassie. It's not as much as you deserve – we really do appreciate how hard you've been working lately. But hopefully it won't be long before we can offer you a bit more – if things keep going the way they are at the moment there are bound to be opportunities for you to move up in the company.'

He was right, the money wasn't fantastic, but I was just delighted to be back in full-time employment – and working at a place where I could see myself moving up the ladder in a year or two's time.

The permanent contract came at an opportune time, offering, as it did, four weeks of paid holiday, one day of which I opted to take that Friday so that I could accompany Ali to the property auction. It was held in a function room at the Royal Garden Hotel on High Street Kensington. Looking around the room, which was packed to the rafters, you wouldn't have thought that we were in the middle of a housing market crash. There were hundreds of people there, and quite a few of them looked more like first-time buyers – young people, some with kids – than property investors or developers.

Ali's house, as I was already referring to it, was lot number twenty-two. The first batch of lots sold for well above their guide price.

'What are we prepared to go up to?' I whispered to Ali, who had found a chair and was sitting at the back of the room wearing her poker face: perfectly impassive.

'I'll go to three twenty,' she said. 'That's the valuation the surveyor put on it. I do love the house but I'm not paying over the odds for it. In any case, anything above that and the mortgage would start to look a bit unmanageable.'

I didn't know how she could manage to be so calm about it. She was about to spend three hundred and twenty thousand pounds. My heart races when I spend a couple of hundred quid on a pair of shoes. But then she is used to dealing with big numbers. When we got to lot twenty-one, a dilapidated pile somewhere in Hounslow, I helped Ali to her feet and we moved through the crowd towards the front.

'Lot twenty-two,' the auctioneer announced, 'is number forty-seven St Mark's Road, W10. The guide price is two hundred and fifty thousand pounds, the reserve price is one hundred and twenty thousand. Can I start the bidding at one hundred and fifty?' We looked around the room. No one bid. My hands were shaking.

'What do we do?' I whispered.

'Nothing,' Ali whispered back. 'We don't open the bidding.'

'Do I see one thirty? Surely I see one thirty? This is a three-bedroom property in excellent condition, in the heart of West London. Do I see one thirty? I do, the bidding is opened at one hundred and thirty thousand pounds. Do I see one forty?'

'Who bid?' I hissed at Ali. 'I didn't see who it was.'

'Shhh. Let me concentrate.'

A bidding war begun between two men, both of whom looked as though they might have been developers – they had bid on other properties already that morning. Ali's house was clearly not their dream home.

'Hopefully, they're not going to be in it all the way,' Ali said to me. 'They're going to want to sell the place on, and since there's not much you can do to the house that hasn't already been done, they need a low price in order to make their margin.'

One of the developers dropped out at two seventy. It was time to make our move.

'Do I see two eighty?' the auctioneer asked. 'The bidding is with you, sir, at two seventy. Do I see two eighty?'

Ali raised her hand. 'We have a new bidder!' the auctioneer announced excitedly. The remaining property developer, who was standing less than ten feet away from us, rolled his eyes and turned to look at us, visibly annoyed. Ali gave him a cold, hard stare. He looked away. He bid two ninety and Ali went to three hundred. The auctioneer asked for three ten. His hand stayed down. She'd done it!

'The bidding is with the young lady, at three hundred thousand pounds,' the auctioneer said. 'Going once, going twice ... I have a new bid! The gentleman at the back bids three hundred and ten thousand.' My heart sank. Ali remained stoical, raising her hand to bid three twenty.

'Do I see three thirty?' Please don't see three thirty, I thought. 'Three hundred and thirty thousand pounds.' That was it. I was devastated, and it wasn't even my dream house. I couldn't imagine what Ali must have been feeling. She'd wanted this so much, but still her face gave nothing away. The auctioneer asked if there were any more bids. There were not. And then, just as he was about to bring the gavel down, Ali raised her hand one more time.

'Three fifty,' she called out. I was so surprised I actually jumped. Three fifty? Where did three fifty come from? What happened to three forty?

'Three hundred and fifty thousand,' the auctioneer

announced. 'Do I see three sixty?'

He did not. 'Going once, going twice . . .' The gavel came down. 'Lot twenty-two is sold to the young lady for three hundred and fifty thousand pounds! Congratulations.' Ali and I were jumping up and down, hugging each other.

'Oh, my God!' I shrieked. 'I can't believe we won! We won!'

'I need to sit down,' Ali said.

'I need a drink,' I said.

'I also need to pee,' Ali said.

When Ali got back from the ladies I'd found a table in the corner of the lobby and ordered a coffee for myself and orange juice for her.

'Christ,' she said, sinking into an armchair, 'I can't believe I just paid thirty thousand over my limit.'

'Neither can I.'

'I just couldn't bear it. I couldn't bear to let it go.'

'What happens now?' I asked her.

'Well, I have to put down a ten per cent deposit today – that won't be a problem, I can get the bank to transfer over the money. Then I have a month – well, twenty working days to be exact – to get the rest of the money together. I'm going to have to go back to my broker and ask for more cash.'

'Do you think you'll be able to get it?'

'I'd better be able to get it – the deposit is non-refundable, so if I don't get it, I'll have just thrown away thirty-five thousand pounds.'

'Jesus, Ali. How can you be so calm about this?'

'Oh, I'm not calm. I'm actually having a nervous breakdown as we speak. But I'm an equities trader – we're good at hiding our true feelings.'

The weekend after the auction was Matt and Jude's engagement party. They had decided on a picnic on the Common for fifty or so of their closest friends. Jude's friends Zara and Lucinda, who are both vegans, did the catering. The food was pretty much inedible. There was plenty to drink and quite a bit to smoke, though, and the combination resulted in a massive outbreak of the munchies. Eventually, Jake led a splinter faction of non-vegetarians on a run to the deli on the high street to stock up on real food.

Vegans or no vegans, it was a glorious day. Jake and I annoyed everyone with our flagrant public displays of affection, and Ali kept everyone amused with horrendous tales of 'the truth about pregnancy'. (She's threatening to write a book on the subject, complete with the low-down on throwing up on the tube, chronic indigestion, stretch marks, swelling, sciatica and strangers feeling free to fondle your stomach in the supermarket.) As the sun started to set, Jude's hippy friends performed a 'blessing ritual' for the happy couple which had the more cynical among us in stitches.

After the blessing, we played a mammoth game of football, involving teams of at least twenty players each, though who was playing for which team never seemed to be completely clear. Several people, myself included, took advantage of the failing light to change sides a few times depending on the score. It finished 23–19. I scored three goals, which should give you a keen sense of what the defending was like.

When the booze finally ran out, the more hardened partygoers among us went back to our flat to open a couple of bottles of Vintage Organics' finest. It was there that Jude dropped her bombshell.

'We have to move out,' she said, gazing mournfully into the middle distance. She was quite stoned. 'We have to leave, Cassie.'

'Why? You and Matt aren't getting married straight away, are you – I thought you were planning on a very long engagement?'

'I'm leaving the country,' she replied. 'In two months' time. As soon as my course is finished.'

'What? Since when? Where are you going? Why?'

'Matt's finally decided he's had enough of being shot at on a regular basis. They've offered him a job at Unicef's headquarters – it's a really good job. And it's in New York.'

'Oh, my God, Jude, that's amazing! New York! That's so exciting.'

'I know,' she said, and burst into tears.

I woke up the following morning with an aching head and only a vague recollection of my conversation with Jude. I staggered into the kitchen, where she and Matt were sitting, drinking tea, looking about as bad as I felt.

'Morning,' I said softly. They both smiled and nodded their heads very gently. 'Anyone got any aspirin?' Matt handed me the box. Jude pointed at the kettle. I nodded. She made me a cup of tea. For ten minutes or so, we sat in silence. Eventually, Jude spoke.

'Did I tell you about the New York thing?' she asked. 'I can't remember.'

'You did, but I can't remember the details. When are you actually going?'

Matt's new job started in June, but they were going to go over in May in order to find themselves somewhere to live and give Jude a chance to start looking for work.

'So we need to give notice pretty much straight away, don't we?'

'I'm really sorry, Cassie, I know you could probably do without this right now. You could always stay here, and just get someone else to rent out the room.'

'It wouldn't be the same without you,' I said. 'In any case, I think I could do with a change. Plus, I happen to know someone who's in the market for a lodger.'

Ali was delighted when I suggested that I should move in with her.

'That'll be perfect, Cassie. I really need someone to help out with the mortgage. And of course that'll mean you're not just renting any more – you'll be buying a piece of my house.'

'No, Ali, I couldn't do that – it's your place.'

'If you're going to be paying part of the mortgage, I

think it should be our place. Yours, mine and little Joe's.'

Oh, my God. I was about to become a homeowner. Or at least, a part-of-a-homeowner. How incredibly grown up of me.

21

Cassie Cavanagh *is moving on to greater things*

If I was going to become a homeowner, remaining in full-time employment was going to be a necessity. And I was starting to worry that I might just find myself out of work yet again if things carried on as they had been recently.

The problem was a gentleman by the name of Alexandre Leveque, the owner of Chateau Saint Martin near St Emilion in Bordeaux. Rupert had sampled his wines when on a tour of the region and had become obsessed with doing a deal with Monsieur Leveque. Unfortunately, M. Leveque was not an easy man to do business with. For starters, he despised *les Anglais*. He was not a fan of Anglo-Saxon corporate culture and he was deeply suspicious of Internet-based businesses. In short, he wanted nothing to do with us.

Peter had been dispatched to France to try to sweet-talk Leveque into doing a deal with us and had returned, chastened.

'Never going to happen, Rupe. The man's a nutter. He blames the English and the Americans for the demise of the great *viticulteurs français*. Apparently the crisis in French wine production is all our fault because we buy cheap stuff from the New World. And of course because we've dared to start producing wine in England, too, which is of course complete sacrilege.'

Rupert refused to accept this. He was determined to get his hands on Leveque's wines and as a result of his obsession, and of Leveque's continued refusal to do business with us, Rupert had become increasingly difficult to please. Because the others were out of the office so much of the time, Melanie and I generally bore the brunt of Rupert's frustration.

After months of feeling that I was a valuable cog in the office machine, I was suddenly made to feel as though everything I did was wrong. It was a bit like working for Nicholas again. The research report I'd written for him on Corsican wines was 'insubstantial'. The delivery company had messed up three orders in two weeks – why had I not got him quotes from new companies? Surely I should have guessed that he would want to look at new delivery firms? My job was to anticipate his needs, not simply to respond to them. And on the subject of anticipating needs, where the hell was his cappuccino?

It was an immense relief to everyone when, at long last, Alexandre Leveque agreed to meet with Rupert. The terms of a deal were agreed, but Leveque refused to sign anything until he'd met Rupert in person: he was to travel out to France that Thursday, taking with him the contract which Leveque would then sign, provided Rupert met with his approval.

On Thursday morning, I skipped into work, anticipating my first relaxing work day in weeks. Rupert would be hysterical about the meeting, but at least he would be hysterical somewhere else. Peter and Fabio were both away on trips and Olly was attending his youngest child's school sports day, so it would be just Melanie, Aidan and me in the office. As it turned out, it was just Aidan and me. Mel called in sick. We were just deciding whether we could afford to nip out to the market for a couple of bacon sarnies when the phone rang.

'Cassie?' It was Rupert. He sounded panicky. 'We have a problem.'

'What's up?' I asked. 'You haven't forgotten your passport, have you?'

'Worse. I've lost the contract.'

'You've what? What do you mean, you've lost the contract?'

'I had to change trains in Paris and I must have left it behind.'

'OK, well, don't panic. I can fax a new copy over to you. Leveque must have a fax machine at his place.'

'Cassie, you don't seem to understand!' His voice rose a couple of octaves. 'This is going to be an incredibly delicate negotiation. I cannot turn up there without the contract. I'll look like a bloody idiot.' *Well, you are a bloody idiot*, I thought. *Who leaves the contract with an important business partner on the train?* 'In any case, Olly had already put his signature on the contract – a faxed signature is no good. It has to be the original.'

'Right. Don't panic. I'll print out a new contract, take it to Olly – where's his son's school, by the way?'

'No idea.' God, he was useless.

'All right, I'll find it. I'll get him to sign and I'll courier the contract out to you.'

'It'll have to be at Leveque's place by eight this evening. We're having dinner.'

'I'm sure it's doable,' I said, sounding a good deal more confident than I felt.

While the new contract was printing, I called around a few courier companies. The news was not good. If you wanted a package delivered to France by that evening, it needed to be collected by eight in the morning. It was now eight thirty. It was the same story with the first three firms. The fourth said they could do it provided that I had the package ready for collection by nine thirty. Hurrah. I rang Olly. His phone went straight to voicemail. Shit. I left a message.

'Olly, you need to ring me back as soon as you get this. It is very urgent.'

I rang again five minutes later, and again five minutes after that. He called back at eight fifty. They were just on their way to the sports day at his son's school in Wimbledon. If I took a cab I could get there in twenty minutes. I rang the courier company again. Could they pick up from the school at nine thirty? Yes, they could. Fantastic.

I hurtled down the stairs, out of the door and up the road to London Bridge station, where you are guaranteed to find a black cab at any time of night or day. There was a queue of around ten people outside the station. Bugger it. I wondered whether I should take my chances on the high street? I decided against it. The queue was moving fairly quickly. It was just after nine when I got into the cab. I could still make it. I would still make it.

The traffic in central London was pretty awful, but once we got past Clapham and out onto the A24 we were picking up pace. It was nine fifteen. It was going to be close.

'You in a hurry, love?' the cabby asked me. He'd obviously seen me looking at my watch every thirty seconds.

'Yes, I really need to get some papers to my boss by nine thirty.'

'We should make it, provided the traffic's like this all the way.' That remark was the kiss of death. Moments after he'd said it, the cars in front of us started to slow. Their speed dropped and dropped and eventually we came to a halt. 'Famous last words,' the cabby said cheerfully. Oh, fuck. I wasn't going to make it.

I got to the school at nine forty. Olly was waiting for me in the car park. I asked the taxi driver to wait and sprinted across to him. He was shaking his head.

'Too late, Cassie. The courier just left.'

'You're joking.'

'I'm not, I'm afraid. I tried to persuade him to wait, but he said nine thirty is the absolute latest they can accept packages for same-day delivery.'

'Oh, Jesus. Rupert's going to kill me.'

'He is,' Olly agreed. I sat down on the pavement, my head in my hands. This was a disaster. What the hell was I going to do? 'We'll have to let him know. Do you want me to ring him? I can tell him that it wasn't your fault.' *Of course it wasn't my bloody fault*, I thought. *He's the one who left the bloody contract on the bloody train.* But somehow I knew that, when it came down to it, I would be the one to carry the can. There was only one thing for it.

'Don't ring him,' I said to Olly, getting to my feet. 'Sign the contract.'

'Cassie, there's no way you can get it to him today.'

'Yes, there is. I can take them to him myself.'

In the taxi on the way back to my flat I rang Air France. There were no direct flights from London to Bordeaux until that evening, but I could get a seat on the twelve o'clock flight from Gatwick which got into Paris at one thirty. From Paris to St Emilion it was about three hundred and seventy miles, so if I hired a car at the airport and put my foot down on the motorway I could be in St Emilion by seven. Although unless I could make it to the airport by ten forty-five, all this was moot.

I left the taxi driver waiting downstairs while I ran up to the flat to grab my passport and a change of clothes – I couldn't get a flight back until Saturday morning unless I was prepared to pay an extortionate fare. I left a hastily scrawled note for Jude, saying, *Gone to France. Back soon.* Then I ran back downstairs, tripped on the second to last step and fell flat on my face, hauled myself up again and flung myself into the back of the cab.

'Gatwick,' I gasped. 'Quick as you can.'

From the taxi I phoned Avis and arranged the car hire. The moment I'd hung up, Rupert rang.

'Is everything sorted, Cassie? Is the contract on its way? What time can I expect it?'

'It'll be delivered to your hotel by seven,' I said.

'You sure about that? The company's guaranteed that, have they?'

'Sorry? I can't really hear you, Rupert,' I lied. 'You're breaking up.' I hung up. Oh, God, please let me get to that hotel by seven.

I made it to the check-in desk at five to eleven.

'You're too late,' the man behind the desk said. 'We've closed check-in.'

'Oh, God, please don't say that. I have to get to Paris. My job is on the line. Please?'

'You're too late,' the man repeated.

'I don't have any luggage to check in,' I said. 'I can go straight to the gate. Please?' I pleaded. He sighed.

'Oh, all right then. But you must go straight to the gate. You don't have time for shopping.'

I was the last person onto the plane. They literally closed the doors behind me as I got on. Then the plane sat on the runway for forty minutes.

'It's your fault, you know,' the prune-faced old woman sitting on the other side of the aisle said to me. 'Because we were waiting for you, we missed our slot.' Miserable old cow.

We landed at Charles de Gaulle just before two. I sprinted to the Avis counter, picked up the keys to my Citroën ZX and purchased a map from a bookshop in the airport terminal. Annoyingly, I discovered that I was on completely the wrong side of the city. I would have to drive all the way around Paris's answer to the M25 – the *Périphérique* – in order to get to the motorway towards Orléans and the south-west. *Le Périph*, as it is known by the locals, is notoriously prone to traffic jams. I was just going to have to pray that today was a good traffic day in Paris.

Fortunately, it was. I made it to the motorway by half past two which, I realised, gave me four and a half hours to drive three hundred and fifty miles. That meant I'd have to average about eighty. Oh, shit. I put my foot down. Vast swathes of France passed by in a blur; I sped past Orléans, Blois and Tours, eventually stopping near Poitiers for a cup of coffee and a ham and cheese baguette. It was quarter to five. I wolfed down my sandwich in under three minutes and got back onto the motorway.

I made it to Rupert's hotel in St Emilion at a quarter to eight. I leapt out of the car, grabbed the contract and my phone and ran into the lobby. There was no one there, but there were seventeen missed calls on my mobile. I didn't bother listening to them;

I rang Rupert straight away.

'Where are you?' I asked.

'On my way to the Chateau Saint Martin. What the fuck happened with the contract? You told me seven o'clock. This is an almighty cock-up, Cassie.' He put the phone down.

Yes, Rupert, it is an almighty cock-up. Your almighty cock-up. I didn't have time to reflect on the injustice of the whole situation, I just had to get over to the chateau. I asked the concierge for directions. He reckoned it wouldn't take more than twenty minutes.

Clutching the concierge's hastily scrawled instructions (which were in passable English), I dashed back to the car and headed off in the direction of the chateau. I got lost twice, but not for any great length of time, and arrived at Chateau Saint Martin at twenty past eight. I hastily reapplied a bit of lipstick and mascara, brushed out my hair, spritzed myself with Chanel and rang the doorbell. An elderly gentleman opened the door. He frowned at me.

'*Oui?*'

'Monsieur Leveque?'

'*C'est moi.*'

'I'm a colleague of Mr Forsythe's. I've brought some papers which he needed.'

He smiled at me.

'We have another guest,' M. Leveque announced. '*Mademoiselle* . . .?'

'Cavanagh,' I said. 'Cassie Cavanagh.'

Rupert gawped at me. The elegant lady got to her feet and offered her hand.

'This is my wife,' M. Leveque said.

'*Bonsoir, Madame,*' I said, shaking her hand. There was a long, awkward pause. M. Leveque was looking at Rupert, expecting an explanation which was not forthcoming. Rupert was still gawping at me.

'Perhaps the young lady would like a drink?' Mme Leveque said eventually. 'We were just tasting the Chateau Saint Martin from 1996. It's really quite good.'

Finally, Rupert spoke. 'I wasn't expecting you this evening, Cassie,' he said.

'Oh, I know,' I replied, accepting a glass of red from M. Leveque, 'I just thought I'd drop the papers round, in case you needed them this evening.' I handed him the contract. He smiled at me, shaking his head ever so slightly.

'Ah. So you *do* have the papers,' M. Leveque said, looking from me to Rupert and back again, his eyebrows raised.

'Yes, of course – I wouldn't come all the way here without the contract, would I?' Rupert said, beaming at the Frenchman.

'But I thought you left them—'

'At the hotel. I left them at the hotel. And my lovely assistant was good enough to bring them across.'

'Well. Thank goodness for your . . . uh . . . lovely assistant. Perhaps not such a bad start after all,' M. Leveque said.

The Leveques invited me to stay for dinner, a delicious rack of lamb with a mustard and rosemary crust. Afterwards, M. Leveque, whom we were by now permitted to refer to as Alexandre, gave us a quick tour of the wine cellars. I was expecting a dank and dusty chamber beneath the chateau; but there were literally miles of tunnels running underneath the vines, lined with hundreds of thousands of bottles, some of them more than fifty years old and worth thousands of pounds. I was sorely tempted to nick one and slip it into my handbag.

The tour completed, Marie-Louise (Madame Leveque) and I had coffee in the living room while Rupert and Alexandre disappeared into the study to talk business. A few minutes later they emerged, Alexandre looking quietly satisfied, Rupert beaming like an overexcited schoolboy. We said goodnight and I drove us back to the hotel.

Rupert babbled excitedly all the way

'How on earth did you get here?' he asked as we pulled out of the gates. 'Christ, I couldn't believe it when I saw you standing in the living room. I thought I was having some sort of psychic episode. What time did you get in to Bordeaux?'

'Actually, I flew to Paris,' I told him. 'Then I drove. Breaking the speed limit all the way.'

'Good for you!' he chortled, slapping me on the back. 'Cassie Cavanagh saves the day!'

'Actually, it seemed as though you were doing pretty well on your own. Leveque wasn't at all what I expected. He didn't seem especially Anglophobic to me.'

'He did warm up as the evening went on, didn't he? But you should have been there at the start. When I told him I didn't have the papers with me I thought he was going to throw me out on my ear. He's definitely a man to be handled with care. You seemed to charm him though. You're good with men, aren't you? Nicholas told me that. He always had a bit of a soft spot for you.'

The next morning I was enjoying a grand crème and a croissant on the terrace – an extremely civilised way to begin one's Friday – when Rupert appeared. He looked bleary eyed and exhausted.

'Ended up closing the bar,' he admitted as he sank down into the chair opposite me. 'The wine list here is fantastic.' He ordered a coffee and smiled wearily at me. 'I've just been on the phone to Olly. We're thinking about making some changes at the office.'

'Really?' I asked, not sure whether to be excited or nervous.

'Sales for the first quarter of this year are looking well ahead of our projections – it is amazing in this climate, but I guess demand for booze is pretty inelastic. Plus, I think we did get the pricing right. In any case, our figures are looking pretty healthy, even if I do say so myself. A lot of the demand is for New World wines – they are cheaper, after all – so we've decided that we're going to give Peter the job of sourcing South American and Australasian wines full-time. Not sure where he'll be based just yet – could be Buenos Aires, could be Sydney – but we're going to need to replace him in London.'

Buenos Aires! Lucky sod. I'd always wanted to go to South America.

'So what do you think?' Rupert asked.

'Sounds fantastic,' I said. 'I'm so pleased that everything's going so well. I'll get onto drafting up a job description and advertisement as soon as we get back to London.'

Rupert laughed. 'No, I mean, would you be interested in taking over Peter's role? I'd need to get you trained up first – you'd probably need to go on a course or two – but it's really a learn-on-the-job type of thing. It would be very hard work, but the money would be better. Quite a lot better.'

I nearly choked on my croissant. Promoted? I was getting promoted? I'd only just got the job full time.

'And of course there would be the opportunity to travel. How's your Spanish?'

'Um . . . non-existent really. I have schoolgirl French . . .'

'Well, you'd have to take some language classes, too. But we'd really like you to take a more challenging role. You've done a great job for us so far. Of course, the first thing you'll have to do when you get back is find someone to replace you – we'll need a new assistant if you're moving on to greater things.'

22

Cassie Cavanagh *parle assez bien le Français mais son Espanol laisse à désirer . . .*

I drove back to Paris the following morning, keeping in the vague vicinity of the speed limit this time, although my mind was racing all the way. I was alternately overwhelmed with excitement and fear. I was no longer just a PA. I was going to have a real job, with real responsibilities. I was going to have to learn all about the wine business. I was going to have to learn Spanish. I was going to have to travel around Europe negotiating with wine makers. It was ridiculous. Me? Negotiating? It was terrifying.

By the time I got back home to Clapham it was after nine and I was exhausted, every last scrap of nervous energy burned out of me. I went straight to bed, depite the fact that it was two o'clock in the afternoon, and fell asleep almost instantly. I dreamed that I was lost in a maze of grapevines. Every time I thought I had found the way out I would turn a corner only to find that there were more vines ahead, stretching out as far as the eye could see.

I was woken by the sound of smashing china followed by loud cursing. I looked at my alarm clock. It was after ten. I'd been asleep for eight hours. I dragged myself out of bed, threw on my robe and staggered into the living room.

'Don't come in!' Jude yelled at me. She was standing in the middle of the room with a dustpan and brush, looking hot and bothered. 'I've just knocked over the table lamp and there are bits of broken china everywhere.'

'What are you doing?' I asked, retreating a couple of steps into the hallway.

'I'm packing.'

'Jude, you're not leaving for two weeks.'

'But we're sending out our stuff on Tuesday – everything that we're not actually carrying, that is. So I have to pack up my books and pictures and things this weekend.' She went back to her sweeping. 'Sorry about the lamp, by the way.'

'That's OK. I never liked it that much anyway. It was a Christmas present from Celia.' I shuffled back to my bedroom, put on my slippers and shuffled back again.

'What was all that business about France?' Jude asked, brandishing my note at me.

'Long story,' I said. 'Do you fancy a cup of tea?'

Over tea and toast I told her all about Rupert losing the contracts, the mad mercy dash to the South of France and about my promotion. She seemed pleased for me, although not as pleased as I would have imagined she would be.

'Have you told Jake?' she asked.

'Not yet,' I said. 'I haven't really had time. I was thinking of taking him out for a celebratory dinner tomorrow.'

'That sounds good,' she said, but she still seemed rather subdued. Perhaps she was just feeling a bit sad about moving out.

I took Jake out to dinner at the Bleeding Heart bistro in Farringdon. We sat out in the candlelit courtyard (where the beautiful Lady Elizabeth Hatton, the toast of seventeenth-century London society, allegedly had her heart ripped out by one of her many suitors) drinking champagne. Jake, like Jude, did not seem quite as delighted about my promotion as I was. He congratulated me, of course, and kissed me and told me how brilliant I was, but he seemed distracted. He also seemed very quiet. I'm all for comfortable silences, but after sitting across the table from him while he pushed his food around the plate, saying nothing for a good five minutes, I asked what was up.

'I've been offered a job,' he said at last.

'That's brilliant news! Why are you looking so miserable about it?' He pushed his hand through his hair and smiled at me, a very sad smile.

'It's not in London,' he said.

'Oh. Well, where is it? Nowhere too northern, I hope.'

'Not northern, no. Southern, actually.'

'What, like Brighton? Brighton would be cool. And it's only about an hour from London.'

He took my hand. 'No, Cassie, not Brighton,' he said. 'It's in Africa.'

'Oh.' Neither of us said anything for a bit.

'It's a really good opportunity for me,' he said eventually.

'Whereabouts in Africa?' I asked. Like it mattered. He might as well have been going to Mars.

'I'd be starting out in West Africa, but I could be travelling around quite a bit. It's for Unicef, you see . . .'

'Matt got this you job, did he?' Bastard.

'Yeah – basically they want a photographer to travel around for six months or so, documenting projects in sub-Saharan Africa. It's going to be for a major report that's published next year.'

'Six months?' I asked, incredulous.

'At least six months. Maybe longer if they decide they want me to cover the Middle East as well. It's a fantastic opportunity for me, Cass.'

'Yeah, you said that.'

'You're pissed off.'

'No! Of course not. I'm disappointed. I don't want you to go away for six months. I don't want you to go away for six days. I particularly don't want you to be travelling around dangerous countries getting shot at and contracting nasty tropical diseases. I can't believe Matt's done this to me. No wonder Jude was weird this morning. She knows, doesn't she?'

'Yeah. He told her. I didn't. I wanted to talk to you first.'

There was another long silence.

'Well, six months isn't for ever, is it? God, Matt and Jude are still together despite seeing each other about twice a year for the past five years,' I pointed out, doing my level best to sound chipper.

'Yeah, that's true,' Jake said. But I could tell what he was thinking. I was thinking it too: Matt and Jude had been together for two years before they were separated. Jake and I had been together a few months. It wasn't the same.

'Although . . . I was thinking . . .' He started to say something but stopped.

'What? What were you thinking?'

'Before you told me about the promotion . . . I was thinking . . . You could come with me.'

'To Africa? What would I do?'

'I don't know. Just take some time off. Travel with me. Have adventures. We could live on next to nothing – we can live on the salary that Unicef are paying me, plus I'll have opportunities to freelance for newspapers, photography agencies, things like that. We could buy a Land Rover, a proper old one, not a Chelsea tractor, drive through jungles, forge rivers . . .'

'. . . Get eaten by lions.'

'Oh, come on,' he said, slipping his fingers through mine. 'Lions very rarely eat people.'

'Jake . . . I don't know. My idea of being adventurous

is mixing high street with couture. I'm not sure I'm cut out for . . . jungles and things. Christ, think of all the insects. I'm horribly arachnophobic, you know.'

'We'll stock up on bug repellent.'

I woke up the next morning at six, my head pounding. Too much champagne. I slipped out of bed and into the shower without waking Jake, dressed quickly and quietly and wrote him a note.

Not feeling too good. Hangover I think. Will call you later xxx

I crept out of the flat into the cool London air and walked up the hill to the tube. I wasn't actually feeling that bad, but for some reason I just couldn't lie there next to him in silence with everything that was going on in my head.

Back at home, I made a cup of coffee for myself and a camomile tea for Jude and knocked softly on her door. I was pretty sure Matt wasn't around, but I didn't want a repeat of the eyeful I'd got last time I walked in on Jude and her boyfriend unannounced. After a moment or two, I heard a muffled response.

'What is it?'

'It's me, Jude. Can I come in?'

'Mmmm.'

I put the cup of tea on the floor and perched on the edge of her bed.

'I need to talk to you,' I said, prodding her softly in the back. She pulled the duvet covers over her head.

'I'm listening,' she mumbled.

'You knew, didn't you? You knew he was planning on leaving.'

She sat up abruptly, peering at me through hooded eyes.

'I'm so sorry, Cassie,' she said sleepily. 'This is all my fault.'

'What do you mean?'

'Well, Matt was talking about how he needed to recruit someone for this job, and like an idiot I said, "Oh, that would be perfect for Jake," and before you know it, Matt's offered Jake the job and Jake's said yes and then you were talking about how great everything was and how excited you were about your new job . . .' She paused for breath, let out a huge sigh. 'I'm sorry, Cass. I didn't mean to mess everything up.' She lay back and pulled the duvet back over her head.

'You didn't mess anything up, Jude.' I sipped my coffee thoughtfully. 'Whether Matt had offered him this job or not . . . it was only going to be a matter of time.'

'Really?' She was sitting up again. I held out the cup of tea, which she accepted gratefully.

'Really. This is what he wants. It's just . . .' Tears sprang to my eyes. 'It's just such bloody bad timing. Less than twenty-four hours ago I was in this state of total exhilaration, I was so excited about my new job – no, my new *career*! I have a career now – can you believe it? Twenty-four hours ago I had it sorted: great job, great new house, great boyfriend. And now I have to make a choice. Do I give up this career opportunity

– my first career opportunity ever, let's not forget – for a man I'm falling in love with, even if I know he's probably not "the one", whatever the hell that means?'

Jude looked at me glumly, for once lost for words.

'I suppose we could do the long-distance thing . . .' I went on.

'Cass, take it from a woman who's been there, the long-distance thing is *not* fun. In fact, it's painful and lonely and depressing. I can't tell you how many times I've thought that I should just call it a day . . . And I *know* Matt's "the one". But there were times when I could see everyone else going out and having fun and meeting new people and I was just waiting, my whole life passing me by . . .'

'Jude,' I said, putting my arm around her. 'God. You never said.'

'No,' she shrugged with a little smile. But I should have known anyway, I thought. 'Anyway, if you do think that it's for keeps with Jake, then I wouldn't even try the long-distance thing. It won't work and one of you will just end up hurting the other one. And I like you both very much. I don't want to have to cut one of you out of my life just yet . . .'

Of course, there was more to think about than just me and Jake. Even if I did want to dash off to Africa to have adventures, even if I was prepared to abandon my great new career for my great new man, I wasn't prepared to abandon my best friend. My single, pregnant best friend who was counting on me. More than that, I didn't want to leave her – I couldn't bear the idea of not being there when she had the baby. The truth was that I'd loved Jake for about five minutes, but I'd loved Ali for years.

Not that I said any of this to him, of course. In fact, I just put the whole issue to the back of my mind and carried on as though nothing were wrong. Faced with the choice of making a decision about my future with Jake and complete denial, I opted for the river in Egypt.

I had plenty of other things to occupy my mind in any case. Intermediate French and beginner's Spanish, for starters, with classes at the Wine Academy every Thursday evening, and antenatal classes with Ali every Friday evening, just for good measure. Plus there was the matter of Jude's impending departure and my imminent move to West London. My relationship with Jake had slipped down my list of priorities a little.

A fact which, it appears, had not escaped his attention. On Jude and Matt's final evening in London, we had dinner together in the flat – Matt, Jude, Jake and I sitting on boxes around the coffee table eating takeaway, with Ali sitting on the sofa (we weren't sure there was a box that would bear her weight). For once, the tension in the room was not between Ali and Jude, who were actually being quite civil to each other. The problems began when Ali started talking about moving dates.

'I can exchange on the fourteenth of April so you could move in any time after that,' she said, helping herself to another enormous serving of chiang mai duck curry.

'I'll move in the very next day,' I said, clinking glasses with her. 'I have got to be out of here by the end of the month, so that's absolutely perfect. God, I can't wait, Al. It's going to be so much fun living together.' Jude gave me a faux-hurt look. 'Almost as much fun as it has been living with you,' I said quickly, and clinked glasses with her, too. Jake got up abruptly from the table and opened another can of cider. It was his fourth so far that evening.

'You've not got plans for the fifteenth, Cassie?' he asked me.

'Not that I can think of . . .' I replied.

'Right.'

'Why, were we supposed to be doing something?'

'Nothing special,' he muttered, turning away from me to rifle through my admittedly rather pitiful CD collection. 'Can I change this music?' he asked, turning it off before anyone replied. 'It's fucking awful.'

I looked questioningly at Jude, who just shrugged.

Things got better as the evening wore on, enlivened by endless anecdotes from Jude about my foibles as a flatmate and a good-natured round-up of the very best barbs and ripostes in the Ali-versus-Jude saga. By the time the third bottle of wine was finished, Jude and I were starting to get a bit weepy.

'You're the best flatmate I've ever had,' she sobbed, as she flung her arms around me. This sent the others into fits of laughter.

'What was it that made her such a great flatmate?' Ali giggled. 'Was it the flooded kitchen, the constant boy drama or the fact that you lived in constant fear of eviction thanks to Cassie's imprudent financial management?'

'She's a lovely flatmate,' Jude insisted, still hugging me. 'At least life's never boring when Cass is about . . . You'll see,' she said, giving Ali a wink.

'I'm living in fear,' Ali said. 'Cassie and a baby. I wonder which one will be more trouble?'

Later on, after I'd helped Ali into a taxi and Matt and Jude had gone to bed, I found Jake skulking in the kitchen, looking for another drink.

'I think we're out,' I said, slipping my hands round his waist. 'Come on, let's go to bed.' 'I'd better not, Cass,' he said, disentangling himself from my arms. 'Early start tomorrow. I should probably just call it a night.'

Later, alone in bed, I realised that the fifteenth of April was the day he was supposed to be leaving.

A few weeks later, I took the day off work and borrowed Ali's car to drive Jake to the airport. Neither of us said much on the way there. When we arrived, a little early, we found a booth in a coffee shop and sat down.

'I'll give you a call when I get there,' Jake said. 'There's no time difference, I don't think. I'll have to check on that.' He took my hand. 'The time's going to fly by, Cass.' I didn't say anything. There was a long and uncomfortable silence. Eventually, he spoke again.

'But . . . you're not that worried about time flying by,

are you?' he asked, staring morosely at his feet. 'Because you want to end this.'

A tear slid down my cheek and landed in my untouched coffee.

'We should have talked about it weeks ago,' I said. 'I should have said something straight away. We can't do the long-distance thing, Jake – you know we can't.'

'It's only six months . . .'

'Maybe. Maybe this trip is six months, maybe it'll be longer. And how long will the next one be? This is what you want to do with your life, Jake. It isn't what I want.' He pulled his hand away from mine. I took it back. 'I love you,' I told him. 'I do, I really do, and I've had such a good time with you. But there's too much here for me to go off on the road with you – work, my family, Ali. And there's too much out there for you to stay here.'

'But we could try . . .'

'Yes, we could try. And I think we'd fail and that one or both of us would end up very hurt. More badly hurt than we are now.'

He leaned over the table and kissed me.

'You're right,' he said, wiping the tears from my cheeks. 'I know you are. I just don't want to let you go, that's all.' He slipped around the table so that he was sitting next to me, and we sat there for a while in silence, our arms around each other.

'You'll still call me when you get there, won't you?' I asked eventually.

'Course I will.' Then he picked up his bag and got to his feet. 'I really ought to get going,' he said.

'Don't,' I pleaded. 'Not yet. Have another coffee.' Neither of us had touched a drop of our first cups.

'Cass, they're calling us to the gate. I need to get through security first. You know how long it takes these days.'

Clinging tightly to his hand, I walked him to security and kissed him goodbye. I waited until he was safely out of sight, then I burst into tears.

It took for ever to get home – there had been an accident on the M4 – and when I got there I felt more depressed than ever. The flat felt so empty, stripped bare of Jude and all her clutter. My things were half-packed – I had until the end of the day to finish it off. The removals van was coming first thing the next day. I couldn't wait. The sooner I got out of the flat and into my new place with Ali, the better.

That night I ate a solitary dinner of cheese on toast made under the grill accompanied by a glass of Chateau Saint Martin '04. It might have been mid-April, but the flat felt so cold I was tempted to put the heating on. It felt horribly quiet, too. I wished I hadn't packed the television away. I sat up until midnight waiting for Jake to ring, but he didn't. I rang Heathrow to make sure his plane hadn't crashed. It hadn't. I called his phone a few times but I just got an odd beeping noise and then silence. I went to bed feeling miserable. I woke briefly at three in the morning. There were three texts on my phone.

Joe is going to be a footballer, no doubt. Won't stop

kicking. See you tomorrow xx Ali

Last night at 6A Venn St? Thinking of you. NY groovy xx Jude

And finally:

Sorry didn't ring earlier. Signal patchy. Hellishly hot here. I miss you xxxxx Jake

When I finally woke up the sun was shining through the blinds and the removals men were ringing the doorbell. I threw on some jeans and a T-shirt and opened the door to two strapping young Australians wishing me a cheery 'G'day'. They were remarkably efficient – the entire place was cleaned out by nine thirty.

I took one last final tour of the place before I left. Oddly enough, it seemed smaller with the furniture gone than it had with everything in it. I was standing in the hallway, staring into the bathroom, remembering the first time I'd ever laid eyes on Jake, the time he'd nearly cracked my head open with the door, when one of the Australians, the particularly attractive one, called out, 'This the last one, love?' He was just picking up the final couple of boxes, one filled with papers and the other, a shoebox containing my Louboutins.

'Oh, leave those,' I said, taking the box from him. 'They're not coming with me.' I thought for a moment about chucking them in the bin, but decided instead to leave them on the kitchen counter. You never know, the next girl to move in might just be my size.

ALSO AVAILABLE IN ARROW

The Popularity Rules

Abby McDonald

Rule 1: All's fair in love, war and popularity . . .

Kat Elliot is no social butterfly: she's spent her life rebelling against phony schmoozing – and it's led her nowhere. Just as she's ready to give up her dreams and admit defeat, in steps Lauren Anderville. One-time allies against their school bullies, Lauren and Kat had been inseparable. Then one year Lauren returned from summer camp blonde, bubbly and suddenly popular, and Kat was left to face the world alone.

Ten years later, Lauren's back. She wants to make amends by teaching Kat the secret to her success: The Popularity Rules. A decades-old rulebook, its secrets transformed Lauren that fateful summer. And so, tempted by Lauren's promises of glitzy parties and the job she's always dreamed of, Kat reluctantly submits to a total makeover – only to find that life with the in-crowd might have something going for it after all.

But while Lauren has sacrificed everything to get ahead, is Kat really ready to accept that popularity is the only prize that counts?

arrow books

ALSO AVAILABLE IN ARROW

The Fabulously Fashionable Life of Isabel Bookbinder

Holly McQueen

When aspiring designer Isabel Bookbinder bags a job with Nancy 'Fashion Aristocracy' Tavistock, she's sure her career is finally on track. Dazzlingly glamorous, this is a world that she feels truly passionate about – after all, she knows her Geiger from her Louboutin, her Primark from her Prada, and she's *always* poring over fashion magazines. Well, ok, the fashion pages of *heat*.

So, learning from the very best, the future's looking bright for Isabel Bookbinder: Top International Fashion Designer. Within days she's putting the final touches to her debut collection, has dreamt up a perfume line, *Isabelissimo*, and is very nearly a friend of John Galliano. And on top of that she might even have fallen in love.

Yet nothing ever runs smoothly for Isabel and fabulously fashionable as her life is, it soon seems to be spiralling a little out of her control . . .

Praise for Holly McQueen:

'Marvellously funny' Jilly Cooper

'Does exactly what it says on the tin: if you like Sophie Kinsella's Shopaholic books and you miss Bridget Jones, then meet Isabel' Louise Bagshawe, *Mail on Sunday*

arrow books

THE POWER OF READING

Visit the Random House website and get connected with information on all our books and authors

EXTRACTS from our recently published books and selected backlist titles

COMPETITIONS AND PRIZE DRAWS Win signed books, audiobooks and more

AUTHOR EVENTS Find out which of our authors are on tour and where you can meet them

LATEST NEWS on bestsellers, awards and new publications

MINISITES with exclusive special features dedicated to our authors and their titles

READING GROUPS Reading guides, special features and all the information you need for your reading group

LISTEN to extracts from the latest audiobook publications

WATCH video clips of interviews and readings with our authors

RANDOM HOUSE INFORMATION including advice for writers, job vacancies and all your general queries answered

Come home to Random House

www.rbooks.co.uk

OKANAGAN REGIONAL LIBRARY
3 3132 03334 2876